THE EVIL THAT
CHRISTY KNOWS

THE EVIL THAT CHRISTY KNOWS

Clare McNally

SEVERN SH HOUSE

This first world edition published in Great Britain 1995 by
SEVERN HOUSE PUBLISHERS LTD of
9–15 High Street, Sutton, Surrey SM1 1DF.
First published in the USA 1995 by
SEVERN HOUSE PUBLISHERS INC of
595 Madison Avenue, New York, NY 10022.
Parts of this book originally appeared in the USA only
under the title of There He Keeps Them Very Well.

British Library Cataloguing in Publication Data
McNally, Clare
  The Evil That Christy Knows
  I. Title
  813.54 [F]

  ISBN 0-7278-4819-4

Typeset by Hewer Text Composition Services, Edinburgh.
Printed and bound in Great Britain by
Hartnolls Ltd, Bodmin, Cornwall.

Prologue

Independence Day was almost over, but the grand finale, the fireworks, had yet to come. A slight figure in a sleeveless white dress sat on the grass that sloped down to Lake Aberdeen, just one of hundreds who had come to the celebration. A little girl sat in the hammock the woman's skirt made over her crossed legs. Christine Burnett Wander kissed the top of her daughter's head. Victoria's bright red hair smelled of bubble gum shampoo from the bath the five-year-old had taken the night before under extreme protest.

Vicki wriggled. "When's Daddy and Joshua coming back?" she asked.

"There must be a long line at the tent where they're selling food, honey. There are an awful lot of people here."

"I'm hungry. I want my Sno-Kone," Vicki said.

She jumped from her mother's lap and shot off into the crowd. Chris was on her feet at once.

"Victoria!"

Vicki ignored her. Lucille Brigham, who was sitting beside Chris, smiled.

"Oh, let her run," she said.

Chris frowned, craning her neck to see through the groups of families. "I just don't like her out of my sight," she said.

"You worry too much," Lucille replied. She uncrossed her legs and got up to stand beside her friend. Lucille was dressed in jeans, her black French braid perfectly aligned with the pleat down the back of her Liz Claiborne shirt. "Must be great to feel so free," she said. "I'm not sure if I ever ran around like that."

"Oh, sure you did," Chris said. "You weren't as wild as Eda, but you had your fun."

"Have you heard from Eda lately?" Eda Crispin had been their friend since childhood. After high school, she'd gone off to New York to become a police officer.

"Just talked to her on the phone last week," Chris replied. "And her partner, Tim Becker, sent a clipping from *New York Newsday*. Eda received a citation for saving a man's life!"

"And she didn't tell us herself," Lucille said. "That's just like Eda, isn't it?"

"You know Eda. She hates a fuss."

The words were scarcely out when Vicki barrelled into her, grabbing Chris at the knees so hard and so fast that she staggered, struggling to keep herself upright. "Victoria Wander, don't run away from me ever again!" Chris said angrily. "Never, ever again!"

"Mommy, there was a really creepy man over there." Vicki's voice was shrill with fear and her

2

finger trembled as she pointed toward the crowd. She turned to look with her mother at the man, but the spot was empty. "He tried to grab me, Mommy."

"Are you sure, honey?" Lucille asked.

"Sure, I'm sure. He sounded like a lion with a real deep roar kind of voice. And he had red hair like Daddy and me, but he wasn't my . . ."

The rest of Vicki's words were drowned out by her brother's voice. "They didn't have any cherry ones," Josh said, shaking a wave of black hair from his eyes as he stretched out his thin arm. Vicki snatched the Sno-Kone from his hand, apparently unconcerned that it wasn't her favourite flavour.

"I got one too, Mom," a blond-haired boy with large brown eyes said to Lucille. "Mr Wander paid for it."

"That was nice, Jerry," Lucille said, glancing over at Brian. "You didn't have to do that."

"No big deal," Brian said.

"What about you, Josh?" Chris asked. "Where's your Sno-Kone?"

"I don't like grape," Josh said. He held a huge pretzel up to his face, peering through it with round, dark eyes. "So I got one of these."

"Looks like they're almost ready," Brian said, pointing to the barge in the middle of the lake.

The fireworks began with a rendition of the National Anthem. Over the next half hour, the sky above the lake was filled with colour, and the cries of the pleased crowd were second only to the

3

massive booms that followed an occasional dud. Vicki kept her hands over her ears. At last, the final Roman candle was set off. Families gathered together and made their way to the parking lot. Brian went ahead, carrying Vicki. She seemed ready to fall asleep. Josh and Jerry ran circles around them.

"Are you busy tomorrow?" Chris asked Lucille. "I thought we could go to the mall for the big sales. We could make a day of it. You know, leave the boys at the video arcade? I wouldn't have to rush home, because Brian's heading out on a business trip."

"Another one?" Lucille asked, a hint of disapproval in her voice.

But Chris wouldn't argue with her. Yes, Brian left her alone for long stretches of time. That was part of being head buyer at Brenley's, the area's biggest department store. Lucille worried too much about her – had been worrying ever since a long-ago day when Chris had crashed into her with her bike. Sometimes, Chris had to remind her friend that she was no longer in the second grade. "Well, it's only overnight this time," she said.

"It's just too bad he has to go away so frequently," Lucille said, grinning mischievously. "Such a handsome man with all that gorgeous auburn hair and those incredible emerald green eyes needs to be kept around the house, my friend. How many times have I said that if my husband was one iota as nice as Brian and as sweet as he is to you, we would never have gotten a divorce?" Serious now, she added: "If you need anything while he's gone . . ."

Chris smiled at her. They'd reached the parking lot, where Lucille's teenaged sons were waiting.

"Hi, Mrs Wander," the fifteen-year-old twins said in unison.

"Hi, Eric," Chris said. "Hi, Robby."

The families parted then. But Lucille's words stayed with Chris, and she was thoughtful during the drive home. Brian did go away a lot these days. He'd only held his position for six months, so she supposed it would take her a while to get used to it. But, still . . .

"I wish you didn't have to leave tomorrow," she said to him, as they drove home. "It would be nice to have a long weekend together."

Brian shrugged. "Business, honey. I have to work my tail off to prove myself to my employers. Eventually, I hope to have enough clout to send someone else in my place once in a while."

He pulled into the driveway and stopped the car. Then he looked at her. "Are you okay?"

"I guess so," she said. "It's just that I love you so much, and I really miss you when you're away."

"I love you too, honey."

"Save it for later!" Josh cried, stopping their kiss before they even got near each other. "Ick!"

"Oh, Josh," Chris sighed. To the ten-year-old, any display of affection was "ick". She opened her door. "Brian, carry Vicki, please? She's out like a light."

5

Even in her sleep, Vicki cuddled lovingly against her father. Chris smiled, feeling warm inside. That was the way a father was supposed to treat a daughter. Not the way her father had; the only times he'd touched her were when he hurt her.

She followed them up the stairs and helped tuck the little girl into bed. Then, impulsively, she turned and gave her husband a big kiss.

Brian smiled and whispered, "What brought that on?"

Chris shrugged. "I guess it's just seeing how sweet you are with kids."

Brian put an arm around her and led her from the room. As they got ready for bed, Chris remembered the strange man Vicki had seen. She told Brian about him.

"Probably just a weirdo," Brian said. "But I'm glad nothing happened. Vicki's too friendly, if you ask me. You've got to have a talk with her about strangers."

"I've done that," Chris said. "It doesn't sink in. But remember, she's only five."

Later, when they climbed into bed, Chris slid close to her husband, resting her head against his chest. She started massaging him. "I had such a good time tonight," she said.

"Me too." Brian kissed the top of her head, then added, "You'll probably dream about red-white-and-blue sparks."

Chris was silent for a moment. Thinking she had fallen asleep, Brian started to pull away from her. But her arm went across his waist and she held him tightly.

"You know I don't dream, Brian. At least, not any more."

For the first two years of their marriage, Chris had woken up many nights screaming in terror. Brian would have to hold her and assure her again and again that nothing was going to hurt her. "I guess you stopped dreaming about the time Josh was born," he said.

About the time she was able to trade the memory of her childhood for the happy childhood of her son. Even if she lived it vicariously, she got great pleasure from seeing Josh's normal, well-adjusted upbringing. She hadn't had a nightmare in ten years.

"Can you hold me until I fall asleep?" she asked.

"Sure," Brian said. "Mind if I ask why? I mean, you usually seem more comfortable on your stomach."

"Guess I need a little loving," she replied. "That man tonight, the one Vicki saw, frightened me. Do you remember when we first met? How that weirdo had been following me?"

"Coincidence," Brian insisted. "Put it out of your mind and get some sleep, babe. You'll probably never see that man again."

"God, I hope not," Chris said, yawning. "I don't know what I'd do if anything happened to the kids."

"Nothing's gonna happen," Brian swore. "I

always tell you that, don't I? Nothing will happen so long as I'm around to keep you safe. I love you so much, Chris, that I. . ."

The arm that had been hugging Brian so tightly went limp. This time, Chris really was asleep. He moved her arm and turned to settle himself. He didn't fall asleep right away. He wouldn't admit it to Chris, because he'd always been the rock she leaned on for support, but he was nervous enough to be tempted to cancel his trip. But it was important; he couldn't put it off.

He gazed at his wife, her face softly illuminated by the moonlight pouring in through the curtains. Brian thought she was as beautiful now as she'd been the day he met her. Maybe even more so. Back then, she'd been the pale, thin child of abuse, dark circles under her lovely brown eyes. He'd wanted to kill her father for hurting her. More than that he'd wanted, still wanted, to keep Christine with him forever, to protect her as one might protect a delicate work of art.

Slowly, he reached through the dim light and stroked her face. Her cheeks had filled out a bit in the last decade, but she had needed the added weight. Brian knew that even real family love, combined with many hours in a therapist's office, couldn't completely eradicate what her father had done to her, what that other childhood trauma had done to her. Sometimes, things would happen that would bring out the fearful child she'd been, and it hurt him almost as much as it hurt her.

Brian finally fell asleep with a growing sense of worry that promised bad dreams.

After Brian left the next morning, Chris met Lucille and headed for Longacre Mall. Armed with Brian's discount card and aided by clearance sales, Chris and Lucille had been able to fill huge shopping bags without spending too much. The day sped by, and Chris didn't think about Brian until she was alone in bed that night. Now, she missed him terribly. Silly, she told herself, rolling over to his side of the bed. His pillow smelled faintly of his aftershave. He'll be back tomorrow.

She fell asleep breathing in the aroma that made her feel as if her husband was near, protecting her, loving her, keeping the demons away.

Sometime near four a.m., she was woken by the barking of the dogs next door. For a moment she lay with her eyes wide open, her heart pounding. She listened as the dogs' owner came out to quieten them, but even after it grew quiet again she couldn't fall asleep. She had a strange feeling something was wrong.

For a long time, she listened to the quiet of the house. When the silence was suddenly interrupted by the sound of Josh coughing, Chris was filled with an overwhelming need to make certain that her kids were okay. She didn't know why she felt nervous, but she pushed her covers aside and went down the hall.

Both Josh and Vicki were sleeping like angels. She adjusted Vicki's covers, tucking her favourite yellow unicorn toy close to her. Then she checked to be certain Josh's breathing was okay. Maybe the cough had been caused by dry air. She hoped he wasn't coming down with a cold.

She was about to go back to bed when she suddenly understood why the barking had unsettled her. Those dogs never barked at night! What had they heard? Had someone been out there?

She thought about the stranger at the Fourth of July festival, and her panic began to rise. Had he come to find Vicki? "Oh, Brian," she whispered. "I wish you were here!"

She hated being alone, especially with two children. The nervous pounding of her heart made it impossible for her to try to sleep again. Instead, she turned manic, rushing from window to door to be certain every lock was secure. The dogs were completely silent now.

She sat on the couch, listening, waiting . . .

And then it was morning, and the day was busy enough to help her temporarily forget her fears. But when she heard the taxi pull up in front of the house, her immediate thought was. *Thank God, Brian's home*!

A smile stretched across her face as she hurried down the front path to meet him. But her heart sank when she saw his face. He looked completely worn out. His eyes were darkly circled as if he hadn't had a wink of sleep. "Oh, honey," she said. "It looks like you had a bad time."

"Terrible," Brian said, simply. He gave her a

perfunctory kiss and barely acknowledged the children.

Chris saw the disappointed looks on their faces and said: "Your father's tired out. Go on and play. I'll call you later." She walked into the house with her husband. "How bad was it?"

"The worst," Brian said. "The client was a real pain in the ass. It took all my effort to convince him I didn't want every single item in his line."

"Oh, Brian," Chris sighed. "Is the hassle worth it?"

"For forty-five thousand dollars a year, it is," Brian snapped. The tone of voice was so unlike him that Chris took a step back. His voice softened. "I'm sorry. I shouldn't take this out on you. If I'm to continue as head buyer of one of Montana's biggest department store chains, I have to get used to hard work. And the occasional annoying supplier."

He rubbed his bloodshot eyes. "I don't want to talk about this now, Chris. I just want to take a nap."

"Okay," she said, "I'll make sure the house is quiet."

She watched him drag up the stairs, his head hanging from exhaustion. It wasn't the first time he'd come home from a trip this way, and the exhaustion was aging him.

But when he came down two hours later, the change was miraculous. He was smiling, his eyes bright. "Let's take the kids to Burger Barn," he suggested.

He opened the front door and called out to Vicki and Josh, who were playing dodgeball with half a dozen friends. When he told them his plans, they started dancing around him.

"Yay! Yay!"

"I know," Chris said as she joined them on the front walk. "Why don't we pick up lunch at the drive-in window? Then we can go down to Lake Aberdeen for a picnic."

"Primo!" Josh cried.

"Yay!"

"Groovy!" Brian said with a big grin.

Bewildered looks crossed the children's faces. Chris began to laugh, ruffling Brian's hair before they scrambled into the car.

"You kids aren't the only ones with a language of your own," she said. "We used to say 'groovy' when something was great."

Josh and Vicki giggled.

"What other silly things did you say?" Josh asked.

Brian straightened himself up with mock indignation. "I beg your pardon," he said. "We did not say silly things."

"Not too silly," Chris said. "Stuff like 'Right On,' and 'Out of Sight.'"

"'Right Arm,'" Brian said, holding up his arm. "And 'Out of State.'"

This, the kids decided, was *definitely* funny. They fell over each other, laughing.

Chris looked back at her rambunctious children and smiled. Brian could see it was a melancholy smile, and wondered if she was thinking of her own childhood. Had she ever laughed like that? He doubted it.

Twenty minutes later, they were sitting at a picnic table by the lake. It was a particularly gorgeous summer day, and many other families had come to enjoy the lush grass and trees and the sparkling water. There was no evidence of the festival that had taken place just a few days earlier, not a burnt-out firecracker or an empty pretzel bag.

"Can we go for a hike?" Josh asked, the minute they had finished lunch.

"Great idea," Chris said.

"Primo idea," Brian amended.

Vicki giggled. "Say 'groovy.'"

Brian pulled her up into his arms and danced around with her, singing a song from the late sixties.

The woods surrounding the lake were huge, and it was easy to get lost in them. The Park Department supplied a free trail map, so for the next two hours they hiked through the woods, admiring the trees and flowers. Vicki often raced ahead, but a quick word from Brian brought her back again. At last, she ran out of steam. Brian carried her piggy-back as they traced the path out of the woods.

They had reached the parking lot when Vicki pointed back at the trees and shouted "Mommy! Daddy! There's the man!"

Chris turned. She could easily make out a man

13

in straggly clothes standing at the tree-line on the far side of the parking lot. Her heart jumped into her throat.

"What man?" Josh asked.

"I don't see anyone," Brian said as he set Vicki down on the ground.

Chris saw the figure had moved back into the shadows of the trees. The hot summer day couldn't keep away the deep chill that gripped her.

"Must have been another hiker, that's all," Brian said. "Let's get in the car now."

When the children were inside, with the doors closed, Brian spoke to Chris. "What are you thinking?"

"Nothing in particular," Chris said weakly.

"Yes, you are," Brian replied. "I'm the one who loves you most, remember? The man Vicki saw upset you, too."

Chris looked at him with imploring eyes. "I'm so afraid that he's back again," she said. "The man who terrorized me so long ago is back again. Only now, he wants my children."

"Chris, that's impossible," Brian exclaimed. "It's been thirty years!"

"He followed me when I was seven," Chris said. "And later, when I was nine."

"But you didn't have me those times."

"I'm just so afraid . . ."

"If you're nervous, why don't you call Dr Romano?"

"My therapist?" She queried. "I haven't seen

14

her in three years. I don't need her, Brian. I need to know that man isn't the same one who was after me when I was a kid."

Brian was about to answer, but Josh cracked the window and called out impatiently, "Some of us are roasting like turkeys!"

"Oh, Josh, I'm sorry!" Chris responded. "It must be beastly in there! Open the windows!"

Brian climbed in on the driver's side. He turned on the engine and flipped the air conditioning to MAX. Josh began to study a collection of small rocks he'd stored in his pocket. Vicki retrieved her yellow unicorn from the car floor and began to march it across the back of the seat.

When they opened their front door at home, the phone was ringing. Chris ran to answer it.

"Hello?"

Silence.

"Hello?" Chris pressed.

"Wrong number," a gruff voice replied, and the line went dead.

Chris trembled. There had been a terrifying familiarity in that voice.

Josh came into the room, asking if he could play with his video games. Vicki wanted juice. Everyday life pushed fearful thoughts out of Chris's mind. By the time she was fixing dinner that evening, cooking chicken on the barbecue, she had all but forgotten the call.

"Garlic potatoes and barbecued chicken," Brian said as he walked across the patio. "My favourite summer dinner. We're eating early, babe. How come?"

"Did you forget?" Chris asked. "I'm teaching at the adult centre tonight."

Brian nodded. "That's right. How could I forget? Your art class starts tonight."

Chris had worked part-time in the local art supplies store for years. Her boss had pointed out her talent for drawing as a potential money-maker, and had offered to display some of her work in exchange for teaching a class. She'd agreed readily, and had been surprised how quickly her drawings sold.

A short time later, the four Wanders sat around their picnic table. The corn-on-the-cob was sweet, the tomatoes, a gift from Lucille's garden, delicious. Vicki made loud noises sucking barbecue sauce off her fingers, setting Josh off to say what a pig she was. But it was good-natured teasing, and the blueberry cobbler Chris had made for dessert put everyone in a good mood.

After dinner, Brian, Vicki and Josh settled in front of the TV. Chris came into the den to say goodbye, pulling her long hair back into a pony tail. She gave them each a kiss and left the house with the happy knowledge her kids were perfectly safe in Brian's loving care.

She enjoyed her first painting class. The students were blessed with a mix of talents, and they all seemed to learn something from her. As she drove home, she was already making plans for the next class.

16

When she pulled her car in behind Brian's, she noticed the house was unusually dark. Brian hadn't left the outside light on for her. Bulb probably went out, she told herself without worry.

But a funny feeling came over her as she entered the house. She had to stop at the door to get her bearings, to understand why an old feeling of dread had come back again. She'd felt it the other night, too, when the dogs had awakened her. She hadn't felt that way since . . .

Chris quickly realized what had set her instincts on edge. It was just a little thing, but *so wrong*: Vicki's yellow unicorn, her favourite toy, was on the steps. She would never have left it there! And Brian wouldn't have tolerated a toy on the stairs. Unless . . . Oh, don't be silly, she told herself.

The command didn't work. She felt trouble in the air as thickly as if it were coming out of the vents. Chris picked up the unicorn, and something wet came off on her hands. Blood.

"Brian?" she called, quietly, nervously. Vicki must have cut herself, that's all.

She waited to hear him call her from the den. When he didn't, she told herself he had probably fallen asleep in front of the TV.

There was a streak of blood on the corridor wall.

"Brian?" A little louder now. Her heart was beginning to pound.

She raced into the den. The TV screen was dark grey, silent. A bowl of popcorn Brian had shared with the kids had been knocked onto the floor, small pieces scattered everywhere. Brian would never have left such a mess.

Her heart beating wildly with fear now, Chris ran for the stairs.

"*Brian!*"

She burst into their bedroom and threw on the light switch. When she saw his red hair peeking out from the edge of the bed spread, she let out a cry of relief that was half laughter, half whimper. "Oh, Brian," she said in a shaking voice. "You wouldn't believe the crazy thoughts that just went through my head."

She climbed onto the bed, kneeling beside her sleeping husband. The movement rocked the mattress, and Brian's head turned.

There, she thought with relief. He's waking up. Then she noticed Brian's head had rolled a little too far. His head, but not his body. His neck was even now with the outline of his right shoulder. But that was impossible . . .

She jumped from the bed. This time, she did not cry out tentatively. She screamed with all her might.

"BRIAN! BRIAN!"

She grabbed for the bedspread and jerked it away. The oriental pattern had hidden the horror beneath: the blanket was soaked with blood. Shaking all over, but unable to stop herself, Chris peeled away the blanket, then the top sheet. Then she stopped screaming, shocked into silence.

Brian was lying on his stomach, dressed only in his briefs. A thick but perfectly even line of blood ran down the valley in the middle of his back, where his muscles joined at the spine. There was a huge puddle of blood on the pillow, just above his neck.

He had been decapitated. His head lay on one side, jiggled a good eight inches from his neck in her frenzied stripping of the bed. His face, turned into the mattress, pointed away from her.

Oh, no, this can't be happening! I'm having bad dreams again! I'm having a nightmare, and I'm going to wake up and Brian's going to be okay and . . .

In the midst of her panic, something in Brian's clenched hand caught her eye. Sobbing, begging herself to wake up, she bent and peered closer. It was a hank of hair from the yellow unicorn.

The children! Terror gripped Chris. She ran from the room, screaming out their names.

"JOSH! VICKI!"

Their beds were empty, never slept in.

She ran through the house, yelling at the top of her lungs. There was no sign of the children. Now she ran outside and crossed the darkened street to Lucille's house. Her friend answered the wild pounding on her front door within moments, the twins standing groggily behind her. "Chris?"

Chris grabbed Lucille by the arms and left blood on her skin. "Someone's killed Brian!" Chris gasped. "Someone's cut off his head and taken my babies . . . Oh, God! Oh, God . . ." She fell into Lucille's arms, sobbing.

"Chris, I don't understand!" Lucille looked back over her shoulder. "Robby, call the police."

To Chris she said, in a voice that was calm and reassuring:

"Slow down. What do you mean someone killed Brian?"

"I . . . I found him in our bed," Chris whimpered. "His head was cut off, just like that guy when we were kids. Josh and Vicki are gone!"

"Oh, no . . ."

"It's a nightmare, Lucille," Chris whispered. "I'm going through hell. But I lived through hell, didn't I? Didn't I live through hell when I was a kid?"

Lucille was dumbstruck. All she could do was hold her friend, offering support.

Chris clutched at her, frantically. "How could it start happening all over again?"

Chapter One

Thirty Years Earlier

Christy Burnett picked up a tray from the stack near the door of the cafeteria and moved through the line. She hadn't had breakfast that morning, and the smell of chicken noodle soup was making her mouth water and her stomach growl.

"Move it, will you, Creepy Christy?" a boy in her second grade class said.

Chrisy moved along compliantly, her eyes fixed on the metal bars that lined the serving area.

"Why don't *you* move, you dumb jerk?" Eda Crispin snapped, pushing ahead of the offending boy.

As she waited her turn, Christy watched her friend. She thought Eda was about the prettiest girl she'd ever met. She had bright blonde hair and eyes that were big and very blue. Her parents bought her the most beautiful clothes. It didn't matter that fidgeting at her desk had wrinkled Eda's dress or that her hair ribbons were pulled loose, or that she'd scuffed the toes of her shoes. Christy still thought she looked perfect, like a doll.

Eda started to fill her tray. She grabbed a hot dog, corn, French fries, and a container of chocolate milk.

Christy's brown eyes grew wider with each addition to the tray. "Gosh," she said, "you must be hungry."

"Guess so," Eda said, poking through the pieces of fresh fruit heaped on a huge stainless steel tray. "I got my allowance today." She chose a banana. "Five dollars."

Five dollars! What a fortune, Christy thought.

"I'll share with you, okay?"

"Thanks," Christy murmured, smiling shyly.

Eda had come to Chandler Elementary School only a month ago. Mrs Mancini had told the class she was from Chicago. During morning break, all the girls had flocked around the pretty newcomer, eager to be her friend, but Christy had kept her distance, knowing she wasn't welcome. Watching intently, she'd wiggled back and forth in a swing.

It hadn't taken the girls long to realize Eda wasn't like them; they were "nice" girls, quiet and well-behaved in starched skirts, their pigtails perfectly braided. Eda had got into a wrestling match with one of the boys and had had to stand in the corner on that very first day at Chandler, and soon all the girls – except Christy – were whispering that Eda was a *tomboy*. And they sure didn't want to have anything to do with a tomboy.

But Christy had been full of admiration. She couldn't imagine anyone being as brave as Eda, who stood up to bigger kids and always did what she wanted to do. She also couldn't figure out why Eda wanted to be her friend when no one else did.

The two girls carried their trays to a table across the room, as far away from the others as they could get. Eda really didn't care about the kids, but Christy couldn't help wishing that they liked her.

Tiffany Simmons, pigtails neatly coiled, plaid dress crisp, came up to the table and handed Eda a small pink envelope. "It's for my birthday party," she said. "My mother met your mother at the Civic Association meeting, and she says I have to invite you." She gave Christy a disapproving once-over and added, "Of course, only *special* kids come to my parties."

Staring down at her soup bowl, Christy took the insult in silence. She knew that "special" meant "rich".

"I don't want to come to your stupid party," Eda said. "I've got better things to do."

"Gee, too bad," Tiffany said, her high voice a squeal of sarcasm. She skipped away, pigtails and plaid skirt bouncing in unison.

"What a dope," Eda said. "I hate snots like that, so stuck up. She acted like she was a princess handing out royal invitations."

23

She peeled the banana and gave half to Christy. "You wanna ride bikes after school?"

"Okay," Christy said. "But I hafta change out of my school clothes. We have a big rule at my house about that."

Probably the biggest rule of all, she thought solemnly as she ate the banana. Her mother, Sarah, had spent an entire paycheck on school clothes for Christy and her brother, Harvey. Harvey Sr had been so mad he'd beaten up Sarah for doing it. Now those clothes had to last as long as possible.

The minute they finished lunch, they went to the playground. Eda's father had given her a new box of coloured chalk, and Eda set it between them on the ground, saying they should draw pictures.

Christy's depicted a mountain lioness with her cubs. "That's so good," Eda said. "I wish I could draw like you. My house looks silly next to your picture."

The school bell rang and the smile on Christy's face vanished. She wanted to go on drawing and talking with Eda, not go back into the prison of the classroom. She hurried to help put the chalk back in the box, then ran with Eda into the school.

As soon as school was over Christy, tightly clutching her bookbag, rushed to find Eda.

"Come on, let's get your bike," Eda said, unchaining hers from the playground fence. Walking her bike beside Christy, they headed across the street. Christy's apartment was over the pizzeria at the corner of Skye and Central streets, in the last of a row of pretty, whitewashed storefronts that made up downtown Aberdeen. The little town was set in the midst of Big Sky Country, a vast stretch of flat land that belied the name of Montana, as it was hundreds of miles to the nearest mountain.

When they reached the pizzeria, Eda stayed on the sidewalk while Christy went inside, calling, "Hi, Mr Venetto. Can I have the key to the garage? I want to get my bike."

"'Course you can," the broad-shouldered man said, looking at the equally broad-shouldered woman behind the counter. An expression of sadness came over both their faces. Christy had seen that look before, but she didn't understand it.

"Wait, *bambina*," Mrs Venetto said. She produced two freshly-made zeppoles. "For you and your little friend."

"Thank you!" Christy said, delighted.

She followed Mr Venetto from the store. His wife watched her, shaking her head. She had heard the screams from upstairs, had seen the bruises on Christy's body. If only there was something more she could do than just give the child a treat once in a while!

And such a pretty child, too, Mrs Venetto thought, despite the almost boyish shortness of her brown hair. She was a frail flower, so delicate she might have been painted with an artist's finest brush.

Outside, Mr Venetto rolled Christy's bike from the garage.

"Thanks, Mr Venetto," Christy said.

"You have fun, *bambina*."

Christy's bike was a rusty, squeaky contraption she'd inherited when Harvey had outgrown it. She felt a little embarrassed bringing it alongside Eda's. *Her* bike was brand new, with the words "PINK LADY" stencilled across the bar in fancy script. Eda didn't seem to notice, but Christy was sure she did. "Watch my bike, while I go upstairs and get out of my school clothes," she said to Eda.

To Christy's surprise, she found a note taped to the locked door. She read it, frowned, and went back downstairs. "I can't go with you," She moped, sitting down on the steps. "Mommy forgot Harvey had a dentist appointment. She says I have to stay here until they get back, and that won't be until five. She didn't have time to get someone to watch me."

Eda made a face, her freckled nose crinkling. "That's so boring! You mean you're just gonna sit here on the stairs for two hours?"

"What else can I do?"

Eda thought for a moment, then smiled. "The dentist's office is only around the corner. Let's find your mom. We'll tell her you want to come to my house."

Christy gnawed her lip, unsure what to do.

"Please, Christy. We could play with my chemistry set. I have a box of Red Hot candies. I'll share."

"Well . . ." Christy looked back at the dimly-lit staircase, where her mother expected to sit for the next two hours. She compared this with the thought of a nice bike ride into Old Winter Hills, Eda's part of town. She wasn't so sure about the chemistry set – it sounded dangerous – but a mouthful of burny, hot cinnamon candies would be wonderful! She nodded. "Okay," she said. "I'll tell her."

They rode through the main part of Aberdeen to the small brick medical building. Christy hopped off her bike. "You wait here," she said.

"I'll come in, too." Eda replied.

"No!" Christy cried.

Eda frowned at her. Christy felt herself growing warm. How could she tell her friend she didn't want her to meet her mother? Christy knew Sarah would be sitting in the waiting room, staring at the wall, moving her lips as if talking to someone no one else could see. If Eda saw her like that, maybe she'd turn against Christy, like the other girls had done.

"I – I mean you need to watch the bikes," Christy stammered.

"Okay," Eda said, still looking puzzled.

Christy pushed her way into the dentist's waiting room. The air was filled with a funny odour, and the chilling sound of a drill issued from the examination room.

Harvey spotted her at once. "What are you doing here?"

Harvey was fifteen years old and had a perpetual scowl on his face. Christy pushed by him, refusing to let him start a fight. "Hi, Mommy," she said, bending down to kiss the woman's cheek.

"Forget it," Harvey said. "She's freaked out again. Too bad she wasn't freaked out enough to forget my appointment."

"Harvey, could you do me a favour?"

"Okay, but you'll owe me," he said grudgingly.

Christy frowned. "I guess so. Harvey, could you tell Mommy I went to Eda Crispin's house? I'll be back before dinner time, before it gets dark, okay? Can you tell her that?"

"Sure," Harvey said.

"You won't forget?"

"I said 'sure,' didn't I?"

Christy nodded, then hurried from the building before he could change his mind.

"I can go," she said. "But I have to be back by five, and I can't do *anything* to get my clothes dirty."

"We'll be careful," Eda said. She knew how strict Christy's father was.

For the next hour and a half, Christy had a great time. Eda had more toys than Christy had ever seen, and she was always willing to share. When it was finally time to go home, Christy felt sad.

"I wish you could stay for dinner," Eda said. "I think the cook is making roast chicken."

28

Christy wondered for a moment what it would be like to have decent meals every night, let alone a cook to prepare them. "Maybe another time," she said.

After saying goodbye, she mounted her bike and sped home. She whizzed by fine brick homes, pink and white azalea bushes no more than flashes to her eyes. These gave way to smaller homes on acre tracts. Christy went by a sump, the drainage from yesterday's storm sending up musty smells. The half block beyond it was solely occupied by a huge grey house. Its front corners were rounded into towers, and old ivy with branches as thick as a man's finger clawed up the rough stone facade.

Christy had always thought the house was haunted. The shades were usually drawn, as if to say, "You are not welcome here." She knew a crazy family lived there. She'd heard grown-ups taling about the Gammels. Christy remembered one time when the mother had been arrested for dumping a bagful of newborn kittens in the middle of Lake Aberdeen. Kittens! How could anyone be so cruel?

She pedalled faster as she approached the house, wanting to be past it as quickly as possible. But as she was speeding by, the front door crashed open, startling her so much that she slammed on her brakes. She slid off the seat, balancing on her toes, as a woman came running towards her, screaming. *"His head! He took off his head!"*

The woman's eyes were wide and crazy, her apron covered with patches of blood. Terrified,

Christy fumbled to get herself mounted again. She wondered frantically if this was Irene Gammel, kitten murderer.

The woman grabbed Christy's blouse. "*Help me! Please! He took off his head!*"

"Lemme go!" Christy pushed the woman away with all her might.

The woman went screaming down the street. Shaking all over, and desperate to get away, Christy got up on her seat, turned, and nearly crashed into a man. He glared at her in a strange way, his eyes full of accusation. Christy felt faint for a moment, fear threatening to black out everything around her. She blinked and the man was gone. Other neighbours had come out to see what was happening.

Christy finally found the strength to pedal away, her heart pounding so wildly she was scared it would burst right through her chest. But the fear from her encounter wasn't nearly as intense as the horror of seeing bloodstains on her blouse, the blouse she was never, ever to get dirty.

She came to a halt across from her apartment, and only then did she feel the sticky warmth against her chest. The blood was all over her blouse, like the red flag a toreador would wave at a bull. It would have that effect on her father, she was certain. He would accuse her of breaking the rules, and he'd beat her within an inch of her life. She just knew it.

As she approached the door that led up to

her apartment, something felt hot in her lower abdomen. She might as well have been a prisoner on death row, heading towards the gas chamber, her young mind was that full of terror. She was sure that if she opened the door and walked up the stairs, she'd wet her pants. Then she'd be whipped twice as hard for doing such a baby thing.

Without much thought, she turned away from the door, got on the bike again, and pedalled down the road. She really didn't know where she was going; only that she had to find some way to make the blouse right again. Ruining an eight-dollar blouse (oh, how many times had her mother quoted that figure) would result in such a bad beating that she'd be wearing long sleeves and dark tights for a week.

She was so blinded by tears that she could hardly see where she was going, and it might have been Divine Guidance that kept her from being killed in rush-hour traffic along Central Street. One pick-up truck barely missed her, the driver shouting something Christy couldn't hear.

The old bike bounced up onto the next curb, rattling down the uneven sidewalk. The town hall sat on this block, a big square brick building with the words *ABERDEEN, EST. 1881* carved into the stone lintel above the door. It was more than a town hall, housing the civic centre, police station, and library as well. It was from the library that a nine-year-old named Lucille Brigham was exiting at the very moment Christy came flying down the street. Just as Christy was blinded by fear, Lucille was completely absorbed by the Dr Seuss book in her hands. She was about to read what happened next on Mulberry Street when she was knocked flat by Christy's speeding bike.

Lucille's pile of books went flying in all directions. She landed on the sidewalk with a scream, long legs poking out from her blue corduroy skirt in a big V. Her black hair hung over her shoulders like a cape. Christy, entangled in the bike, began to sob even louder and harder. And then, in a moment of anger, she began to rip at the blouse. It was a hateful thing now, the cause of so much trouble.

Startled but not really hurt, Lucille was amazed at the smaller girl's tantrum. But when she saw the blood, she had the presence of mind to reach out and grab Christy's arm. "Stop it!" she cried. "Just stop!"

Christy, still howling, ignored her. But Lucille was big for her age, (some people guessed it was closer to thirteen than nine), and she quickly overpowered the distraught girl. "You'll get in trouble if you do that!"

The words were so ironic that they cut through Christy's fury. She sniffed hard and blubbered: "I'm – I'm already in t-trouble!"

Lucille stood up, brushing dirt and grass from her outfit. She looked down at Christy, wide-eyed. Then she carefully pulled the bike from her. "You got hurt," she said. "You should go into the library and let Mrs Greenstrom help you."

"N – no."

"But you're all covered with blood!"

"Not mine. A crazy lady did it to me. She had blood on her hands and then she wiped them on my blouse and now I'm gonna get a . . . get a . . . wh – whipping!"

"Oh, of course you won't!" Lucille insisted. "It wasn't your fault. Your mom and dad can't be that mean, can they?"

The look on Christy's tearful face told the older girl they very well could be. Lucille sighed. She gathered up the fallen books, then helped Christy to her feet. "I live just around the corner," she said. "You can come to my house and we'll wash the blouse."

"But that'll take forever."

"You can say you fell off the bike," Lucille said. A story was forming in her mind. In it, this little girl with the big brown eyes and boy-like brown hair was a princess, held captive by evil people pretending to be her parents. It was up to Lucille to save her. "Yeah," she said, a gleam in her eyes. "You could say you fell off the bike and got knocked unconcious. Maybe you'll still be in trouble, but maybe your mom will be so glad she won't hit you."

Christy sighed, considering this. It was unbelievable even to her young ears, but this other girl was so much older and bigger that it had to be a good idea. She nodded.

She and Lucille began to walk together, the bike between them.

"What's your name?"

33

"Christy Burnett. I'm seven and a half."

"My name's Lucille Brigham. I'm in the fourth grade and I'm head of Student Council."

That didn't mean much to Christy, but she "oohed" appropriately.

"Tell me about the lady with the blood on her hands."

Christy related the story as best as she could, although much of it was a blur.

Lucille's eyes went round with fascination. "I bet she murdered somebody!" she said with something akin to glee. "Everyone in town knows that the whole Gammel family is nuts. She said something about a head? I bet she decapitated someone!"

"Decapi . . .?"

"Means she chopped off someone's head," Lucille said, proud to know the big word. "Can you show me the house tomorrow? Can you?"

"I don't think I'll be going out tomorrow."

They reached a farm, where a yellow house stood back from the road.

"This is my house," Lucille said, leading her along the gravel path. "Come on in, and I'll wash your blouse."

When they entered, Christy's eyes were immediately drawn past the dining room entrance to the sliding doors at the back of the house. They offered view of a large yard. Christy froze for a moment, staring at the horse that ran about a paddock.

"Isn't she cute?" Lucille asked. "She's my

mom's, but I'm allowed to ride her if I'm especially good. Like when I help Daddy with the sugar beets. We grow sugar beets, you know. Daddy's the biggest sugar beet farmer in the county."

"Wow," was all Christy could say.

"Come on," Lucille said. "The washing machine is downstairs. I help my mom with the wash all the time."

They descended the wooden staircase to the basement, entering a dark and damp cellar that smelled a lot like turpentine. It was just a jumble of old clothes and paint cans and boxes to Christy. All she really saw was the gleaming white knight that was the washing machine.

"Your blouse will be as good as new," Lucille said. "Except for that button you tore off."

The button wasn't the worst of it. Christy could live with that. "You sure are nice."

"Thanks."

It was a strange start to a lifelong friendship. It was over an hour later that Christy returned home, and when she did, Harvey Jr. was sitting on the stairs with a grin spread across his face. "Boy, are you gonna get it," he said.

"I – I fell off my bike," Christy lied. "A nice girl took me in to help me, and . . ."

"Save it," Harvey said. "You were supposed to be waiting here on the steps when we got home."

Christy's eyes went round. "Why didn't you tell Mommy I was at Eda's house? You said you would!"

"Did I say that?" Harvey was completely guileless.

"You stupid drip," Christy said. "I really hate you." She pushed by him roughly.

Harvey sneered, "Dad's got the paddle out."

Christy's heart skipped a beat. She wanted to run away again, but she knew there was no escape this time. Trembling all over, her head hanging, she went in to face her punishment.

Her father was a massively big man, and the sight of him towering over her was terrifying. "Where the hell have you been?"

"Daddy, Harvey was supposed to tell . . ."

"Don't make excuses!" Harvey Sr. roared. "You made your mother crazy with worry! She's got enough problems!"

"But, I . . ."

"Enough talk," her father said. "Get in your room. I'll be there in a minute."

Christy ran to her room and sat on the edge of the bed, crying, terrified. She had no idea there was a much greater threat hanging over her. The woman who had wiped blood on her had just run from the scene of a gruesome murder. She was Irene Gammel, and the victim was her husband, Darren. The blood was from the open pipe of his neck, where his head had been just moments earlier.

The crazy expression Christy had seen was probably the most animated Irene had been in years. She was a painfully introverted woman who rarely left her house, and certainly never had anyone to visit. Her neighbours all whispered about the Gammel family and how strange they were. Sometimes, they spoke with pity of Irene and Darren's children, ten-year-old Teddy and four-year-old Adrian.

That evening, the boys were the subject of an intensive search. They had disappeared without a trace, perhaps kidnapped by the same person who had murdered their father.

"I'll bet the old bitch did something to those kids," Harvey Sr. said. He was relaxing in front of the TV, as if he hadn't just finished thrashing his daughter.

"You think she killed 'em?" Harvey Jr. asked with gory fascination.

"Chopped their friggin' little heads right off!" Both father and son laughed out loud.

Christy heard the conversation from her bedroom, and tried to cover her ears, but her mind kept replaying her father's words. Irene had chopped off her little boys' heads. Some grown-ups beat kids up, and some chop off their heads. She fell asleep thinking those horrible thoughts and began to dream.

In the dream, her father was chasing her with the biggest paddle she'd ever seen. It was bigger than a tennis racket and covered with spikes! Christy ran as fast as she could, but she didn't go anywhere. She took a great leap, her legs scrambling in mid-air, but she didn't land. Panic filled her as she desperately tried to make contact with the sidewalk below her. Somehow, in the dream, the inside of the apartment had turned to the street where the Gammel family lived.

Something grabbed her. Christy screamed soundlessly as her father swung her around. But it wasn't her father any more. It was a complete stranger, who pulled her up close to his face and glared at her with the ugly green eyes of a devil. "Keep your mouth shut, girl." He pushed a knife right up to her face, the blade gleaming in light from an unseen source. "Keep it shut or I'll rip your face right off!"

Christy woke up screaming. Her father ran to her, called her a hysterical little bitch because she'd interrupted his TV show, and threatened her with another beating if she didn't keep quiet.

Christy bit her lip, and lay there in silence.

Chapter Two

Eda met Christy on the swings at the schoolyard the next day. Christy was kneeling on the seat, not sitting, and she was wearing long sleeves even though it was very warm out. Eda's hands tightened into fists. She knew what those long sleeves meant. She hated Christy's parents for being so mean. But Christy was smiling.

Eda climbed on the swing next to her and pushed off.

"I made a new friend yesterday," Christy said. "Her name is Lucille and she's in the fourth grade."

"Wow!" Eda cried from up high. She came down and let her heels brake in the sand. "You made friends with a big kid?"

Eda jumped off and ran for the empty seesaw. When she reached it before another kid, she stuck out her tongue in triumph. Christy came up after her and climbed on. Eda saw her wince as her thighs rubbed the wood, but Christy didn't complain. Eda was certain if her daddy walloped her like that she'd complain a whole *lot*.

"Lucille's great," Christy said as they teeter-tottered. She explained how the bigger girl had come to her rescue the day before.

"Didn't keep your daddy from hitting you," Eda grumbled.

Christy lowered her eyes and didn't respond.

"Well, I'm glad that lady didn't get you," Eda went on. "It must have been real scary."

"It was," Christy said with an emphatic nod.

"Gee, my parents were talking about that crazy woman this morning," Eda said. "Her neighbours called the police because she was running around screaming. It's on the front page of Daddy's newspaper."

Eda's father was publisher of the *Aberdeen Chronicle*. About a month earlier, he'd decided life in Chicago was too hectic. He'd spent his childhood in Montana, and when the opportunity came to buy a chain of small-town newspapers there, he took it. It was a big change for Eda, especially having to say goodbye to her friends. Meeting Christy had been the best thing about the move.

"Did your father tell you about the story, Eda?"

Eda shrugged. "Well, not really. Mom says it's grown-up stuff. I wish I could read better, so I could look at it myself."

Christy pouted. "I really want to find out about that Irene Gammel. I got into trouble because of that dummy!"

"But the paper has too many big words to read."

They seesawed for a few more moments. Then Christy's eyes got big.

"Lucille!" she cried. "We can ask Lucille to read the paper to us!"

"Yeah!" Eda said. "I bet a fourth-grader knows lots of big words." She was so excited about the idea that she jumped from the high end of the seesaw, making Christy crash to the ground. Christy gasped in pain. "I'm sorry, Christy!" Eda said, running to her friend's side. "I'm so sorry! Here, here, you can pinch my arm real hard."

"Huh?"

"I mean it," Eda said, holding out her bare arm. There was no need for Eda to wear long sleeves on a warm day. "Pinch it, and we'll be even-Steven."

"Never!" Christy insisted. "Come on, let's find Lucille."

There were two recreation areas at Chandler – one for first, second and third grades, and the other for older children. Long before any of these children had started school, invisible barriers had been set up between the divisions. As Christy and Eda crossed into fourth grade territory, a few kids turned to stare at them. One girl even started walking toward them. Eda saw she had a mean look on her face, but she wasn't afraid. She glared at the big girl, who, much to her surprise, turned away.

"Do you see Lucille?" Eda asked.

Christy looked around. Lucille was taller than

the other girls in her group, and easy to spot. She smiled when she saw her younger friend.

"Hi, Christy," she said. "How'd it go yesterday?"

"Okay," Christy lied. "This is my friend, Eda."

Lucille said hi. Eda mumbled a reply as she gazed at the tall girl. She couldn't take her eyes off Lucille's long, straight, black hair.

"Lucille, can you do us a favour?" Christy asked. "Can you buy one of Eda's daddy's newspapers? There's stuff about Irene Gammel in there, but no one will tell us the story."

Lucille's eyes rounded with glee. "I don't have to buy a paper. I know the story. I wasn't supposed to hear it, either, but my big brother Tom is really cool, and he told me everything.

"What did he say?" Eda asked, excited.

"It was a murrrderrrr," Lucille drawled in a voice that made her sound like the announcer on "Chiller Theater"

Both girls gasped.

"Tom says she went upstairs to her bedroom and found her husband there," Lucille said. "Only it wasn't his whole body. Just his head. And there was blood all over the place!"

Eda turned to Christy, who looked very sick. It was murder blood that woman had rubbed on her yesterday!

But Lucille was talking again: "That's not the worst part," she said. "The worst part is that they had two kids and no one knows where they are!"

A fifth-grader named Eddie, who was playing nearby, added his two-cents worth: "She cut the body in little pieces and made the kids eat 'em!"

"Stop talking like that!" Christy begged.

Lucille made a bored face. "Flake off, Eddie."

"Squares," Eddie said, gathering up his marbles to put them in a leather sack.

Eda looked up at Lucille. Boy, she sure was big. Maybe seven feet tall. "What's the rest of the story?"

"Well, the police are looking everywhere for Teddy and Adrian Gammel, of course. And they've got that woman in jail. But Tom says she'll probably get out because she probably didn't do it."

"What do you think, Lucille?"

"I think," she said, "that the kids are either dead or far, far away. They'll look and look, but they'll never find them. Well, maybe not for years and years. It's like the little princes in England."

"Who?"

"A long, long time ago," Lucille explained, "there were these two little princes in England. One of them was supposed to grow up and be king. Anyway, they disappeared one night. Nobody found them until years later, when they were doing some work in the palace. They tore down a wall and found two little skeletons behind it."

"Yuck," Eda said, making a face.

43

"I don't want to talk about this any more," Christy said. "It scares me."

The bell rang, and the children lined up to return to their classrooms. It seemed to Eda that the day dragged on *forever*, but at last the final bell rang.

"Can we go to your house today?" Eda asked as they walked out of the school yard. Eda rolled her bike between them.

"I don't know," Christy said. "I have to see if Mommy's okay."

Eda wasn't exactly sure why Christy had to see if Mrs Burnett was okay every time she wanted to play.

"All right," Eda said. "If she isn't okay, you can come to my house again."

Christy smiled. "I like your house better. You have so many toys."

Christy had very few playthings, but Eda didn't care. She lived over a pizzeria, and that was *neat*.

Eda *had* noticed some bad things about the Burnett apartment, but she was too nice to say so. It was always so *dark* in there. And it smelled funny. One time when she was living in Chicago, her father had brought her down to the police station with him. He went there a lot to do newspaper stories, so when he took her it had been a big treat. She loved watching the policemen at work. The captain even let her sit on his desk and got ice cream for her. But a scary thing had happened. An ugly man with filthy clothes came up to her. He smiled a smile with no teeth, and tried to touch her. Eda wasn't usually afraid, but she was glad when her daddy pulled her into his arms and a policeman took the man away. He had smelled *terrible*. That was the smell she sometimes noticed in Christy's apartment.

But when Christy opened the door and led Eda inside, she was completely surprised. Today, the apartment was immaculately clean and smelled like Christmas trees. All the windows were opened, letting in fresh air.

"Gee," Christy said. She was as surprised as Eda.

Sarah Burnett was busy dusting the coffee table. She was wearing a crisp white apron over a lavender dress, and her hair was combed into a flip. She looked up and smiled.

"Hello, sweet angel," she said to Christy. "Hello, Eda."

"Hi, Mrs Burnett," Eda said. She couldn't say more. It was the first time Christy's mother had ever greeted her.

"It smells good in here, Mommy," Christy said.

Sarah put her hands on her hips and looked around the room with a satisfied expression. "Yep, been pretty busy. Place sure needed cleanin'." She turned and went back to work.

Christy led Eda into her room, where she changed out of her school clothes, carefully hanging up her blouse and jumper. Then she sat on her bed and pulled off her stockings. Eda gasped to see the purple bruises that covered her friend's legs. "Oh, Christy, does it hurt a lot?"

"Only if I touch them," Christy said, blushing. She quickly pulled on a pair of jeans. She was usually embarrassed to wear castoffs from Goodwill in front of Eda, but today she was just grateful they were loose enough not to bind her legs. As she fastened a safety pin at the waist, she asked: "What do you want to do?"

"I dunno," Eda said. "Play dolls?"

"I only have one doll," Christy said. "I have lots of paper and crayons. Want to draw?"

Eda didn't like drawing very much, because she wasn't good at it, but she knew it would make Christy happy. They stretched out on the floor and began to sketch with crayons.

"You know what?" Christy asked after a while. "I don't think Lucille knew the whole story."

"Why?"

"Well, I think something more happened."

Eda sat up, Indian-style. She leaned forward and reached for a green crayon to scribble leaves on a tree. "How come?"

"I'm not sure. I had a real bad dream last night, and in it a man tried to hurt me with a knife." She shivered. The dream came back vaguely, nothing more than a pair of ugly green eyes and a flash of metal.

"Maybe you were just scared," Eda suggested. "Like when you watch 'Chiller Theater' or 'Twilight Zone'. Those shows give me nightmares."

"I don't watch them." Christy coloured for a few more moments, filling in a rainbow.

"Well," Eda said, "I sure hope you don't dream them again."

"Me too."

Eda picked up a red crayon and coloured apple blobs on her tree. Christy found a black crayon and started to draw clouds over her pretty rainbow. She made them really dark, really big, and really scary looking. Soon, they blocked out the rainbow completely.

On Saturday morning, Christy moved very quietly through the apartment. It was her father's day to sleep in after a long week at the Cable and Wire Factory. Waking him up, even by accident, was a great way to invite a whipping. She tiptoed to the front door and carefully opened it. She walked slowly down the creaky staircase. First step, second step, skip the third that made a loud sound. She couldn't risk it. One time she'd made a noise on the stairs, waking her father. He'd come out and knocked her down the whole flight.

As soon as she got out the door, however, a grin spread across her face and she broke into a run. Just as she was crossing the street, she saw someone appear from behind a tree. She slammed to a stop and gaped at the man. He was staring hard at her, one hand raised high as if to strike. Christy's eyes were drawn to something that glittered in the sunlight. A knife? She didn't wait to find out.

"Chrisssteee," the man breathed.

With a scream, Christy ran into the school playground. Eda and Lucille were taking turns on the slide. Lucille jumped off, her blue shoes kicking up sand; when she saw Christy running towards them.

"Someone's after me!" Christy yelled.

Eda and Lucille hurried to her. Christy pointed behind herself. "There's a crazy man after me, and he has a knife!"

Her two friends looked beyond her, then at each other. Seeing the confused look on their faces, she looked herself to see an empty street. It was as if no one had been there at all. "He was *there*." Christy insisted. "He said my name in a real scary way and came after me with a sharp knife!"

"Maybe he's hiding," Lucille said, fascination in her voice.

"Oh, let's get out of here," Christy said. "He scares me!"

"Maybe you should tell someone," Eda suggested. "My dad's best friend is a cop, and . . ."

Christy shook her head vigorously. "Oh, no," she said. "Then he'd talk to my father, and my father would hit me for bringing a police officer up to the apartment. My father hates the police ever since that time he got . . ." She was going to say "arrested", but the word was almost as shameful as the night her father had got so drunk he had beaten up two men at Shrank's Bar & Grill.

"Well, okay then," Eda said. "But you shouldn't

48

let that guy scare you and not tell a grown-up. Maybe you can talk to our teacher on Monday."

"Maybe," Christy said half-heartedly.

Lucille adusted her pink gingham headband and changed the subject rather abruptly. "Well, are you ready?" she asked.

"For what?" Christy asked.

"Eda and I were talking. We want to go to the murder house."

Christy backed away, shaking her head. "Oh, no! I'm not going to that terrible place again!"

"Don't be such a baby," Eda said. "We just want to look at it."

"It's empty, anyhow," Lucille said. "That lady is in jail. What could happen?"

"Besides, you're the only one of us who knows where it is."

Christy shifted from one foot to the other. "I don't remember," she lied. "Besides, the pizzeria is still closed. I can't get my bike."

"We walked this morning," Eda said. "Now, come on, Christy. We're just going to walk past it, okay?"

"Please?" Lucille implored.

Christy looked from one to the other. How could she disappoint the only people who really cared about her? She'd met Lucille only two days ago. Maybe if Lucille thought she was a baby, she wouldn't want to be her friend. And the house *was* empty now . . . An image flashed in her mind: eyes, hateful and staring. They were the eyes she'd seen in her dream.

"Christy?" Lucille pressed.

Christy rubbed her arms and forced the image away. "Oh, okay! But I'm staying across the street."

She did exactly that when they reached the house, but Lucille and Eda ran ahead, stopping at the end of the walkway.

"I'm going to take a closer look!" Lucille announced. "I'll bet there's blood!"

"Oh, don't!" Christy yelled, but Lucille was already walking up the path to the house, Eda closely behind her. "Please, come back!" She was terrified something would grab her friends. *But that's silly* she told herself. *There's no one there*!

Suddenly, she felt a hand clamp around her arm. She was turned around, and faced a man with faded blue eyes. His breath had a spicy smell, like the beefsticks her father chewed when he watched "The Red Skelton Show".

"You and your little pals oughta stay away from that devil house," he said. "Weird place, weird family. Always had the shades drawn, never acted friendly. And those noises at night, out in that big field in back. Big bulldozer digging. Probably buryin' something . . ."

Christy finally found enough voice to let out a small scream. The man let her go as Eda and Lucille came running across the street.

"Get away!" Eda cried, fists raised.

"You get away!" the old man retorted. "Get away from that devil house!"

Christy broke into a run. Her thoughts were so

wild she didn't hear Eda and Lucille begging her to wait up. Maybe the man with the ugly green eyes was watching her, maybe he would grab her as easily as the old man had, maybe there really was blood all over the house . . .

"*Christeee*"

Eda's shout cut through her panic, but Christy didn't stop until she reached the park near the lake. She plunked down into a swing, tears spilling from her eyes. "I told you I didn't want to go there!"

"Well, we didn't know an old guy was going to grab you!" Eda said defensively.

"Are you okay, Christy?" Lucille asked. "He didn't hurt you, did he?"

Christy thought a moment, then shook her head. "I guess not. He just talked about that family. He said they were weird and did funny things at night.

"Like what?" Eda asked.

"I don't know," Christy said. She gazed down the hill to the water. It was speckled with fallen leaves of red, orange and yellow and looked pretty. "You want to take a walk along the lake?"

But Lucille wasn't going to let her off that easily. "Maybe they were witches," she said, a gleam coming into her eyes. "Maybe they had a coven and they danced naked in the moonlight and made blood sacrifices . . ."

"Stop it, Lucille!" Christy begged.

"What's a coven?" Eda wanted to know.

Another voice cut into their conversation.

"Aww, there's no such thing as witches."

The girls stared up at the young police officer who'd suddenly appeared. He tried to look stern, but his face was too handsome and his eyes too bright to succeed.

"Hi, Officer Mike!" Eda cried.

Mike Hewlett looked around. "I'm surprised your parents let you out alone."

Eda giggled. "I always go out by myself. I'm nearly eight, you know."

"I know you're a big girl, Eda," Mike said. "But it's dangerous to wander around without an adult these days."

"'Cause of the murder?" Eda asked.

"And the kidnappings," Mike replied.

"Do you think they'll find those boys?" Christy inquired. She wanted to ask if they'd caught the man with the mean eyes, but she was afraid of sounding silly. It had just been a dream, hadn't it?

"I hope so," Mike said. "We're certainly doing all we can."

As if to prove the point, the sound of a dog barking came from the nearby woods. The children looked across the lake to see half a dozen hounds exiting the trees, closely followed by their trainers.

"Those men are looking for the missing kids, aren't they?" Lucille asked.

"That's right," Mike said. "Teddy and Adrian Gammel. Teddy is in the fifth grade in your school. Do you know him?"

The girls shook their heads.

"Adrian is just a baby, barely four years old," Mike continued. "You kids would do well to say a prayer in church for their safety."

"You know I can't go to church," Eda said. "I'm Jewish."

"Then go to temple," Mike said. "But listen, no matter where you go, stay in a group. We don't know what happened to the Gammel boys. The kidnapper could be far away, or right here in Aberdeen."

"But . . . but we thought their mother . . ." Eda said.

"Irene Gammel was let out of jail this morning," Mike replied. "There was another . . . a similar killing last night. She's innocent."

"Where was the killing?" Lucille asked. "Did any other kids disappear?"

"Never mind where it was," Mike said. "And no, no kids disappeared this time. Let's keep it that way. You walk back to town together, okay?"

He headed toward the squad car that was parked in the nearby lot, casting a farewell smile over his shoulders.

"Mike's okay," Eda said. "He treats me like a grown-up, not a baby."

"How come you call him Mike?" Christy asked. "He's an adult!"

The girls started to walk.

"He's my father's friend. When we moved to Aberdeen, and Daddy wanted to do a story on

53

houses that were robbed, Mike's the one who helped him."

"He's real cute," Lucille said.

Eda shrugged. She hadn't really noticed. Now she looked around. "Well, what do you want to do now?"

"Let's get our bikes," Lucille suggested. "We can ride around town a little, then stop at The Ice Cream Cottage. My treat, guys."

"It's safe there," Christy agreed, "with so many people."

"My house is nearest," Lucille said. "We'll get mine first."

The girls enjoyed riding through town, stopping to look at the new display in the toy store window, "oohing" over rabbits in the pet store window. They circled the town square several times and rode in and out of alleys. Eda was always way ahead of the others. They called to her to wait up, but no sooner did they reach her than she was off again. Finally, Lucille got tired of the chase and sped up herself. Christy didn't dare force her rickety old bike to do more work, and so she had to wait until her friends circled around and met her again. She stopped in front of the bakery and wished she could eat everything in the window.

As she was admiring an apple strudel, someone came up behind her. It was a man, and he stood very close to her. Christy's eyes were brought up to his head, his flat-top haircut making it look very square. But it was his eyes that grabbed her. Even in their reflection they were ugly eyes, like in her dream. She was about to move away when he raised his hand – and something flashed in the sunlight.

Christy was sure it was a knife. He'd been following her ever since she saw him earlier, and now he was going to kill her!

Fear choked off any attempt at a scream. Instead, she stumbled up onto her bike, not daring to look back, racing until she reached her friends. She was so upset she nearly crashed into the back of Eda's bike.

"What's the big idea?"

"There was that man again . . . that man with a knife, and . . ."

"Catch your breath, Christy," Lucille suggested.

Christy gulped in big bubbles of air, then finally calmed down enough to tell what had happened.

"We better find Officer Mike," Eda said.

"We'll ride back down to the lake," Lucille said. "But first, Christy, we'll take a look."

Christy led them back to the main part of town. She looked up and down the road, trying to spot the man who'd tried to kill her. Finally, to her terror, she saw him walking slowly by the medical building. "There he is!" she cried, pointing.

Lucille and Eda looked carefully in that direction. Then Lucille began to laugh.

"It isn't funny, Lucille!" Eda said.

"Oh, yes it is," Lucille insisted. "Christy,

you're a nut. That's old man Pierpont. Mother says he's a drunk, but Daddy says he wouldn't hurt a fly."

The old man raised a hand, as he had done near Christy, and metal flashed in the sunlight. With a cry, she covered her eyes.

Lucille put a hand on her arm. "Christy, that isn't a knife," she said. "That's the thing he drinks out of. It's okay."

Christy didn't uncover her face. Was this what she was going to feel like until they caught the murderer? Was every man who came close to her, every flash of metal, suspect?

"Come on, Christy," Lucille said. "I think it's time we stopped to have that ice cream."

"Sounds good to me," Eda agreed.

Christy tried to push thoughts of the evil man aside as they went to the Ice Cream Cottage. They parked their bikes out front, then took seats along the counter. Soon, Christy was enjoying a butterscotch sundae. For a few moments, she was able to forget the scare she'd had. "Thanks, Lucille," she said. "This is great."

Lucille smiled at her. Just then, the bells over the door jingled, and another group of girls came in. Eda moaned to see Tiffany Simmons among them.

"Oh, brother," she said. "Here comes the snob of the ages." She caught Tiffany's reflection in the mirror and made a face. Tiffany sneered at her.

"Ewww," she said. "There's white trash in here! Maybe we better leave."

"Do us a favour," Eda shot back.

Tiffany indicated a plump girl standing at her side. "Miranda saw Christy running to the school playground this morning, screaming like she was crazy. Maybe we'll call her Crazy Christy, instead of Creepy Christy."

"Just ignore her," Lucille whispered.

Tiffany and her friends headed to an empty table. She brushed very close to Christy, causing her to drop a spoonful of ice cream in her lap.

"Oh, no!" Christy yelped.

"Sorry," Tiffany singsonged. "It was an accident."

Eda was off her chair in an instant. "Was not! You did that on purpose!"

Lucille grabbed her arm. "No, Eda! You can't fight in here!"

Eda glared at the other little girl. Tiffany was the picture of innocence. "I'll get you," she vowed.

Christy got off her seat. "I've got to clean this up," she said. "I'll be right back."

She went to the rest room at the back of the store. As she was standing at the sink, dabbing her sweater with a paper towel, she thought she heard something move in the stall. She looked over and saw two legs in faded jeans, and a pair of old boots. This was a girls' room, but that was no girl in there.

"Christy . . ." It was a man's voice, deep and evil. And deadly familiar. Christy froze.

"I've come for you, Christy . . ."

The door started to open. Christy found her voice and began to scream, turning to run from the room. "He's in there! He's in there!"

Lucille and Eda ran to her. Tiffany and her friends watched from their table with disdain. The owner of the store hurried to see what was wrong.

"There's a man in there," Christy said. "It's the man who took the Gammel boys! He's after me now!"

Quickly, the manager ran into the bathroom. He came back a few moments later, shaking his head. "There's no one there at all," he said. "Maybe you better leave now."

"But I heard him!"

Lucille put a firm hand around Christy's elbow. Together, the three girls left the ice cream parlour.

"I did hear him," Christy insisted, tears streaming down her face. "He said he'd come for me! What am I gonna do?"

Eda and Lucille looked at each other. They just didn't know what to say to make their friend feel better.

"They're planning to drag the lake this afternoon."

A week had passed since the Gammel boys' disappearance. Christy was spending Saturday afternoon at Eda's house. They sat in the middle of a bedroom that seemed as big as the Burnett's apartment, surrounded by Barbie and all her accessories. But the dolls lay forgotten on the floor as the girls knelt down close to an air vent and eavesdropped. Eda's parents were talking in the parlour, directly connected by a heating vent to her bedroom.

The children leaned closer to the vent.

"Oh, Dean," Eda's mother said. "Do you really think those poor little things are . . . dead?"

"If you ask me, Rita," Dean Crispin told his wife, "I think they're alive someplace."

"Well!" Rita said. "I refuse to fall into a false sense of security just because there was no kidnapping with the second murder. What's Sheriff Barnard doing to protect our children?"

Eda had to clasp a hand over her mouth to keep from giggling. Through the vent, the sheriff's name sounded like "Barnyard".

Christy put a finger to her lips.

"We'll find out at the rally tonight," Dean said. "Now, Rita, I've got the *Sunday Gazette* to print. I'll be back by dinner."

When it seemed obvious the conversation was over, the girls crawled away from the vent. Christy took hold of a teddy bear and held it tightly. She hoped Mr Crispin was right. She hoped the Gammel boys were alive. It wasn't *their* fault their family was weird. They were just kids! But if they were alive, where were they? What was happening to them, right now, right at the same time she was safe and sound in a pretty room? "Eda?" she asked softly. "What does 'drag the lake' mean? It sounds scary."

"They're looking for bodies under the water," Eda replied, making a disgusted face. "But I think Daddy's right. I think Teddy and Adrian are alive."

Christy felt icy across the back of her neck. She didn't like talking about dead kids; even kids who, maybe, weren't dead at all. "I saw posters for that rally," she said. "Your Daddy put them up all over town."

"Are your parents going?"

Christy shrugged, then slowly shook her head. What would her parents care about protecting children? They did a pretty good job hurting their own right at home.

"Well, mine are, of course," Eda said. "And you know what? I'm going, too."

"What do you mean you're going?" Christy asked in disbelief. "It's at night. You can't go out at night."

"I'm gonna sneak out," Eda said. "My parents won't be here, and the servants will all be busy."

Christy's eyes were full of worry. "But if you get caught," she said, "you'll be whipped for sure!"

"I won't get caught," Eda insisted.

The terrified look on Christy's face told Eda she'd need more reassurance. It wasn't enough to say that her parents never laid a hand on her.

"I'll keep hidden in the bushes," she said, "and I'll come home long before anyone knows I'm gone."

"But why do you want to go?"

"Because no one will tell us a thing," Eda said. "And I bet the grown-ups do plenty of talking tonight." She jumped up. "Come on, let's check the kitchen," she said. "I'm hungry."

Christy followed her out into the hall and down a huge staircase, hoping there would be something delicious to eat. Christy planned to take all that was offered. It might be the best she had to eat all day.

That night, Eda gave her parents fifteen minutes' head start, then snuck out of the house. It was slightly less than a mile's walk into town, but the crisscross of shadows and light from the street lamps made the roads seem to stretch forever. Eda wasn't afraid of the dark, but out here in the night, out where a killer might be hiding, she felt strange.

She turned a corner and saw a pair of glowing eyes peering out from behind some bushes. Yellow eyes, like the devil might have. Eda stopped short, staring at the pinpoints of light. Were they staring back, she wondered? Was something going to pounce?

Then one light disappeared, quickly followed

by the other. The devil was gone. Eda started to walk faster, wanting to get to town right *now*. In minutes, she reached the relative safety of the bushes surrounding the town hall.

It seemed to her, as she gazed through the branches, that every single mom and dad in town was in front of those wide steps. Eda's father stood high above the others, a hand resting on the head of a stone lion. People were carrying signs. Just beginning second grade, there were many that Eda couldn't read, but she could make out words like "SAVE OUR CHILDREN".

Her father waved both hands over his head to silence the crowd, then began to speak. Eda thought he looked very handsome, and very important, in his best grey suit.

"We have come here tonight," Dean Crispin began, "to demand action! We demand to know what is being done to protect our loved ones, especially our children, from the madman who stalks our town! Two murders have been committed, will there be more?"

Shouts from the crowd; Eda wished she could understand what they were yelling.

"An innocent boy has vanished! Will there be more?"

More shouts.

"We must protect our homes and families!"

Signs bounced up and down and fists waved in fury. Eda watched her father in fascination.

"WHERE ARE THOSE CHILDREN, SHER-
IFF BARNARD?"

A hand fell lightly on the back of Eda's neck.
She froze, her shoulders pulling up, her eyes
widening.

"I know where those boys are," a voice whispered. "Do you want to see them? I think I'd like
you to see them."

Eda was too frightened to answer.

"But I don't want you, little girl," the voice
said. "I want your friend. They call her 'Creepy
Christy', don't they? Cruel children! Such a
beauty! So perfect for . . ."

Eda found her strength at last, and ducked
down quickly. Free of the stranger's grasp, she
stumbled away and started to run as fast as she
could. In her fear, it didn't even occur to her
that her parents were right there, right near a
police station. She just ran blindly, certain the
killer was right behind her. She'd never reach
home in time! He'd catch her, and maybe cut
off her head, or make her disappear like Teddy
and Adrian Gammel, or . . .

She suddenly remembered that Christy lived
nearby. The safety of her apartment was much
closer than Eda's own home, so she headed in
that direction. She was relieved to see a light on
in Christy's room.

Eda tucked herself into the doorway of the
pizzeria. She looked down the street, only to find
it completely deserted. With a sigh of relief, she
stepped onto the sidewalk again and went up to

the Burnetts' apartment door. But she stopped, thinking: what if Christy's parents were home? Did she dare knock on the door? How would she explain what she was doing there?

She danced from one sneaker to the other – it was getting cold out here. Then a smile spread across her face. She could climb up to Christy's window! It would be easy – first she'd use the stones in the wall as footholds, then she'd catch the fire escape and go up that way. It would be as easy as climbing monkey bars.

In minutes, Eda was tapping at Christy's window.

Inside the house, Christy looked up from the picture she was drawing. Someone was tapping at her window! She turned to look at the curtains, drawn tightly now. If she opened them, would a pair of ugly green eyes be looking at her? Then, faintly, she heard: "*Christy! Open up! It's Eda!*"

Eda? Christy jumped up and hurried to the window. Carefully, she pulled a tiny bit of the curtain back. When she saw her friend, she opened the window. "What are you doing out there?"

"Christy, the killer almost got me!" Eda said breathlessly, climbing through the window.

"Oh, no!"

Eda took a deep breath. "Where are your parents?" she asked, sitting on the edge of the bed. "I didn't see them at the rally."

"Mom's inside, watching 'Bewitched'," Christy said. "Daddy's . . . out."

Eda nodded, and told her friend what had happened. When she finished, Christy said: "Maybe you should tell that policeman."

"Officer Mike?" Eda asked. "Are you kidding? My parents would *kill* me if they knew I snuck out."

Christy lowered her eyes.

"Oh, well, they wouldn't really kill me," Eda amended quickly. "But I'd be grounded forever. Besides which, well, I didn't really get a good look at him. They wouldn't know who to look for. But Christy, he asked about *you*. Why would he do that? Is he the guy you dreamed about?"

"I . . . I don't know," Christy said. *Green eyes, flashes of metal . . .* She looked at Eda with fear in her eyes. "Maybe he knows I saw that woman," she said. "What am I going to do, Eda? No one would believe me now."

Eda bounced on the edge of the bed. "Gee, I wish I could have heard more at the rally!" She said.

Christy went to the window and looked out, half-expecting to see someone lurking under the street lamp.

Eda leaned down and picked up the picture Christy had been drawing. "This is good," she said. "Those look just like real leaves."

"It's the tree across the street," Christy replied.

"I wish I could draw like you," Eda said. "Hey, Christy, I gotta go home now."

"All by yourself?"

"You sure can't walk me," Eda replied. "Don't worry, I'll be okay. I'll run as fast as I can."

Christy was worried for Eda, but could see there was no other choice. "Wait a second," she said.

She left the room, then came back with a pocket knife. "Harvey keeps it in his dresser," she said. She didn't tell her friend that Harvey's dresser was actually the bottom drawer of his parents' bureau.

"Won't he be mad?"

"He won't even know it's gone," Christy said. "Grandpa gave it to him for Christmas a few years ago. He never even uses it. Says pocket knives are for wimps."

She leaned closer to her friend and whispered, even though no one could hear them. "He's got a switch blade."

"Wow!"

Eda put the pocket knife inside her jacket. Then she turned and opened the window. As she climbed out she said: "I'll call you tomorrow morning."

"Let's call Lucille, too," Christy said. "Maybe she'll want to play with us again."

Eda nodded, then disappeared down the fire escape. Christy held her breath as she jumped from the bottom, but Eda landed squarely on her feet. She waved her hands over her head, then ran off.

Across the street, a stranger waited until

Christy's curtain was drawn before stepping out of the darkened doorway of the hardware store. He smiled with satisfaction. He now knew exactly where Christy lived.

Chapter Three

Now that Eda had also seen, or rather heard, the man, Christy didn't feel quite so alone. She tried to tell her mother about the man, but Sarah was even quieter than ever and didn't seem to hear her. Harvey only laughed at her, saying he'd heard people were calling her Crazy Christy now. Someone had seen her running across the street, screaming. Another kid had heard her tell her friends someone was after her, but there had been no one in the street at all. *No one at all.*

"But Eda saw him, too!"

"When?" Harvey demanded. "When did she see him?"

Christy was about to tell, but suddenly remembered Eda's worry she'd be punished if her parents found out she'd gone out at night. She'd never actually seen Eda's parents hit her, and they didn't seem to be mean people. But hitting was what parents did when they were mad, and if Eda got a beating it would be her fault for tattling. She clamped her mouth shut. Harvey only sneered in disdain, accusing her of making things up.

It was the time of the Cuban Missile Crisis, and

the new topic on everyone's lips was Communism. People still talked about Teddy and Adrian, but not as much as before. It was almost as if, now that their mother had gone off to Washington State, that there was no one left to care about them. But Christy cared. She thought of them quite often.

All the children were learning "Duck and Cover" from a film featuring a little turtle in an army helmet. Seeing those blasts of light terrified Christy, but Eda thought it was all very silly.

"Like ducking under a picnic blanket is going to keep you from being burned up by a bomb," she scoffed.

"I'm glad they're all the way off in Cuba," Lucille had said. "I'm glad we don't live in Florida."

Most of the time, Christy didn't think about the impending Communist threat. At seven, she was really too young to understand. But she wasn't too young to understand that two little boys were missing and it seemed they'd never be found. And now someone seemed determined to snatch her, too, to make her disappear.

She used to drag her feet on the way to school, unwilling to face the teasing of her classmates. Even with Eda there, kids like Tiffany could be terribly cruel. But nowadays, after that man had nearly grabbed her in the street, she raced towards the relative safety of the schoolyard.

She was in such a hurry one morning that she tripped over an untied shoelace and slammed hard on one knee. To her horror, her stocking knee had ripped open when it made contact with the rough pavement. Christy stared at it, sitting in the middle of the road. She was going to get a whipping!

A car's horn honked wildly, and at the last moment Christy looked up. She froze in terror at the sight of the oncoming vehicle. It swerved to avoid her, but at the same instant someone picked her up. She turned her head quickly to see her saviour, but one look at red hair and green eyes made her thrash and kick.

The man held fast to her. "Just wanted to remind you," he whispered. "My axe is still sharp."

Christy gave him a hard kick and ran into the school. She nearly slammed into the principal, who scolded her without even seeing how distraught the child was. Christy couldn't stop crying, and it was the school nurse who finally helped her relax. She explained what had happened. The janitor, a burly man, went outside to look. When he came back, he spoke softly on the other side of the curtain that surrounded Christy's cot. She heard him say none of the other children had seen a thing, except that Christy was nearly run over because she was sitting in the middle of Central Street. There was talk of her mother being crazy, and something about apples not falling far from trees. Finally, the principal had assured her that although they were all worried about many things these days, there was no point in hysteria. Nobody had grabbed Christy. She was to be a big girl and stop her nonsense.

But she couldn't be big. They were watching another turtle movie when something made her look through a crack in the shade. The man was standing across the street, the shining blade of his knife held high. He slashed it through the air, as if he knew she was watching him.

Christy started screaming, and no amount of cajoling could quiet her. She finally had to be sent home. Because her mother was in no shape to watch her, her father had been called from work. He pretended to be very concerned when the principal stood talking to him, but the moment she left he took out the ping pong paddle and began to beat Christy for making him miss the money earned for an afternoon's work.

She vowed at that moment she'd never talk to another adult about her fears again. What was the point, when no one believed her? There was only Eda and Lucille, and only they would know the truth.

The Brigham's station wagon was pulling out of the driveway just as Christy and Eda rode up on their bikes about a week later. Lucille poked her head out the window and waved. "We're going to get fabric for costumes!" she said. "Wanna come? Can they come, Mom?"

"If they want to squeeze in," Mrs Brigham said.

The girls parked their bikes behind the house,

then wiggled in next to Lucille. Her brother, five-year-old Stannie, groaned and pushed himself as close to the window as possible to avoid touching his sister. Eda leaned over and stuck out her tongue at him. Stannie crossed his eyes in response.

"Halloween's coming up pretty fast," Mrs Brigham said. "Have you girls decided what you're going to be?"

"I saw a cowgirl costume in the Sears catalogue," Eda said. "It's got fringe and little silver buttons."

"Mom's making all our costumes," Lucille said. "I'm going to be a witch this year."

"I'm gonna be a cat!" said three-year-old Greta.

Mrs Brigham tilted her head back a little as she drove. "How about you, dear?" she asked Christy. "Have you decided on your costume?"

Christy hadn't even thought about Halloween. How could she tell them she didn't have a costume, that she probably never would? "Not really," she said, softly.

There was silence in the car for a few minutes, except for the baby's babbling. Then, as she turned into downtown Aberdeen, Mrs Brigham said: "Maybe Lucille could lend you a costume. What about that pink costume you wore to your recital a few years ago?"

"Oh, Mom, that's perfect," Lucille responded. She held up both hands. "It is *so* beautiful, Christy. You can be a fairy princess."

73

A shy smile spread across Christy's face. Maybe she could have fun on Halloween, after all.

They parked in front of Wittig's Five-and-Ten and got out. Entering the store, Mrs Brigham wheeled the baby to the pattern books, her children following like little ducks. The store was the biggest in town, with rows and rows of shelves cluttered with merchandise. While her mother was looking at fabric, Lucille led her friends to the candy and toy counter. Glass apothecary jars lined the wall near the cash register, each one brimming with treats. Christy stared up at them, wishing she had a penny or two. Those malt balls looked delicious, or maybe the licorice, or the MaryJanes . . .

A whirring noise made her turn. Stannie had found a friction gun. A blue and red wheel shot sparks as he pulled the trigger.

"Get lost, Stannie," Lucille said. She reached into her pocket. "Let's pick out some candy. We can each have one thing. Then I'll have two pennies left for Stannie and Greta."

They were looking at the candy when two women, laden with bags, stopped near them.

"Did you hear that Gammel woman left town?" one said. "As if her boys don't matter none!"

"I still say she's guilty," said the second. "She had blood all over her. You mark my words, they'll . . ."

Eda poked Christy in the ribs. "They're talking about the murder," she whispered.

74

They pretended to be busy choosing candy while they eavesdropped.

"Well, my sister's beautician lives down the block from them," the first woman was saying, "and she told my sister that they were the most unfriendly family. Her son is in Teddy Gammel's class. Said the boy was always dirty. He was sent home with head lice! I wouldn't be surprised if Irene Gammel beat those poor children."

"Who knows what her husband was like?"

"Well, it's just disgraceful," the first said, "her leaving town like that. If my children had vanished, I'd stay right here until they were found. It just proves, in my mind, that she's guilty."

"But what about the other murder?"

Lucille's younger sister, Greta came running into the aisle. "Mommy's ready to go," she said.

"Now?" Lucille whined, disappointed.

"Yes, now," Mrs Brigham called from across the store.

Lucille looked at her friends with surprise. How could her mother have such good hearing? Disappointed they couldn't hear more about Irene Gammel, the children made their candy choices, and Lucille paid. Then they all went out to the car, enjoying their treats. Christy had picked a jawbreaker because she thought it would last the longest. Besides, it was fun to take it out of her mouth every few minutes to see the colour change.

In the car, Lucille told her mother what they'd overheard. "Why would Teddy and Adrian's mother leave them?" she asked as she tied knots in a candy shoestring.

"I think that poor Mrs Gammel was trying to get away from gossips like those women," Mrs Brigham said. "Let's not talk about it. Does anyone want ice cream?"

The vote was unanimous, and by the time they pulled up to the ice cream parlour, the Gammels were forgotten.

On Halloween night, Christy pulled on the pink leotard and sparkling silver-pink tutu Lucille had given her. It was a little big, but Mrs Brigham had taken it in in a few places, and Christy couldn't help feeling pretty.

She wanted to have fun tonight. She hadn't had the dream about ugly green eyes or flashes of metal in several weeks, and thoughts of murder and kidnappings were all but gone from her mind.

She walked into the living room, where her father slouched in his chair. He was drinking beer and watching a football game.

She tried to sneak by him, but he turned and said: "Where'd you find that get-up?"

Christy swallowed, her heart beginning to race. Was her night going to be ruined? "Lucille Brigham gave it to me," she said softly.

Harvey Sr. grunted. "No loss to her."

Wanting to get away before he could say more, Christy hurried from the apartment. Eda and Lucille were waiting on the corner. Blonde braids peeked out from under Eda's pale blue cowgirl hat, the silver fringe of her jacket ruffled in the wind. Lucille wore a funny nose and a wig. "You look great, Christy!" she cackled in her best witch voice.

"Thanks," Christy replied.

Her brother seemed to appear from nowhere, a pillowcase in his hand. Christy could only guess what nasty tricks were hidden there.

"This Halloween business is all bull, y'know," Harvey said. "It said on the news the Russians are building missile bases all over Cuba. I bet they'll bomb us any day now."

"Don't talk like that!" Christy begged. He was spoiling her fun with such scary talk.

"Oh, just ignore him," Lucille said.

Just then, an older boy came running across the street.

"Mrs Garone just made fresh popcorn!"

"Oh, boy!" Eda cried.

The children raced across the street, trick or treat bags flying.

As the night progressed, their bags grew heavier and heavier. They moved from the main part of town to the nearby streets, knocking on door after door. When they came to the block where the Gammels had lived, some of the older kids started to tease the little ones.

"Darren's gonna getcha! Darren's gonna getcha!"

"Look at the woods! I see someone without a head!"

A little girl screamed. Christy looked across the street to see Tiffany Simmons, dressed up as a bunny rabbit. She had her hands over her eyes.

"Figures it's Tiffany," Eda scoffed. "What a baby! I'm not afraid of anything."

But Christy couldn't blame Tiffany for screaming. She was afraid, too. Somehow, this street seemed darker than all the others. "Can we get away from here?" She asked. "I don't like it. It gives me the creeps."

"Yeah, there aren't any houses lit up here, anyway," Lucille said.

The girls turned the corner, unaware they were being watched. Inside the Gammel garage, a stranger hid in the shadows and watched the children parading by. He'd been waiting all night for one particular child, Christy Burnett. There would be no chance to get her tonight, not with all these people around, but he hoped that following her would give him the clue that would help him snatch her one day soon.

He had used a pair of garden shears to poke holes in a tarpaulin he'd found piled in a corner. When he saw Christy and her friends, he pulled the makeshift ghost costume over his head and snuck out of the garage. He looked just like any other adult accompanying the kids on their rounds. No one paid attention to him. He moved quickly, searching for the little girl he had made his prey. A boy in a skeleton mask and costume jumped in front of him. He roared in anger, but the kid only laughed. Scary noises were part of the night's fun.

Christy and a group of other children were walking away from a house, laughing.

"I got a Tootsie Roll Pop!" Lucille cried.

"Nestlé bars are my favourite," Eda said. "I think I have eight."

Harvey, coming up the walk, said: "Christy! What've you got in that bag?"

Christy's fist tightened protectively around the handle. "Nothing," she said, her eyes wary.

Eda stepped forward, looking defiant. She pulled herself up as tall as she could, barely reaching Harvey's shoulders, and said: "Don't you even think about stealing Christy's loot!"

"Huh, big talker!" Harvey sneered. "What're you gonna do, Brill-O head? Shoot me with a water pistol?"

"Someday I'll have a real gun," Eda vowed, "then you'll get it."

"Oh, forget him," Lucille said. "Come on, it's getting late. Let's go home. We'll walk Christy back first."

The children headed back into town, unaware that their exchange had told the stranger exactly how he was going to get Christy Burnett.

Halloween candy was quickly gobbled up, and soon talk of spooky things gave way to Thanksgiving plans. After school one day, Christy changed from her dress to corduroy pants and a turtleneck sweater. As she headed for the kitchen, hoping there was a snack, her mother came into the apartment with two bags of groceries.

"Hi, Mommy."

"I can't hear you," Sarah said. She put a hand to her ear. "The voices are too loud." She looked around the dark little room with worry in her eyes. "I wonder why Dr Markel doesn't make the noises stop?"

Christy didn't know what to say.

Sarah went into the kitchen, ignoring her daughter. Christy followed, setting up her papers on the table, and tried to busy herself with a Thanksgiving drawing. Her mother flitted about the kitchen, pulling food from the refrigerator to prepare dinner. After a few minutes, she stopped and leaned over Christy's shoulder. "What a pretty Indian maiden," she said. "Thanksgiving is coming, isn't it? I have to make plans. Oh, yes, I have to make lots of plans! I have to buy a goose. No, a turkey. It's turkey for Turkey Day! Turkey with stuffing. Might use the stuffing from the couch. Daddy won't yell, oh, no, he won't, because the stuffing from the couch is so cheap."

Sarah ranted on like that for twenty minutes, then lapsed into silence again. Most of what she said made little sense, and frightened Christy. By the time her mother was finished, she was so sad that tears had spilled on her drawing.

The Burnett family celebrated Thanksgiving two days late, on Saturday. *Celebrate* wasn't the word

80

in Christy's mind as her family ate roast chicken, potatoes and canned corn in silence. Her mother had awakened in one of her "moods" and had sent Harvey Jr. to the butcher for a turkey. By now there were none available, but he'd chosen the biggest chicken he could find.

"Chicken," Harvey Sr. grumbled, washing the meat down with a beer. "Supposed to be turkey on Thanksgiving. Supposed to be Thanksgiving on Thursday."

Harvey Jr. and Christy exchanged glances, but knew better than to speak. Sarah, however, smiled brightly. Christy took a bite of stuffing and gazed at her mother. She looked pretty today. Her light brown hair was pulled into a neat bun, and she was wearing a little make-up. Christy wished her mother could always look this way.

"Well, isn't this nice?" Sarah said, as if Harvey Sr. hadn't spoken at all. "All of us together. And just the family. None of those . . . others."

Somehow, Christy managed to survive the weekend with neither Eda nor Lucille. Eda had gone to Chicago, Lucille was at an aunt's house. Christy imagined both of them were laughing and having a grand time. By the time dinner was over, her father was snoring on the couch with a half-empty beer can dangling from his hand, her mother had announced that she was tired, and Christy knew Sarah's good mood was over. Harvey Jr. helped her wash dishes, then disappeared from the apartment. Christy thought about leaving herself, but where would she go? Besides, what if that man was still out there?

When she saw Eda in school on Monday, she was so happy she hugged her. After school, they rode bikes to Eda's house. They found Mrs Crispin in Eda's bedroom, going through piles of old clothes with the housekeeper. Eda bounced up onto the bed, scattering dresses.

"Eda Crispin!" Rita cried in exasperation. "Get off the bed! Can't you see Mrs Slocombe and I are busy?"

"Did you have a nice day at school, dear?" the housekeeper asked.

"It was okay," Eda said, jumping off the bed. "Watcha doing?"

"Gathering up some of your outgrown clothes," Rita said. "We're boxing them up for Rabbi Horn to distribute among the poor children in town."

She turned around with a pile of blouses that Mrs Slocombe had just neatly folded. For just a moment, she stared at Christy. Having one of those "poor children" right here made her uncomfortable.

She turned quickly and put the blouses down in a box. Then she picked up a coat and started to fold it. "You know, Eda outgrew this coat so quickly," she said to Christy. "I wonder if it might fit you? Would you like to have it?" Rita watched Christy's expression, expecting her to be insulted. Instead, the little girl nodded eagerly.

She took the coat, royal blue with silver buttons, and ran her fingers over the fur collar. "Oh, thank you!"

"Try it on, Christy," Eda said.

Christy did so. The coat fitted perfectly, and unlike the coats she'd received other winters from charities, this one didn't have holes in the pockets. She twirled around in it. "Thanks!"

"You're quite welcome, dear," Rita said.

"How pretty it makes you look," Mrs Slocombe added.

"That was my Hanukkah coat last year," Eda said. "Oh! Mommy? Can Christy come for Hanukkah dinner? And can my friend Lucille, come too?"

"Certainly," Rita said. "You just tell Cook, all right? And be sure to let Daddy and me know what night they'll be coming."

Christy frowned. They'd be coming on Hanukkah, wouldn't they? She asked Eda about this as they headed towards the kitchen.

"Hanukkah's eight days long," Eda said. "I get a present every night, but on the first and last nights I get extra stuff."

"Eight nights!" Christy cried in wonderment. She couldn't imagine anyone being that lucky. Like Thanksgiving, Christmas was something she didn't dare get her hopes up about.

They entered the kitchen, where Eda told the cook about her plans. Christy breathed deeply, taking in the aroma of pumpkin pie. She hoped someone would offer her a piece, but instead Eda said: "Let's go outside. I saw a nest in a tree and I want to try to get it."

Eda's backyard was so big that Christy could hardly see the trees at the other end. Her friend raced ahead of her, blonde hair bouncing crazily in the wind. The sky was grey with the promise of rain. The air was crisp, but in her "new" coat, Christy didn't notice. She ran after her friend, laughing.

"Look up there," Eda said. "Do you see it?"

Christy tilted her head back and gazed through the bare branches of a huge oak tree. She spotted a dark clump. "That's really high, Eda."

"Oh, it is not," Eda insisted. She braced her sneaker on the side of the tree and hoisted herself up. "I'll throw it down. You catch it!"

Christy held her breath as she watched Eda shimmy up the tree, certain she was going to kill herself. She was so absorbed that she nearly jumped out of her skin when she felt a tap on her shoulder.

"Lucille!" she cried as she swung around.

"Wait 'til you hear what happened!" Lucille gasped.

She looked up into the tree. Eda was almost to the bird's nest. She watched as Eda grabbed the nest, working it loose from a tangle of branches. "CHRISTY! CATCH!"

Eda let the nest drop, but it was Lucille who caught it. "COME ON DOWN!" Lucille cried. "I'VE GOT NEWS!"

By the time Eda jumped to the ground, Lucille

was almost breathless with excitment. "Listen to this," she said. "One of my mother's friends called to tell her – they found Teddy Gammel's jacket!"

"Where?" Christy asked.

"Behind a gas station just outside of town."

By coincidence, the annual holiday party at the Cable and Wire Factory fell on the same night as the Crispins' Hanukkah celebration. Harvey Sr. dressed in his one and only good suit, and saw to it that his wife put on her best dress. Sarah moved like a robot, never smiling, simply staring into the mirror as her husband zipped up her dress.

"The party's over at eleven," Harvey Sr. told his kids.

They were sitting together on the living room couch, as ordered. Christy was wearing a red dress her mother had purchased during one of her "high" moods. Harvey, by contrast, had on jeans and a sweatshirt. He was shoeless, and a toe poked through the end of one white sock.

"That means I expect you home at ten," their father said as he opened a bottle of cologne. "And don't think you can pull a fast one on me. I might come home for a bit just to check on you."

"It'll be dark then," Sarah said in a quiet voice. "How will they walk home in the dark, with all the snow? Things hide in the dark, bad things . . ."

"I'm going to a party right near Christy's," Harvey Jr volunteered. "I'll pick her up on the way home and we'll walk together."

85

"Fine," his father said. "Come on, Sarah. We'll be late."

He helped his wife into her coat, then steered her to the door. Before leaving, he turned and pointed an intimidating finger at his kids. "Ten o'clock," he said. The threat was clear. He didn't need to say more.

When they heard the downstairs door shut, Harvey and Christy jumped from the couch.

"Are you really gonna walk me home?" Christy asked.

"Why not?" Harvey replied. "Is it a crime?"

"Well, no," Christy said, uncertain. "But . . ."

"Forget it," Harvey said. "Let's go. The guys are waiting for me."

They put on their coats and left the apartment. As they sat on the bottom steps and pulled on their boots, Christy asked: "What kind of party are you going to? Is it for Hanukkah, too?"

Harvey snorted. "Don't ask so many questions."

Christy pulled on her gloves. Then the children walked out into the night. For a second, the sight of downtown Aberdeen, decorated for the holidays, made Christy stop and stare. "Oh, Harvey, look!" she cried. "Isn't it beautiful!"

"I guess so," Harvey said, his breath making a cloud of mist. Arches of coloured lights had been strung over Central Street, beginning and ending at lampposts that had been wrapped to look like candy canes. The storefronts were decorated with their own lights, all blinking merrily. In the distance, someone was playing a recording of Bing Crosby's "White Christmas".

Christy sighed. "I love Christmas. I think it's going to be great this year. I think we're going to get presents."

"Yeah, sure," Harvey said sarcastically. "We probably won't get shit."

"Harvey!" Christy cried. "Don't talk like that!"

"Come on, will you?"

Christy followed him, climbing over an embankment of snow. The going was easier in the streets, and they walked right down the middle. Once in a while a car would come, crunching on the freshly plowed snow, and they'd separate to let it pass. The snow made it difficult to hurry – it was a full twenty minutes before they reached the gates of the Crispin house. Not a word was spoken in that time, although Christy softly sang Christmas carols.

"Here it is," she said. "Thanks for walking with me, Harvey." She realized then that she hadn't thought of the stranger even once during their walk. It was going to be a good night!

"I'll pick you up at nine-thirty," Harvey said. "Be ready. I don't want a whipping just 'cause of you."

"I'll be ready."

She pushed open the gate and started toward the house. About halfway up, she turned to wave to her brother. But the road in front of the house was empty. Shaking her head in wonder at her brother's speed, she turned and hurried up to the front door.

There were no wreaths or coloured lights on the Crispin's front door, but every window held a candle that flickered warmly in the darkness. Christy rang the bell. A man pulled open the door. He smiled at Christy and welcomed her into the house. He was wearing a suit with a short coat and white gloves.

"The guests are in the parlour," he said. His words sounded strange to Christy, unlike any she'd ever heard. They were beautiful words, warm and rounded.

"What's a parlour?"

The man laughed, a baritone laugh. "Like a living room, *ma cherie*," he said. "You come with Jean-Robert. He will show you the party."

She followed him, and in a few moments heard music. It wasn't Christmas music, of course, and for a second that didn't seem right. Christy had to remind herself that Jewish people didn't celebrate Christmas. She couldn't wait to see how they *did* celebrate.

Jean-Robert pushed open a pair of doors and showed her into the parlour. Eda came running up to her, all smiles. She was wearing the most beautiful blue dress Christy had ever seen. The top part was satin; the bottom hung in tier after tier of lace. "Here you are!" she cried.

Rita Crispin came up behind her daughter. She reminded Christy of pictures she'd seen of Elizabeth Taylor as Cleopatra. Rita wore a long, flowing dress clasped with a gold sunburst at one shoulder. A thick fringe came down to her darkly-lined eyes, and her hair was perfectly straight and cut just to her chin. A smile lit up her face. "Did your parents drive you, dear?"

"My brother walked me," Christy said, a hint of pride in her voice. Having Harvey as an escort was something amazing.

For a second, Rita's expression faltered. But her smile quickly reappeared. "What a nice brother," she said. "And it must be so cold out!"

"It's okay," Christy said. She'd been too excited to notice the cold.

"You look pretty," Eda said.

"So do you."

Eda made a face that showed she'd rather be in play clothes. Then she took hold of Christy's hand and pulled her towards a table full of presents. They were wrapped in blue, gold and silver. Eda pointed to a few of them. "That one's mine, and that one, and that one," she said. "I don't know which one I get to open tonight, but I hope it's the big one."

Christy's eyes widened. Eda was so lucky to get all these presents!

Her friend pulled out a small box. "Guess who this one is for?"

"I dunno."

"You!"

"Really?" Christy looked at the box, no bigger than the palm of Eda's hand, and wondered what it could possibly be. She was about to ask when the big double doors opened and Lucille came into the room. Eda put down the box, and the two girls ran to greet their friend.

Lucille's long black hair had been pulled back in a French braid, a stark contrast to the white dress she wore. The three little girls giggled with each other.

"You kids look more like Independence Day than Hanukkah," Dean Crispin said as he came up to them. "Red, white and blue!"

Christy thought Eda's father looked like a prince in his black tuxedo. Through his glasses, she could see a sparkle in his eyes – or maybe that was the tiny lights that had been strung across the ceiling. He had a drink in one hand, and something golden in the other. Christy tried to see what it was, but Eda jumped at her father and took his hand.

"Gold coins! Gold coins!" she cried.

Dean laughed heartily, then passed bags of gold-foil-wrapped coins to the children. "come sit down, everyone," he said. "It's time for the Hanukkah Story."

Christy sat mesmerized as Eda's father told the Hanukkah story. She thought the Syrians were really mean to keep the Jews from practising their religion.

"But for three years," Dean Crispin said, "an army of rebels struggled to free their home. When at last they succeeded, they had to make the temple holy again. That meant lighting a lamp for eight days. But did they have enough oil for eight days?"

In a chorus, the children around the room yelled: "NO!"

"They lit the lamp anyway," Dean went on, "and what happened? It burned for eight days!"

Christy was amazed. How could a little oil light a lamp for that long? It was just like magic!

"Now we'll light the menorah," Dean said. "If you'll follow me . . ."

Christy leaned over to Eda and whispered: "What's a menorah?"

"A special candlestick with eight candles," Eda said. "You light one each night with a *shammash*. I don't get to light it tonight, though. The youngest one goes first. That's my cousin Martha. She's just three years old."

The family and their guests watched as Martha was lifted to light the candle. A prayer was said, and then everyone was called in to dinner. There were many kinds of food that Christy had never seen before. Her eyes widened at the sight of bow-shaped noodles being spooned into her dish.

"That's kasha varnishkes," Eda told her.

Christy smiled. Everything was delicious – pot roast with fruit sauce, honey cakes, challah, noodle pudding.

Her fourth helping of potato pancakes didn't go unnoticed. Rita saw the butler stop at the child's place and serve more of the treats. Her heart went out to the little girl. She ate as if

91

she was starved! Rita thought perhaps she might have been. The type of family Christy came from was common knowledge in town. Everyone at the beauty parlour had something to say about crazy Sarah Burnett. And her husband! Well, if ever there was a man who belonged in jail . . .

"Who's for presents?" Dean announced.

"Me! Me!" Eda cried.

Rita, embarrassed by her daughter's lack of decorum, tried to say something, but Eda was already bounding out of the dining room.

"Christy! Lucille! Come on!"

The children gathered in the parlour, laughing and talking excitedly as the first night's gifts were brought out. Christy hadn't been expecting a gift, and she thought she'd burst wide open if someone didn't give her the package Eda had shown her. At last, it was handed over the sea of raised hands. Christy hurried to find a seat. The silver paper was torn off in a matter of seconds.

Christy gasped when she pulled a charm bracelet from the box. There was a little dog on it, and a key, and a small object she didn't recognize. "Oh, it's so pretty!"

"Look what I got," Lucille said. "It's a necklace. Look at the colours in the stone!"

"That's an opal," someone said.

Lucille and Christy turned to see Mike Hewlett behind the couch. The police officer, still in uniform, smiled at them.

"Hi, Officer Mike!" Eda cried. She held up a gold locket. "Look what I got!"

"That's great," Mike said.

"How come you didn't come to dinner?"

"Sorry, I was on duty," Mike replied. He looked across the room. "You have a nice time, kids. I've got to talk to your father."

When he left, the three girls gathered on a couch and compared gifts. Christy asked about the unusual charm.

"That's a dreidel," Eda said. "It's a game. My uncle has a big wooden one."

Just then, the butler came over to Christy. "A young man is waiting for Miss Burnett."

"That's Harvey," Christy said. "He's going to walk me home."

Rita frowned at her husband. "Should they be walking, Dean?" she asked. "It's late, and so dark . . ."

"Harvey's strong," Christy said. "We have to be home by ten – we promised our father. And it's just a short walk." She knew Harvey would never accept a ride home, and was afraid they might both get in trouble if she didn't join him.

"I'll walk you to the front door," Eda offered.

"Me, too!" said Lucille.

After the butler helped Christy into her coat and boots, she hugged her two friends. Then she carefully pulled the cuff of her glove over her new bracelet to keep it safe.

"I had a super time," she said. "Hanukkah's a great holiday, Eda! You're so lucky it's eight days long!"

"Maybe we can do something at my house for

Christmas," Lucille suggested. "Maybe we can have hot chocolate and bake sugar cookies."

"Yeah!" cried Eda.

They hugged again, and Christy went out the door, hurrying down the snow-covered sidewalk to her brother. Harvey was jumping back and forth to keep himself warm. His cheeks were bright red under the lamplight, and there was frost on his eyebrows.

"Hi, Harvey!" Christy greeted. "Did you have a good time at your party?"

"It was okay," Harvey grunted.

"My party was like a story," Christy said dreamily. She gazed up at the stars. "I wish this night could last forever!"

They walked a block before Harvey answered. "I know a way we can make it last longer," he said. "I heard they're giving away toys and things to poor kids at the Salvation Army. You know, that brick building behind the high school?"

"Gee, it's kinda late," Christy said. "Do you think they'd be open? And do you think we'd get home in time?"

"Aww, those places stay open all night," Harvey said. "And we've got plenty of time, if we hurry. I know a shortcut that'll save us ten minutes."

Christy made an indecisive little moaning noise.

"Well, do you want a present or don'tcha?" Harvey demanded.

His sister thought about the beautiful charm bracelet she'd received. It didn't seem fair that

94

she got something and her brother didn't, so she nodded eagerly.

"Then let's go!" Harvey cried, breaking into a run.

Christy raced after him, slip-sliding on the snow, yelling for him to wait. He took a turn down the road that led to the industrial part of town. Aberdeen's biggest employers were its cable and wire and furniture factories. Right now, the huge stone building that housed Glemby's Furniture was dark. Harvey pointed to the lights shining in the top window of the Cable and Wire Factory.

"That's where our parents are," he said. "You really think they'll know we got home at ten? Dad's probably stinking drunk by now."

Christy could hear muffled laughter and music. She wondered if the people inside that big, brick building were having as much fun as she'd had tonight. Still, it was dark and creepy down here on the street. "Can we hurry?" she said. "I don't like it here."

"This is the quickest way," Harvey said. "Come on, just around the corner." He disappeared into the shadows.

"Harvey, don't go away!" Christy cried, chasing him. She followed him around the side of the building. Suddenly, a man jumped out from behind a big dumpster. Christy screamed. "Haaarrrveee!

The man grabbed her, leaning close to press something that smelled bad against her face. Her last vision before passing out was a pair of mean, hateful eyes.

Sometime later, she came around with the sense of being tied up. She couldn't see in the dark, but she could feel the rough texture of rope against her wrists, cutting into her, tighter and tighter. "My bracelet," Christy whispered.

Another voice spoke, but she didn't understand. Then she heard: "Shut your mouth, Harvey." A man's voice. A man was tying her up.

"Harvey?" she tried to say her brother's name, but her mouth felt funny.

Laughter.

"Shh!" said the man.

"What're you gonna do?"

That was Harvey's voice.

"Take her to the boys. Take her to stay with Teddy and Adrian, forever. She saw. She knows. They have to stay together."

Something was being pressed against her face. Something wet and cold.

"Christy? Christ, oh shit, please wake up!"

Christy obeyed the voice with a terrified yelp. She backcrawled across the snow. Her eyes gazed up in fright at the figure towering over her, the golden lamplight behind it making it look like a ghost. "Go away!"

"Christy, it's me," Harvey yelled. "Can you get up? I thought that guy had killed you!"

Christy lay in the snow a few moments, her wits slowly returning. The sensation of being tied up, the pressure against her face, the voices – were they all a dream? "What . . . what . . .?"

"Some creep jumped us in the alley," Harvey said, holding out his hand. "I found an old hubcap in the trash and clocked him over the head. I had to hit him three times, but I finally knocked him out! Then I dragged you away as fast as I could. But you got heavy, Christy. I had to rub snow on your face to wake you up."

Christy accepted her brother's hand and let him help her to her feet. "I . . . I heard him talking to you," she said. "He called you 'Harvey'. Who was it?"

"Nobody!" Harvey snapped. "You dreamed it. You were delirious."

"Del . . ."

"You were zonked," Harvey said. "Look, I rescued you, okay? That guy didn't know my name! You were just hearing things! It was a stranger. You oughta be glad I was here!"

"But, Harvey . . ." Things didn't seem right.

"I saved your life," Harvey insisted.

Christy brought her hands up to her face. As she did so, she saw the charm bracelet still safely locked around her wrist – but her gloves were gone. She buried her face in her hands and began to cry.

"Don't do that," Harvey said. "It's okay. We hafta hurry, though. It's getting late and I'm afraid we won't get home in time."

Christy went on crying. She hurt all over. What would happen now? Would her parents believe her? Or would she get another beating?

Harvey hooked his hand around her elbow. "Come *on*," he urged. "We may just make it in time."

"I – I thought they weren't gonna be home until eleven!"

"It's almost that now," Harvey said. "I told you, it was hard fighting that guy and then pulling you through the snow. I think he drugged you. I couldn't wake you up!"

Christy sobbed as she stumbled along the street, her arm still caught in her brother's tight grasp. It wasn't fair! This was the best night of her life and now it was ruined! "Harvey! Harvey, slow down!"

"We can't!"

A few moments later, Christy said: "Do you think it was the kidnapper?"

"I dunno. Look, there's the pizzeria. Oh, *damn*!"

"What!" Christy didn't think she could stand more trouble.

"They're already home!" Harvey whispered. He pointed up to the lighted window. "*Shit*! I thought we'd beat them!"

He pulled her toward the door. Before he opened it, Christy looked into his eyes and saw they were full of fear. "Harvey, I'm so scared," she said. "I don't want to be hurt."

Harvey breathed deeply. "I'll tell Dad everything that happened," he said. "He won't hurt you."

"You can't stop him!"

"Oh, I can – " Harvey stopped talking, and became more like his nasty self. "Just get inside!"

They sat together on the bottom steps and removed their wet boots. Then, in stockinged feet, they dragged themselves upstairs to face the unknown.

The living room was empty. Harvey leaned close to his sister. "Make a dash for your room," he whispered. "I'll do what I can."

"Harvey – "

"Go!"

Christy shot across the room. She closed her door, then sank down on the floor in the dark and listened. Moments later, she heard her father's footsteps thumping over the wooden floor. "You're late."

"We . . . we had some trouble, Daddy."

Harvey never called their father "Daddy."

"You were told to be home by ten. It's almost eleven. Where the hell have you been?"

"We would'a been home by ten," Harvey said. "Even earlier. We were walking when all of a sudden this man jumped out from behind a building. He tried to hurt Christy! I tried to stop him, Daddy! But he was bigger than me. I think maybe it was the kidnapper, the guy who took those Gammel boys – "

"*Shut the hell up!*"

Behind her door, Christy jumped.

"You expect me to believe that cock-and-bull story? You *liar*! Tell me the truth, Harvey! Tell me what you've really been up to! You're fifteen now, huh? I know what fifteen is like. More brains between your legs than in your head. Did you get any tonight, Harvey? Did you? Was she worth . . . this?"

Christy started at the sound of a face being slapped.

"I'm telling the truth!"

"Liar! Li-ar!"

A blow with each syllable. Screaming, yelling. Christy flinched with each slapping sound as if the blows were hitting her. Something thundered across the floor. A piece of furniture?

Why wouldn't her father believe Harvey? Harvey had saved her life! He was a hero!

"Stinkin' liar!"

"Lemme go!"

Crashes, more screams . . .

And, finally, a door slamming. Christy froze, listening as footsteps raced down the stairs. She jumped away from the door and climbed up on her bed to look out the window. In a few moments, her brother's silhouette stumbled into the road. He turned and raised a fist, shaking it. With the streetlamp shining down on him, making his face as bright as the moon, he shouted: "I ain't your son no more! *No more!*"

"Harvey!" Christy shouted through the glass, but her brother couldn't hear her. By the time she worked the lock and opened it, he had disappeared down the street.

"Shut that damned window," her father's gruff

voice said from behind her. "You want to heat the neighborhood?"

Christy obeyed at once. Then she turned slowly, grabbing a pillow to clutch against herself, as if it could offer her protection.

Her father looked like a giant, standing in the doorway with his fists clenched. A shadow fell across his face, almost hiding his angry expression. "Had to come home early tonight," he said. "Your crazy mother started in with her voices. Said they were singin' Christmas carols. So someone kids around and asks what they're singing. Your mother tells them 'Oh Little Town of Bethlehem'. And she starts singin' herself, only she puts in dirty words. My boss had invited his minister to the party. I'm probably gonna lose my job because of your mother."

Christy didn't say a word. Sometimes, silence was her only defence. She'd heard what had happened when Harvey tried to tell the truth.

"Bad enough my wife is crazy," Harvey Sr. went on. "But now I got a looney for a daughter. And you're makin' your brother lie for you. Well, the hell with him. If he can't take his medicine like a man, good riddance."

He isn't a man! He isn't big like you!

Harvey Sr. took another step into the room. "But then, maybe you talk like that because that's what you want," he said. "Maybe you want some guy to take you away because anyone, even a killer, is better than your stinkin' drunk of a father! *Right*?"

101

Christy shook her head vigorously, eyes widening with terror.

"Maybe you *want* him to get you," Harvey Sr. said, moving closer and closer. "You think it'd be fun to be in all the papers, don't you? Just like Teddy and Adrian Gammel? Bet their heads are on the mantel in that old house, propping up their father's. All nice and cosy."

With that, he reached out and grabbed Christy by her ears. She yelped with pain, but didn't dare struggle. Her father was strong enough, and drunk enough, to rip them right off her head. "What would he do with *your* head, Christy?" he asked, his alcohol breath like poisonous gas. He began to shake her back and forth. "It's such a pretty head. Bet he's got heads in all his rooms. Maybe he'd put yours in the kitchen, right in the middle of the table. With flowers all around. Real pretty, huh? *Huh*?"

The bed creaked noisily beneath them. Christy squeezed her eyes shut, silently begging him to stop.

"Or maybe he'll put you on the back of the toilet seat," he ranted. "Right there with the *crap* where you belong!" He gave her a hard shove that bounced the back of her head against the windowsill. Christy lay there, frozen. Her bed rose up as her father got off it. For a few moments, there was such silence in the room that Christy dared to believe he'd gone. Slowly, she opened her eyes.

He was standing in the middle of the room,

his eyes darting about. He looked like a wolf in search of something, ready to pounce when he found it.

The room was quiet. Christy cried in silence, the only noise an occasional hiccup that escaped her. Finally, her father grabbed a little plastic doll her mother had bought from the drug store. "If you don't stop this talk about a man chasing you," he said, "I'm gonna see to it that he does get you. I'm gonna take you out one night and leave you for him, right by that gas station where they found that kid's bloody jacket. Then the killer will have you, and he'll make you look just like *this*." He gave the doll's head a quick turn, pulling the head from the socket. Then he threw the pieces at Christy. The body struck the wall, but the head hit her cheek and left a stinging pain.

"Not another word," her father warned. He turned and left the room, switching off the light.

Christy stared at her closed door for a few moments. Then she crawled under her blanket and lay for a long time with her eyes open. It seemed the wonderful time at the Crispins' house had never happened. But it *had* happened, and she had to think about that. Not about the killer, or heads, or her father. She squeezed her eyes shut and imagined the party all over again, wishing with all her might that she could be Eda's sister and live with the Crispins forever and ever . . .

Chapter Four

The Present Day

Lieutenant Eda Crispin was walking from the locker room of her Queens, N.Y. police station when her partner called to her from across the room.

"Hey, Cowgirl!" Tim Becker said. "There's a fax coming in for you."

Eda had learned long ago not to react to the nickname her colleagues had given her when they learned she was a native of Montana.

Tim pulled the paper out of the machine and handed it to her.

As she read it, the colour drained from her face and she began swearing under her breath.

"Eda, what's wrong?" Tim asked.

Eda crumpled the fax and threw it on the floor. She just couldn't believe what it said. Brian Wander was dead? Chris's two kids were missing? That was just like the Gammel crime.

But what did something that happened thirty years ago have to do with Chris now?

Tim picked up the paper and read it for himself. He whistled softly. "Sounds like you need to get out to Montana," he said.

Eda nodded. "My friend needs me. Tim, can you cover for me with the Captain? I can't waste any time."

"You bet," Tim said. He put his arms around her and wished her luck.

Then Eda hurried out of the precinct. She made a quick stop at her apartment to throw a few things in an overnight bag, then headed to LaGuardia Airport. While waiting for her flight, she called Lucille to say she was on her way.

Lucille met her at the airport.

"How is Chris?" Eda asked.

"Heavily sedated," Lucille answered. "She was completely hysterical last night, and the hours in the police station wore her out completely. I'm glad you're here. Chris is going to be grateful you came so quickly."

They walked out to Lucille's car together. As she got in, Eda said:

"I hear Mike Hewlett is Chief of Police now. You remember how nice he was to us kids when he was a rookie? He was my father's good friend. I bet he'll talk to me about all this."

They drove in silence for a while, until finally Eda slammed a fist down on the seat. "Damn! I'm so worried about those kids! If anything happened to them, it would destroy Chris."

"She's pretty near destroyed already," Lucille said. "Brian was her life. You know how things turned around for her when she married him. He rescued her from such a horrible existence."

Eda nodded. "Her knight in shining armour. Who would want to hurt such a great guy?"

"I'm afraid the killer might still be nearby," Lucille said. "I sent my own kids to stay with their grandparents in Rose Park. The twins weren't too happy about it, but I don't care as long as they're safe."

"I'm going to do some sleuthing of my own while I'm here," Eda said. "There must be some connection between those long-ago crimes and what happened now. I'm sure the police are pursuing that route, but I want to see what I can learn on my own."

They finally pulled up to Lucille's house. Eda wasn't surprised to see a crowd of people in front of Chris's place, held back by a yellow police banner. There were reporters, gawkers and thrill-seekers.

"What a bunch of ghouls," she said.

"They keep trying to interview me," Lucille said. "They won't take a hint I don't know anything. Come on, let's go in the back door."

They hurried inside, to find Chris sitting at the kitchen table.

"Chris!" Lucille cried. "What are you doing up?"

"Did they find my babies?"

Lucille and Eda looked at each other.

"I haven't heard anything, honey," Lucille said.

Eda had to blink back tears of shock at the sight of her friend. While Lucille had been the exotic beauty of the trio, Chris had always had a gentle, Victorian quality about her. But this was no innocent sitting in the yellow and orange kitchen. This was someone who had once lived in hell, and had just been sent back there. Someone who had seen her husband's headless body. Someone who might never seen her children again.

"Hi, Chris," Eda said. "I came as soon as I heard what happened."

"Do you hear that?" Lucille asked, as if to a child. "Your two best friends are here to help you. We're going to get through this, Chris!"

Chris stared at her, but the sedative she'd been given kept her from reacting to Eda's presence. "They're never going to find them," she whispered.

Quickly, her two friends moved to her side.

"Don't you worry," Lucille said. "They *will* find them. You have to keep hoping!"

"Chris," Eda said, "I know it must be hard for you to talk about what happened, but . . ."

"They made me tell the story over and over again at the police station," Chris said wearily. "If my art students hadn't verified where I'd been when . . . when it happened . . ." She covered her face, but didn't cry.

"I thought the three of us could brainstorm," Eda went on. She knew there was little time to waste being overly gentle with her friend. "Somehow, there's a connection between this and the Gammel crime."

Chris's head snapped up. "They keep asking me about that!" she said. "I couldn't tell them a thing. What could I possibly know? I was only seven!"

"But if there was anything that happened to us back then," Eda said, "anything at all to help us make sense of this, we have to try to remember it."

Lucille frowned at her. "You're upsetting her, Eda. That isn't what you came here to do, I'm sure."

"Of course not," Eda said. "But I just can't sit back and let the local police go off on their own. If there is a link, I want to do my part to find it."

Chris pulled her hand gently from Lucille's. She nodded, rubbing her eyes. "I don't remember much," she said. "But maybe, if we start talking, something will come to me."

She turned to stare out the window. For a moment, the blank look on her face made Lucille think the sedative was kicking in again. But Chris wasn't going into a fugue state. She was remembering, her mind racing back to a long-ago day in the school playground. "We wanted to read articles in Eda's father's newspaper," she said.

Lucille nodded eagerly. "That's right! You were only in second grade and couldn't handle the bigger words yet. So you wanted me to read."

"We've got to remember it all," she said. "We've got to figure it out, to help find my children."

The women went on talking for hours, moving on to the living room. The coffee table in front of them grew crammed with empty cups and a partly-finished plate of cookies. Lucille had a pad of paper on her lap, nearly filled with notes.

"I got four dolls for Christmas the year it happened," Chris said in a quiet voice. She shifted in the chair where she was sitting, tucking one thin leg beneath her. "My mother had gone on a crazy shopping spree. My father beat her up for it, but he never made her take the gifts back."

"I remember that Christmas," Lucille said. "It was the year I got my first horse. I was so excited about him. I named him Wenceslas, after the king in that Christmas carol. Only I couldn't spell it, so I called him Wency." She looked at Chris, who sat with her head resting against the side of a wing-backed chair. Her eyes were red, the skin beneath them darkly circled.

"There's something else I remember," Lucille went on. "I rode Wency to your apartment to see if you wanted a ride. I was amazed at all the presents you got, because I thought you were poor. But you didn't seem happy at all. You were surrounded by boxes and boxes, but you didn't seem pleased."

Eda leaned forward. "You did seem more miserable than usual that Christmas. And every holiday season after that, you were a changed

110

person. I would invite you to Hanukkah dinner, but you always refused."

Chris closed her eyes. Someone was staring back in her mind. She opened them quickly. "I couldn't stop thinking about my father's promise to give me to the killer," she said. "I was just a kid, so I believed him."

"You thought you couldn't even tell your friends about it," Lucille said with sympathy.

"I thought . . ." Chris breathed, "I thought he had spies everywhere. People watching me, listening. My mother kept telling me there were bad people everywhere. I started believing they were working for my father. I became more afraid of them than the man who was following me."

"What a rotten thing to do to a little kid," Eda said. "Your father has a place in hell, I'm sure."

Lucille stood up, collecting the dishes. "Harvey really did run away, didn't he?" she asked. "I think I remember that."

"Who could forget when he came back?" Eda said.

Chris turned to look out the window. "It was on my tenth birthday. I was so surprised to find out he'd married! His wife's name was Felicity. She was pregnant. She was a hippie; a little flaky, but very sweet to me. I think we could have hit it off if they'd stuck around a while. Harvey was nice, too. But even more surprising, so was my father. It felt so wrong, somehow, but I couldn't understand why." A rough shudder racked her body.

111

Lucille decided she'd had enough, and said: "Let's talk about it later. Are you hungry? I could start an early dinner. Nothing fancy, but . . ."

"I'm not hungry," Chris said.

"You have to keep up your strength, Chris," Lucille insisted. "Maybe in a little while . . ."

Chris picked up her own coffee cup and followed Lucille to the kitchen. As she went to put the mug in the sink, it slipped from her hands and crashed to the floor. That was all the catalyst needed to send her into hysterics. Quickly, both Eda and Lucille put their arms around her. They let her cry for a few moments, then helped her sit down.

"What if he's back again?" Chris asked. "What if, somehow, he's kept track of me all these years? He's got my kids now! He's got Josh and Vicki and I'll never see them again the way no one ever saw the Gammel boys!" She put her head down in the crook of her elbow and began to pound the table with her fist. "I'll never see my babies again! *Never!*"

"*Oh, Chris, of course you will!*" Lucille insisted.

"*Damn him! Damn him to hell!*" Chris slammed her fist on the table.

Eda stood back. Chris continued to bang the table top, her brown hair falling over her like a shroud, Lucille trying to comfort her. They'd been talking for hours, and through it all Chris had shown an extraordinary range of emotion. But she'd never shown anger the way she was doing so now.

112

Eda was about to say something when the phone rang. Still keeping an eye on Chris, Lucille answered. She spoke quietly, but Eda could hear the concern in her voice. When she hung up, she took a deep breath. "That was Mike Hewlett," she said. "They're searching the woods around Lake Aberdeen."

"That's good, Chris," Eda said by way of encouragement. "They're not wasting any time."

Chris rubbed away the last of her tears. She stood up and ran her fingers through her hair. "I have to be there. Can you drive me, Lucille? I have to help look for my children."

"Oh, Chris!" Lucille cried. "I don't think you should!"

But Chris wasn't listening. As if she was propelled by some unseen force, she was already heading toward the back door. Eda moved quickly to stop her.

"Please, let me go," Chris said. From the time she'd come home from the police station, Chris had felt completely helpless. Talking about the past, trying to find some connection to her missing children, had helped a little. But she needed to do more than sit around doped up on sedatives.

"I know you need help," Eda said.

"But if you walk out that door now, you'll be bombarded with reporters. And it will be even worse down at the lake!" Lucille protested.

"Mike Hewlett will be there to protect her," Eda said. "Come on, Lucille. Find a pair of dark glasses. Do you still have one of those big hats you used to wear?"

Lucille sighed, but reluctantly gave in and worked on helping Chris go incognito. When they pulled out of the driveway a few minutes later, a few of the reporters looked their way, but no one seemed to realize the woman they wanted to talk to was just a few yards away.

"We went to Lake Aberdeen just yesterday," Chris said, staring out the window. Through the dark glasses, everything had a gloomy cast of grey. "The kids had a great time."

Lucille and Eda kept silent. It was only a few minutes' ride to the lake, and when they arrived Lucille circled the parking lot until she found a pair of squad cars. "There's Sheriff Hewlett," she said. "Maybe you ought to talk to him, Eda."

Eda got out of the car and walked over to the group of volunteers. Although there were several hours until sundown, many of the searchers were equipped with flashlights. A half dozen dogs sat obediently to the sides of their trainers, waiting for the signal to begin.

Mike had finished giving instructions, and the group was dispersing. Eda went over to him, her blue eyes wide with inquiry. She hadn't seen him in years. Would he recognize her? He'd certainly changed himself. His face was a little more wrinkled than she remembered. But when he saw her, his eyes filled with the kindness that had endeared the children of Aberdeen to him, and without a word he opened his arms. Years

114

of hard work had tightened his muscles, and he seemed strong as an oak when he hugged Eda tightly. "Welcome home, Eda," he said. "Chris must have been pleased to see you."

"I'm not sure if *pleased* is the right word, Mike," Eda said. She looked back towards Lucille's car. "She's here. She wanted to be part of the search. Lucille didn't think it was such a good idea, though."

Mike took off his cap and wiped sweat from his forehead with a light blue handkerchief. "I'm not sure it is, either," he said. "But I don't see how it can hurt any more than finding her husband like that."

Eda felt a shiver run down her arms, despite the July heat. "I'll get her, then."

She went to the car and told her friends Mike had given his approval. Chris looked all around as she approached the sheriff, as if she might see Josh and Vicki at any moment. He greeted her, but she didn't acknowledge him.

"I don't see any media," Lucille commented.

"We kept this as quiet as possible," Mike said. "I'm sure someone will show up, but hopefully we'll be done by then."

Chris looked at him now. "What should I do?"

It was Eda who answered: "Maybe Chris and Lucille can have an area to reconnoiter. I'd like to walk with you, if I can, Mike."

He smiled. "I'd be glad to have a fellow cop at my side, Eda." He pointed towards a narrow

115

path on the other side of the lake. "Walk around to there," he said. "It cuts through to a field about a mile back. Look in every branch, near every leaf and stone on the ground. Anything at all, a cigarette butt, a piece of fabric, can be a clue."

"We understand," Lucille said. She was impatient, wanting to get through this and have Chris safely home again.

After they left, Eda walked along with Mike. He watched the other two women for a few minutes, his expression troubled. "I wish I knew what to say to her."

"She knows you're doing your best," Eda said. "But she's fluctuating between shock and hysterics. We spent the last few hours talking about the Gammel murder and kidnappings. I'm sure you haven't missed the bizarre similarities. We can't help recalling that Teddy and Adrian Gammel were never found."

"Not for lack of trying," Mike said, taking off his cap again and running his fingers through hair that had gone from black to almost steel-grey. "That case is still open, and we've gone through those files again and again. The forensics team spent hours going over the Wander house. We've sent samples to the lab in Marylborne, and we hope to get results back quickly."

As he walked along the lakeside, his eyes scrutinized every inch of the ground. A bottle cap caught his eye, and he bent for a closer look. Eda saw that it was rusted; a piece of litter that had probably been stamped into the dirt years earlier.

"It's a good thing your friend had an alibi," he said. "I'm sorry to say it, but she was a prime suspect. Having those six people from her art class verify her whereabouts certainly helped her."

"I don't see how anyone could accuse Chris of such a horrible crime," Eda said, almost indignant. "She's the most gentle soul I've ever known. And she loved Brian and the kids almost to the point of obsession."

"I was just thinking of the parallel between the two crimes," Mike said. "To this day, there are a lot of us who believe Irene Gammel is somehow implicated. Of course, evidence proved she didn't exactly commit the crimes. Remember the second murder, the one that took place while she was still in jail? That helped clear her of any suspicion. Still, the whole thing seemed strange."

"Mike, do you think those boys might have survived?"

Mike shrugged. "I don't know. It was wishful thinking in the town for years. But, since this is a copy, knowing the fate of those kids would help. We're trying to locate Irene Gammel."

"She left town not too long after the kids vanished," Eda recalled. "My mother's friends used to gossip about it. They thought she was a horrible mother, leaving her children like that. Where was it she went? Oregon?"

"Washington," Mike corrected. "We knew where she was thirty years ago, but today? You can't keep tabs on a person forever. Irene

Gammel wasn't found guilty of any crime. Following her for the rest of her life would be tantamount to harassment." He put a hand on her arm and steered her into the section of woods he'd chosen for his own search.

"You don't even know that she's alive," Eda said.

"We're hoping she is," Mike answered, "and that she can fill us in."

"Well, that's one reason I wanted to talk to you," Eda said. "I have some details, myself."

Although he was still carefully scrutinizing his surroundings, Mike listened attentively as Eda told him an abridged version of the story the three women had pieced together. He interrupted once in a while, asking for clarification or more detail, but for the most part he was a captive audience.

When she had finished, he mumbled words of amazement. "I don't understand why Christy didn't tell anyone she was being followed," he said. After hearing of the woman as a child, he couldn't help using her nickname.

"How could she?" Eda asked. "She was a lonely little girl being terrorized by both her father and brother. Her mother was certifiable – probably schizophrenic now that I think of it. If she couldn't trust her own family, who could she trust?"

"She had you and Lucille, at least," Mike said.

"That's probably what kept her from going insane herself," Eda said. "That, and meeting a great guy like Brian Wander. He was her saviour."

"Well, someone wanted that saviour dead," Mike reminded her. "And we've got to find out who. What you've told me is certainly going to help. You've got quite a memory for particulars. No wonder your father was always very proud of you."

Eda laughed. "I think Dad would have been prouder if I'd taken over the newspaper when he decided to retire. He never was too happy about me being a cop."

"Oh, yes he was," Mike said. "He subscribed to every New York City newspaper, just to see if there was a story about you in one of them. If he could have taken them on his world tour, he would have."

He sighed. "I wish Dean was still here. He was my mentor, Eda. We were good friends, even though he was ten years my senior. I never met such a man for bouncing ideas off. If he was here now, things might go more smoothly."

He smiled at Eda, and she recalled how handsome she'd thought he was when she was little. He was still just as attractive, in a more mature way.

"But I'm glad I've got his daughter," Mike said. "Eda, if there's anything you can do for us, we'd appreciate it."

"I'll do whatever I can."

Something bright blue caught their attention. Mike moved towards it and crouched down. He held up a bluejay's feather. When he got up again, his weary sigh spoke of the hard work he'd been doing. "I hope," he said, "that we can prevent another thirty year mystery from haunting Aberdeen."

The search team moved ahead slowly, carefully scrutinizing everything in sight. Forty minutes later, Chris was stopping to rest when a dog's bark made her look through the trees. A few yards away, a woman held fast to a German Shepherd's leash. Something bright yellow was sticking out of her pocket. Chris gazed at it for a few moments. "Lucille?" she called.

Lucille was a few yards ahead. She turned and came back to Chris.

"Look at the woman with that dog," Chris said. "Do you see her pocket? She's got Vicki's unicorn!"

"Well, I think . . ."

But Chris was already plowing through the trees, her steps made awkward by roots and branches. Lucille called for her to wait, but Chris didn't seem to hear.

"What are you doing with Vicki's unicorn?" she demanded. "That's her favourite stuffed animal! Why do you have it?"

The woman backed up, taking the leash half-way down with her free hand to steady the dog. The German Shepherd gazed up at Chris, it's expression seemingly full of curiosity.

"I was given it for my dog," the woman said. "It helps him pick up the scent."

Lucille came up to them. "Chris, it's okay," she said, putting an arm around the smaller woman's shoulders.

Exhaustion and frustration combined with the residual effects of the sedative she'd been given, and Chris began to cry.

"It's Vicki's favourite toy! She loved that! She must miss it so much right now!"

The woman with the dog gave Lucille an inquiring look.

"She's the mother," Lucille said. She didn't wait for the woman's reaction, but turned Chris around and led her down the path. "You've had enough," she insisted. "We're going home."

"I didn't find anything," Chris said weakly.

"There must be thirty people combing these woods," Lucille pointed out. "If anything's here, they'll find it."

When they reached the car, Lucille helped Chris inside. Then she leaned into the open door and said: "I'm just going to tell Eda we're going home."

Eda and Mike were on their way back when Lucille caught up with them. They both looked very tired and dejected.

"We didn't find a thing," Eda said.

"I'm sure the kids aren't here," Mike put in. "But a second team will come in later to see if we missed anything."

Lucille pointed back at the car. "Eda, Chris is hysterical. She saw a dog trainer with one of

Vicki's toys, and it set her off. I'm taking her home."

Eda looked at Mike. "I think I'd like to stay and discuss things further."

"You can come back to the station with me," Mike said. "And I'll drive you home later."

"Just don't be too long, okay?" Lucille asked. She felt a little annoyed that Eda had let Chris come here. "Chris needs both of us now."

Eda nodded and watched Lucille stride back to her car. Had it been wrong to bring Chris here? "It's my fault she's upset," she said.

"Of course it isn't," Mike insisted. "You're just doing what you think is right. You're just being a friend."

Chapter Five

Josh awakened into a fog that seemed more like a dream than reality. His entire body hurt, he was shivering with cold, and it was dark. Shaky, he moved slowly until he was in a sitting position. He was on some kind of cot, he guessed through the mush of his thoughts. He could feel the cold metal of its frame through his cotton pajamas. "What's this place?" he demanded, although he sensed no one could hear him.

He tried to get up. Bad idea – his legs buckled under him. Josh thought he might get sick, but he closed his eyes and chewed on his lip until the nausea passed. Then he tucked his head between his knees and tried to remember what had happened.

They'd been watching TV, he knew. Mom had gone out teaching, and they had decided to play video games. Dad had just made popcorn for everyone when the doorbell rang. He'd gone to answer it. Josh had seen a scruffy-looking man at the door. Then, for some reason, Vicki had screamed.

Then . . . then . . .

123

Josh sat up slowly. That was all he could remember. He knew something bad had happened, but not what it had been. He thought, for now, he didn't want to remember. He just wanted to get the heck out of here.

"The bad man, Daddy! *The bad man*!" Somewhere in the darkness, Vicki was screaming.

"Vicki!" Josh cried. He groped around until he found her. The little girl was thrashing about on another cot, her arms waving wildly.

"The bad man!"

"Vicki, wake up!" Josh commanded.

As if his words were magic, she snapped awake, then sobbed loudly in the darkness. Josh felt awkward, wishing his mother were here to help. Mom always hugged Vicki when she had a bad dream, until she calmed down. But the idea of hugging his little sister was, well . . . gross.

"Are you gonna cry forever?" he asked.

"It was the bad man, Josh," Vicki blubbered. "The bad man I saw at the fireworks."

Josh had no idea what she was talking about. She'd seen him at the fireworks? The guy who rang the doorbell?

"Where did Daddy go?" Vicki asked. "Did the bad man hurt him? Why is it so dark, Josh? Where's my unicorn? Where's Mommy? I WANT MOMMY!"

Josh got up. He couldn't answer most of her questions, but there was something he could do right now, no matter how crummy he felt. He could find a light. "I don't know where we are," he said, although Vicki was crying too hard to hear him. "But there's gotta be a light switch somewhere."

He reached out, walking slowly until his hands hit a wall. He slid along it, feeling the rough, cold cement. When he bumped into what seemed to be metal shelves, the resulting rattle made Vicki scream again.

"Be quiet!" He found a switch just beyond the shelves, and flipped it up. His eyes squinted shut in protest to the bright overhead light. After a few moments he opened them again, to find himself looking up at three big racks of food. "Look at all this stuff!" he cried, reaching for a bag of potato chips. "Wow!"

"I don't want food," Vicki grumbled. "I want to go *home*."

Josh returned the chips. He didn't want food, either. "Let's look for a door," he said, turning around.

They seemed to be in a cellar of some kind, spartanly furnished with two cots, a table and chairs, and a pantry. An opened door revealed a bathroom. The floor in both rooms was made of cement. But Josh felt something was wrong. It took him only an instant to realize what it was. There were no windows.

"Where are we, Josh?" Vicki asked, more calm for now.

"Looks like a basement," Josh said.

Vicki stood up and shuffled over to him. "My feet are cold," she said. "I want my slippers."

Josh ignored her. He had spotted a door all the way at the back of the room; a big black door with a rusted knob. "Come on!" He hurried to the door, expecting to push it open and make a run for it. "Hurry, Vicki!" he urged. "That guy might be coming back! Maybe this is our only chance!"

Vicki raced to his side. Josh took hold of the knob and tried to turn it. It stuck. "Oh, no!"

"Josh, open it!"

He tried again. And again. And even when he knew the door was locked, he went on trying. "We're stuck," he moaned. "There's no way out."

"Yes, there is!" Vicki insisted. "I want out of here. I want OUT! *Lemme out!*"

Vicki threw herself on the floor and began kicking the door, screaming and crying. Josh watched her for a moment, screaming and crying, amazed, in spite of their predicament, at how his sister could scream. Then he picked up his fists and began to shout himself, pounding the metal door, hoping someone was out there to hear them.

Chapter Six

Chris was so tired when she came home that she collapsed into bed without needing another sedative. And in her dreams, her mind played tricks on her: Everything was just fine. Brian was with her. and the children slept soundly in their beds. As she lay sleeping, a smile spread over her careworn face as her dreams carried her to one of the happiest times of her life.

"Come see your new baby sister, Joshua," she told her then five-year-old son. He'd been staying with Lucille while she was in the hospital, and she'd just brought him home.

Victoria Rose Wander lay in a beautifully decorated bassinette, one tiny fist curled up towards her chubby little face. Chris watched with a smile as Josh leaned into the crib.

"Can I touch her?"

"Of course," Chris said. "Vicki's your baby, too."

"Wow . . ." Josh said in awe. He reached into the bassinette, then looked up at his mother, beaming. "I like her," he said.

Chris looked at Lucille, who gave a knowing wink.

"And you thought he'd be jealous," she said.

"Hey, Josh!"

It was Brian, calling from outside. Josh ran out of the front door. Chris looked out the window to see Brian holding a shiny red bicycle. She went outside herself, shaking her head.

"Brian, that's much too big!" she protested. "Josh is only five!"

"Chris, Josh is seven," Brian said.

When she looked at her son, he'd grown older. Chris's dream-self accepted this.

"Come on, Josh," Brian said. "Hop on. I'm going to teach you to ride."

"Yay!" Josh cried. "No more training wheels!"

Brian held the bike steady as Josh climbed on the seat. He looked over his son's head and said to Chris: "His other bike was getting too small." It was his way of explaining the expensive purchase.

"It's fine, Brian," Chris said. "He really needed a new bike, now that summer's here."

But it wasn't summer any longer. It was early spring, and they were all watching through the living room window as snow fell.

"I wish winter would go away," Vicki said. She was nearly five now.

"Well, long winters are part of life in Montana," Brian told her as he picked her up. "But it'll be spring before you know it."

"I'm glad Easter is late this year," Chris

said. "We should be seeing some flowers by then."

"How come Easter changes all the time," Josh asked, "but Christmas is the same day every year?"

Brian put Vicki down and took Josh into the kitchen, where a calendar hung near the telephone. Chris followed them. He turned the page to April and pointed. "See that white circle?"

"Yeah?"

"That's a full moon," Brian said. "It's the first full moon after the first day of Spring. Now, you go to the next Sunday. See?"

"Easter!" Josh cried.

"Right," Brian said. "Easter falls on the first Sunday after the first full moon after the first day of Spring."

"Oh, brother," Josh said. "I'm glad Christmas and Halloween and my birthday aren't so crazy to remember."

"It is crazy, isn't it?" Chris said. "But that's just the way the Church decided to do it."

"Crazy like Christy," an unfamiliar voice said.

Chris swung around. Her house was gone, her family was gone. She was in her old apartment, facing her brother. He was a young man, his wife Felicity at his side.

"You don't want to think about it," Harvey Jr. said cryptically.

And in that instant, Chris woke up to reality. Her heart beat rapidly as she lay in bed, Harvey Jr.'s image fading slowly from her mind. But the other images, the memories of things that had really happened, stayed with her. Things had been so wonderful all these years, but now it seemed her idyllic life was a dream itself.

She climbed slowly from the bed, rubbing the back of her neck. She didn't cry for those lost memories. She was beyond tears. The sun was already bright outside the window, and the clock told her it was nearly nine in the morning.

Eda was reading the morning paper when Chris entered the kitchen.

"Where's Lucille?" Chris asked, heading to the coffee maker.

"She went to run an errand," Eda replied "and to check up on her kids. She made corn muffins before she left."

Eda pushed the basket towards Chris as she sat down with her coffee. Chris was surprised to find she was very hungry. The muffins were delicious.

"How'd you sleep?" Eda asked.

"Okay, I guess," Chris replied, "I dreamt about nice things, like Brian teaching Josh how to ride a bike. It was only when Harvey showed up at the end that things turned bad."

"Harvey would do that, wouldn't he?" Eda said. "How did he figure into a nice dream?"

Chris sipped her coffee. "I don't know. He was just there. He said something strange to me. He said: 'You don't want to think about it.' I wonder what it meant?"

"Could be your subconscious sending you a message," Eda said.

Chris laughed a little. "That sounds like something Lucille would say."

"It makes sense. You have a lot on your mind. My God, do you ever! But there must be some missing pieces, some things that haven't come to you yet. What about the time when Harvey returned? The fact that he appeared so suddenly in your dream must mean something."

The back door opened and Lucille came in, bearing a bundle of papers. She set them on the table. Chris took one and studied the side-by-side pictures of her children. Underneath, three-inch-high letters declared: "MISSING."

"Eda and I are going to paste them up all over town," she announced. "And some of the people who work on the school newsletter have volunteered to saturate the county. If there could possibly be anyone who doesn't know what happened, after all the media attention, they'll know now."

"I never did like that picture of Josh," Chris said softly. She put the paper back on the pile and stood up to give her friend a hug. "Thank you so much."

"It's the least we can do," Eda said. "Lucille told me she's already contacted ChildFind and the Center for Missing and Exploited Children. It's possible they're still in the area, Chris. Kidnappers usually stick around for about forty-eight hours."

"Not all kidnappers are murderers," Chris pointed out.

131

Lucille picked up half of the papers and handed them to Eda. "Don't think about that now. We're all doing our best to find Josh and Vicki."

"And we will!" Eda insisted.

Chris held out her hand. "Let me have some of those."

"No," Lucille said, simply. "Chris, I didn't like the idea of you going out on that search last night. I don't like the idea of you riding around town, either."

"For heaven's sake, Lucille," Eda said, "she's a grown woman."

Lucille gazed at Eda for a moment, then at Chris. "Am I being Mother Hen again?"

Chris managed a smile. "It's okay. I really don't feel up to it, anyway."

"You can stay by the phone," Eda offered, "in case someone calls." She knew Chris hated being helpless.

"Good idea," Lucille said. "But listen to the answering machine first. That way you can screen out any weirdos."

Chris frowned. "Why would weirdos call here? No one knows I'm here!"

"But my number is on these posters," Lucille pointed out. "And tragedy brings out the worst people. Still, we could also get a hopeful call!"

So Chris stayed at home, staring at the telephone. It never rang, and soon the silence became so frustrating that she switched on the television. Tiffany Simmons was on Cable 75, and two pictures of Josh and Vicki were behind her. Chris stared at the pictures, hardly hearing Tiffany at all. She could only hear the sound of her breathing, as tears fell once more.

Eda spent an hour at the police station looking over files from the original Gammel case. Mike was more than happy to have her help, not only as a fellow police officer, but as a good friend of Chris's. When she finally decided to quit for the day, he drove her back to Lucille's house. The sight of a police car attracted reporters like ants to honey, but Eda waved them all away impatiently. "Sheriff Hewlett gave me a lift," she said. "I don't have any information."

"But aren't you Chris Wander's old friend?" someone asked.

"Of course. I'm here to offer emotional support, that's all."

"Where is she staying?" another reporter demanded.

Mike was out of the squad car, holding up both arms. "Leave her alone. Mrs Wander is in protective custody."

Everyone turned to Mike with more questions. Eda shot him a grateful look, then hurried up Lucille's driveway. She was halfway to the kitchen door at the back when she heard someone calling her name. She turned to see a woman, smartly dressed in a suit with a bow at her neck, hurrying up the driveway. Her heels clicked softly on the cement.

"Eda? Eda Crispin, is that you?"

Eda stifled an urge to make a face. Acting like a kid wouldn't do for a decorated officer of the N.Y.P.D. But it was difficult to maintain her composure at the sight of Tiffany Simmons. She knew that Tiffany was now a reporter for a local news station, and braced herself for questions. "Hello, Tiffany," she said.

Tiffany's hair was as fussily coifed as ever, each strand exactly in place. It irked Eda. She wished she *was* seven again, just so she could reach out and mess it up.

"What do you want?"

"Oh, I'm so sorry about Christy's husband. Poor Christy! And those children! Have you talked to Christy? Is that why you're here?"

Eda nodded. "I flew in to be with her."

"What a great friend you are. Christy must appreciate you."

A great enough friend to know we haven't called her "Christy" in years. "She does," Eda said. "Look, I'm tired. Goodbye, Tiffany."

"Wait! Would you mind if I asked a few questions? You know, old friend to old friend?"

Eda's growing exhaustion was exacerbated by a slight case of jet lag. She breathed in deeply, like a bull readying itself for the fight. "You are not my old friend," she said evenly. "You hated Chris thirty years ago, and you probably hate her as much today. You're just as bad as those other ghouls across the street!"

She left Tiffany standing open-mouthed, and walked up the stairs to the back door. Finally,

134

just before she entered the house, she heard Tiffany gasp, and then shout: "Having money didn't keep you from being trash! All I wanted to ask was where Christy is staying!"

"I wouldn't tell you," Eda said, closing the door behind her.

Lucille was in the kitchen. She looked at Eda with an inquiring gaze. "I heard shouting."

"Oh, Tiffany Simmons was outside."

Lucille smiled. "I've seen her on Cable 75 News. She's as obnoxious as ever."

"Little Miss Perfect. Where's Chris? Resting, I hope?"

"It took some effort," Lucille said. "Did you learn anything?"

Eda told Lucille about her conversation with Mike. Together, they decided it wasn't worth waking Chris up.

Outside, Tiffany stared at the house for a long time. She thought Christy Wander would be crazy to hide so near the scene of the crime. But then, where better to hide than under everyone else's nose? She slid on a pair of sunglasses, then walked to her car. She knew she wouldn't get a story today. But she was patient. She could wait until the others had given up. Then she'd confront that bitch Eda. And she'd find Christy, and have her story.

The cameraman, suddenly aware she'd left the crowd, hurried up to her. "What's up, Ms Simmons?"

"There's no story here, Frank," Tiffany said. "Let's call it a day."

"But what about . . .?"

"Never mind," Tiffany said. She waved a hand, like a queen dismissing a servant. "Go on home. I'll call you when I need you." She got into her car before he could say a word.

The following morning, as soon as the coffee maker had brewed a pot, Lucille went up to Chris's room to wake her. Chris was curled in a foetal position, her arms wrapped tightly around a pillow. Lucille wondered whom she was hugging in her dreams. She put a hand on her shoulder and shook her gently. "Chris, wake up! Do you want breakfast?"

There was a knock at the door, and Lucille glanced back to see Eda enter the room.

"I heard her get up in the middle of the night," Eda said. "She's probably exhausted. Maybe you should let her sleep."

Agreeing, Lucille followed Eda from the room and softly closed the door. While Lucille prepared breakfast, Eda went outside for the newspaper. She felt a twinge of nostalgia to see the paper's banner: "*Aberdeen Chronicle.*" It hadn't been in the family for nearly a decade, but she recalled vividly the days when her father first bought it. That had been at the time of the original murders. Strange how things came around again.

Dean Crispin had sold the *Chronicle* after her mother had died, and he was spending his retirement years travelling the world. The last she had heard, he was in Singapore. She wondered what he'd have to say about this latest turn of events.

"Good morning!"

Eda winced at the familiar-sounding voice. "Don't you ever go home?"

"Not until I get my story," Tiffany said. She was dressed in a sky-blue linen suit. "Eda, please talk to me. I'm not stupid. I know that you're here because of Christy, and I also know where she's staying."

Eda looked the other woman in the eye. "You do? That's a pretty good trick."

"Oh, come off it," Tiffany said, sounding annoyed. "You were like three peas in a pod when we were growing up. I can't imagine that you'd dump Christy in a strange place at a time like this. She's in there with you, isn't she?"

Eda shook her head and turned away.

"Don't you walk away from me!" Tiffany snapped. "Who do you think you are?"

Eda still didn't answer. She thought that if she opened her mouth, she'd explode and Tiffany might end up all over the sidewalk.

"You listen to me, Eda Crispin!" Tiffany cried. "I thought I'd do a sympathetic piece on this crime! But everyone in town knows what kind of background Christy comes from! Everyone knows what kind of man her father was! An abused child grows up to be an abusing

137

parent. People are talking, Eda! They're getting suspicious!"

That was too much for Eda to take. With a cry, she turned and ran down the driveway, hands outstretched. In training to be a police officer, she'd studied combat techniques and martial arts. But all those skills were forgotten as the little girl she'd been came to the surface; the little girl who hated Tiffany and all snobs like her. "You *bitch*!"

"Eda, no!" Tiffany turned to run.

Eda came up behind the woman, one hand reaching out to grab her. She almost had her by the collar when someone got *her* from behind.

It was Lucille. "Eda, stop! She isn't worth it!"

"She's a lying, cruel-mouthed bitch!"

"I'll have my story, Eda Crispin!" Tiffany backed across the street. "I'll see Christy if I have to haunt you day and night!"

Eda was about to yell out a choice epithet when Lucille gave her a yank and pulled her back to the house.

"Calm down," she said in a gentle voice. "You aren't helping Chris this way."

"You should have heard what she said," Eda replied as they entered the house. "She knows Chris is here, and she won't let us alone until she talks to her."

"Well, we certainly can't allow that."

Eda went to the coffee maker and poured herself a cup she didn't really want.

138

"I'll talk to Mike again," she said. "I'll have him talk to her, threaten her with harassment."

"I don't think you can," Tiffany said. "The First Amendment protects witches like Tiffany."

Eda sat down, setting her cup down hard on the table. "Then I'll find another way to stop her."

Lucille shook her head, sitting herself. "You're amazing. You haven't changed a bit. I never met anyone who could fly off the handle one minute, then be sweet the next, like you!"

"It's gotten me in some trouble at the precinct," Eda said. "But I guess they're getting used to me by now. Oh, that reminds me. Do you mind if I make a long-distance call?"

"Go ahead," Lucille said. "I've got some writing to catch up on."

"A new mystery?" Eda said. "I really loved *The Clock Struck One*."

"Thanks," Lucille said. "I've been working on my latest book for months now. But nothing in fiction compares to real life, does it?"

"I guess not," Eda agreed.

Lucille went to her office while Eda dialled the phone. She knew Tim had today off, and was pleased when he answered.

"Eda! How are you, Cowgirl? How's your friend?"

"I'm okay; Chris isn't. It's a horrible situation, Tim. I don't think I'm going to be back any time soon." She gave him an update.

When she had finished, Tim said:

139

"What about her husband? Could there be a connection?"

"The police are working on it."

"And you're just going to leave it at that?"

"You know me better than that, Tim. Of course I plan to check up on Brian Wander."

"Talking about the past seems to have been a good idea. You should go on doing it."

"Well, Chris is resting now," Eda said, "but when she wakes up we plan to continue."

Lucille came into the room.

"Hey, Tim, I have to go," Eda said, although Lucille signalled it was okay to stay on the line. "I'll keep you posted. Tell the Captain I'm using my vacation time."

"Goodbye, Eda."

Eda hung up the phone.

"I'm heading into town," Lucille said. "I need printer paper, and I thought I'd pick up a few groceries. Are you going to call Mike about Tiffany?"

"You bet I am. If she has any ideas about harassing Chris, you can bet there'll be others."

A worried look crossed Lucille's face. "I just hope we don't have to leave," she said.

Her father had been right.

There was a whole collection of heads at the Gammel house. Heads on tables, heads decorating bedposts, heads in pots on the stove . . . Chris walked slowly, staring at every head, looking

140

for familiar ones. Josh and Vicki were here somewhere.

She heard a footstep behind her. "I'm so glad you've come, Christy. Now I can add you to my collection."

Chris woke up with a gasp. It was dark in the room and silent except for a low hum from the clock. She turned to look at the time, and frowned to see it was eight-thirty. In that short space of time, the dream was forgotten. But not the real nightmare that had caused it.

Groggily, Chris tried to make sense of the time. It had been midnight when she went to bed. Had she slept through the whole day? Bewildered, she threw her covers aside and got up. Without putting on the robe Lucille had left for her, she hurried downstairs to find her friends drinking coffee at the table. "Why didn't you wake me up?" she demanded. "Why did you let me sleep?"

"Chris, there was no waking you up," Lucille said. "We tried a few times during the day, but I guess the sedative you took was stronger than we imagined. Besides, you needed your sleep."

"But a whole day!"

"There wasn't any news," Eda told her. "We would have tried harder to wake you if there had been. I spoke to Mike Hewlett again, and he says they're working round-the-clock. But right now, there isn't anything to tell you."

Lucille regarded her friend with concern. "Are you hungry? I made a nice shepherd's pie for dinner. I could heat it in the microwave."

141

Chris shook her head. "I don't think I could eat. But I could use a cup of coffee."

Instantly, Lucille was on her feet, fulfilling the request.

Chris accepted the cup gratefully. She drank nearly half before speaking again. "I can't understand why there hasn't been a phone call," she said. "I mean, the children were kidnapped. Why hasn't there been a ransom call?"

"I don't know, Chris," Lucille said. "Maybe . . . well, maybe the kidnapper is biding his time. Anyone cruel enough to do what he did . . ."

"I don't want to think about that," Chris interrupted. "I just want to get my children back! Eda, did Mike say anything at all that I should know?"

Eda thought a moment. "He was interested in the man who had been following you. He'll probably want to ask questions, Chris."

"I don't know." Chris ran a hand through her hair, looking worried. "A lot of people believed it was only my imagination."

"A lot of people?" Eda echoed. "Just some mean kids and your father, Chris. And who the hell cares what he thought? He was a vicious child abuser."

Chris moved uncomfortably in her chair. Lucille watched as an expression of fear crossed her features, one she'd seen many times in their childhood. But she wasn't about to let Chris get caught up in thoughts of her father, not when there was work to do. She shot Eda a warning glance, then stood up and took Chris's cup.

"Refill?" she asked in a cheerful tone that was only slightly forced.

"Please."

"I think," Lucille said, "that we should continue talking about the past. What we remember from long ago may provide important clues for the police to follow."

Eda nodded in agreement.

"Chris, if you try to remember the times you saw that man," she said, "we may be able to establish a pattern."

"Let's sit in the living room," Lucille said. "It's much more comfortable there. Chris, are you sure you won't have any dinner?"

"Not now."

The three women left the kitchen. Chris had always felt instantly comfortable when she entered Lucille's living room, where the floral print couch and ruffled curtains invited visitors to relax. But tonight, when she sank amongst the overstuffed curtains and put her cup on the coffee table, she only felt tense. Resting an arm across the back of the couch, she turned to look out the window. "They're still out there."

"Don't look, Chris," Lucille said. "There isn't anything to see. And if anyone looks over here and sees you, you'll never have any peace." She was thinking of Tiffany. Did the woman really know Chris was here? She was tempted to peek herself, to see if Tiffany had come back. The woman had rung her doorbell earlier that day, but Lucille had refused to answer.

"So, let's get started," Eda said.

Chris reached for her coffee cup. "I just wish we could do more than talk."

"It's the best place to start," Lucille said. "Chris, let's talk about the night after Hanukkah dinner at Eda's house."

"Your brother was with you that night," Eda said.

Chris stared at a reproduction Remington on the table, focusing her eyes on the fierce look of the horse's face. "Harvey kept saying he saved my life," she recalled. "But I never felt quite right about that. He ran away, remember, so I couldn't question him further."

Eda jotted down some notes to herself. Something about this whole story was suspicious, and she planned to do a little research of her own regarding Harvey Burnett, Jr.

"But he came back three years later," Lucille said. "Did you talk to him then?"

"There was no time," Chris replied. "My father treated him like the Prodigal Son. They spent most of Harvey Jr.'s time in Aberdeen together. It was as if nothing bad had happened between them. Then Harvey Jr. left, and I never saw him or his new wife Felicity, again. Felicity was expecting, you know. I never even learned about the baby, whether I have a niece or a nephew. But, somehow, I think Harvey knows the truth. I think he knew it when he came home."

Wearily, Chris rubbed her eyes. Lucille gave her hand a squeeze, while Eda watched them. Eda vowed that, somehow, she had to try to find out what Harvey Jr. knew about the terrible night Chris was attacked in that alley.

Chapter Seven

Vicki looked down at her bowl of soup and made a face. "It tastes funny," she said.

"You're just saying that 'cause I cooked it," Josh retorted. "Sorry if I can't do it the way Mom does." But when he lifted a spoonful to his own mouth, he spit it back into the bowl. "Gross!"

They'd found a portable stove in the room, and a can opener. After dumping noodle soup concentrate into a pot, Josh had realized there was no sink in the room. Investigation found a large water tank in one corner, with a tap at the bottom. He'd filled the soup can with that. "It tastes rusty," he said. "I guess I should'a let it drain a little. Forget it – there's potato chips over there. They've got to be okay." He took a bag down from the shelf and popped it open, spilling crumbs on the floor. Then he and Vicki sat on the edge of a cot, sharing them.

"Does your tummy still hurt?" the little girl asked.

"Not so much."

Vicki took another potato chip and stuffed

it whole into her mouth. "What're we gonna do, Josh?"

"Gee, I don't know," Josh admitted. "If it's really late at night, there's nothing we can do. It's stupid to yell for help if no one can hear you. We can't get out as long as the door is locked."

Vicki yawned noisily. "I'm tired. I wanna go to sleep again."

"Maybe one of us should stay awake," Josh said. "I mean, if anyone comes." He didn't admit his fear that "anyone" could be the kidnapper. Having had time to think, he was convinced that that was what had happened. He had some vague memories of his father fighting with someone, but he was afraid to push the recollection further. The underlying sense of something horrible was too much for him to take. Vicki had stopped talking about the bad man, and he was glad. She scared him when she screamed like that.

"I don't wanna," Vicki said, yawning again.

"Then don't," Josh said. "I'll wake you up if help comes."

Vicki stretched out on the cot, pulling a green army-issue blanket over herself. "Wish I had my unicorn," she mumbled drowsily.

Josh got up and cleaned the soup bowls. The soup was gross enough as it was, he thought, without letting it sit around. There was a bent and rusted can on the other side of the room, where he dumped the inedible noodles. He rinsed the bowls and spoons under the tap of the water tank and stacked them on the table again.

Once finished, he started another trip around the room. He hoped he'd find something he'd missed before; some way out of this strange place. He was convinced they were in a basement, since there were no windows. There *were* vents, and he wondered if he might be able to unscrew the covers of one to crawl through. Then he shook his head. The vents were too small.

The lights flickered suddenly. Vicki, not quite asleep yet, bolted upright. "Josh?"

"It's okay," Josh said, although he wasn't so sure himself. What would happen if the lights went out? What would he do then? He hadn't been afraid of the dark for a couple of years now, but . . .

"*Are you awake?*"

The voice sounded far away, like a radio just off a station. Josh didn't answer.

"*I asked: are you awake?*"

"Yeah!" Josh yelled back, looking all around. "Let us out of here, will you?"

"*In time,*" the voice said. "*Did you eat?*"

"The water is gross," Josh said.

"*What did you eat?*"

"Soup," Josh answered. "And potato chips."

"*What kind of soup?*"

Josh gave his sister a look that said: "what kind of question is that? Who cares?"

"Just let us out of here!" he shouted. "You better let us out, or our father . . ."

"*What kind of soup*?" It was almost a scream.

"Chicken noodle," Josh said, raising his eyebrows at Vicki.

She twisted her mouth. This guy was *weird*. "You open that door!" she yelled. "You open that door and let us out, you *criminal*!"

There was a long silence. Finally: "*What door*?"

"The door that's locked, stupid!" Josh snapped. "The way out of here!"

The unseen figure burst into laughter. The sound of it bounced around the stone room, growing more maniacal by the minute. Josh lost his bravado, and suddenly hugging his sister didn't seem so repulsive. They looked around themselves. Where was the voice coming from? It seemed to be everywhere!

At last the hideous laughter stopped.

"*I'll be back in the morning*," it said. "*I'll bring the key*."

"*We want out now*!" Vicki shouted.

They waited for a few minutes, but there was no answer. Vicki cuddled more tightly against her brother. "Josh, why won't he let us out?"

"I don't know why," Josh said. He pulled away. "What makes you think I know everything?"

He hurried away from her, feeling bad that he couldn't save them. He was the big brother, the smart one, the brave one. If this was a video game, he'd know what to do. He'd know where to find weapons, a secret door to another level, a special code to make him invincible. But this wasn't a video game. This was real, and it was scarier than anything he'd ever experienced.

As Vicki watched, Josh went into the small bathroom and shut the door. He didn't want her looking at him when he felt so little and helpless. He plonked himself down on the floor and gazed for a moment at the cracked toilet bowl. There was no water in it, and it didn't flush. The back had no lid, and a spider had long ago abandoned a web inside the tank.

Josh stared a little longer, as an idea began to form in his head. Slowly, he rose. He could stand on the tank and reach the ceiling, couldn't he? He'd watched a house being built once, and he knew there was space between the ceiling and the floor above. Not much space, but probably the right size for a kid. If he could get up in there, if he could find a weak spot in the floor above . . . No, it was a crazy idea.

He looked up at the ceiling. It was covered with dingy tile, spotted brown and black with water stains and mildew. "What the heck," he said out loud, standing up. It was worth a try. He climbed onto the tank. Then he reached up and started pulling the tiles away. One by one they crumbled to the floor. He had to avert his eyes, and he sneezed a few times, but after the dust settled he looked up at his handiwork.

He expected to see a network of pipes and wires, or perhaps just some wooden beams. Instead, there was solid cement, just like the walls around him.

Defeated he jumped down to the floor. And in the privacy of that dingy, winterless bathroom, he buried his face between his knees and began to cry.

The things the children used had to be replaced. Everything down there had to be precise or terrible things would happen. There had to be fifteen cans of soup, fifteen bags of chips, fifteen of everything. Fifteen was a very important number.

He knew he couldn't buy anything in town. The people of Aberdeen were certainly on the lookout for strangers, and in a town this small he'd be spotted. So he drove into the next town, Longacre, and bought what he needed there. He parked his car at the bus station on the edge of Aberdeen and walked the rest of the way. He kept away from the main roads, kept his head ducked down so no one would see his face.

When he reached the corner nearest his lair, he waited for half an hour to be sure he was alone. Then he raced across the street, cutting across nearly two acres of tall grass until he reached his destination. Even then, he waited at the door another ten minutes, breathing hard from the run. Then, very, very slowly, he opened the door.

He peered at the children, who huddled together on a cot, sound asleep. Moving carefully, (like a stalking tiger, he thought), he entered the room and replaced the soup and chips. He was about to leave when he remembered the boy had asked about a key. A laugh tried to escape, and he covered his mouth with a dirty hand. Then he reached into his pocket and pulled out a rusty old key. He put it on the table and left.

The sound of a door slamming pulled Josh from sleep so abruptly he fell from the cot. He sat holding his head for a few moments, dazed, unable to comprehend his surroundings. Finally, he realized where he was and that what he'd hoped was a nightmare was all too real.

He stood up and looked around. Had he heard a door slam? He looked back at his sister, who slept curled up like a baby. He wondered how long they'd been asleep and if it was morning yet. A terrible ache turned his attentions to the bathroom, and with great reluctance he used the old toilet. "Gross," he mumbled.

When he came out again, he noticed something on the table. A key! He hurried to pick it up. It didn't look like any key he'd ever seen. It was rusted and very heavy. Josh didn't care, though. He just wanted to try it. "Vicki!" he called. "Wake up! He left the key, just like he said he would!"

Maybe it was all a joke, and maybe now it was over. "Vicki!"

The little girl sat up and began to whine. "I want Mommy!"

"Can it!" Josh said, holding up the key. "Look what I've got."

Vicki's eyes widened. "Yay! Are we goin' home?"

"Soon as I get the door open."

Vicki walked with him to the door and watched as he pushed the key in the lock. At first, it wouldn't turn. Josh bit his lip, and tried harder.

"Are we stuck?" Vicki asked. "Are we stuck?"

"No!" Josh snapped. They couldn't be stuck! He was sick of this game and he wanted to go home!

He wrapped both hands around the key and put his weight into the effort. At last, with a pop, it turned the lock. Vicki's look of apprehension turned into a wide grin. Josh pushed the door open . . . and walked into a closet. "What the . . .?"

"Josh," Vicki said softly, "this isn't the way out."

"I can see that!" Josh said, trying hard to fight tears. What kind of cruel trick was this?

The closet measured about four-by-four feet. The walls were cement, without windows or vents. The room was completely empty.

Vicki turned and ran to the middle of the room. She turned in circles, shouting: "I want out! I want out! I want ooouuut!"

"Vicki, shut up!" Josh snapped. Her voice was bouncing off the walls. "Nobody can hear you!"

"Hey, you stupid people out there! You make a door for us!"

Josh sat on the edge of the cot and covered his ears. As Vicki went on shouting, he thought about her words. *Make a door.* There had to be a door! There had to be a way out of here! Maybe it was just blocked off. "Hey, Vicki!" he called.

By now his little sister was jumping up and down, her fists flailing angrily.

"Vicki, let's find a door!"

Somehow, that cut through her tantrum. She stopped, took a few deep breaths, and stared at him.

"Let's find a door," he said again. "We got in, we'll get out."

"Okay," Vicki said, almost calmly. It was as if she hadn't had a fit of temper at all.

"Let's look very carefully," Josh said. "Like detectives. You know, like Encyclopedia Brown would look. The door has to be hidden."

"Yeah, hidden," Vicki agreed.

"We'll start over there," Josh said, pointing to a wall.

They walked along, feeling carefully for any sign of an exit.

"It's cold," Vicki said.

Josh didn't answer. He was concentrating too deeply, peering at every little crack, checking the places between the cement blocks. There was a way out of this place, and if it took him a million hours, he'd find it.

Vicki walked over to the shelves. She felt hungry suddenly, and took down a bag of pretzels. As she ate them, she peered carefully behind shelves of food. It was silly for a door to be behind shelves, she thought. She kept looking, and kept seeing nothing but solid wall. Finally, she came to the end of the shelves. She was about to turn back to her brother when the light flickered.

"Not again!" Josh moaned.

Vicki looked up at the flickering bulb. And as she did so, she noticed something they hadn't seen before. "Josh, look!" she cried. "What's that ladder doing up there?"

Josh turned to see at the same time she ran across the room. There really was a ladder, and it was bolted to the wall. Vicki reached up, but couldn't grab the end of it.

"How come it's on the wall like that?" she asked. "How come it's so high?"

At once, Josh knew the answer. They hadn't been able to find the door because it was over-head! The ladder led to a trapdoor! "Help me push the table over!"

The two children pushed the table to the wall. When he stood on it, Josh could see that it was an extension ladder and that it had been pulled up and hooked in place. All he had to do was unhook it and climb right up to the trapdoor above. He took hold of a rung and tried to lift the ladder. But it was much too heavy. Josh studied it, scratching his head in thought.

Well, why did he need to unhook it? He could reach the bottom rung right from the table! He climbed onto it, then looked over his shoulder. "We'll be outta here in a minute. Then we'll go home and tell Mom and Dad what happened."

"Yeah," Vicki said, "Daddy'll beat up the bad man who put us here!"

Josh paused. Something about the words *beat up* brought back that vague, frightening memory that had been trying to surface since he woke up down here. But he pushed it away. Whatever it was, it didn't matter so long as they got out of here.

He started up. "I'll climb out," he called down. "And then I'll unhook the ladder and you can climb up."

"Okay!"

The ladder shook slightly with each step, but Josh held tightly and kept ascending. He had no idea that his weight was working the latch free until it was too late.

Suddenly, the lower half of the ladder came loose. It shot towards the floor with lightening-like speed. The clanking blended with the sound of the children's screams. When the ladder hit the floor a few seconds later, the impact threw Josh off. He fell backwards, smashed his head on the table edge, and passed out.

Vicki stood staring at him for just a moment. Then she started to shake him. "Josh, wake up!" she begged. "Please!"

But Josh wouldn't wake up. Vicki stared at the ladder that had hurt him. How could they get out if the ladder hurt them? She went to the ladder and grabbed it. Shaking it with all her might, she gazed up at the ceiling. She could see the door now, a funny round door. "Open up!" she shouted. *Open up! Open up! Open up!*" But no one heard her.

Chapter Eight

Chris sat on Lucille's couch with her head in her hands, weary after long conversation.

"We need to talk to Harvey Jr.," Eda said. "Do you have *any* idea where we can trace him?"

Chris shook her head. "When Harvey was visiting, his wife Felicity suddenly went into labour. They rushed off to the hospital. That's the last I ever saw of either of them."

"Another dead end," Lucille sighed.

"I refuse to believe that," Eda said.

Chris stood up and tried to busy herself clearing the cups away.

"Forget those," Lucille said. "Let's just go to bed."

They walked upstairs together. Eda said goodnight when she reached her bedroom. They'd spent a long time talking, reminiscing, but tomorrow morning she wanted to do something more active. She planned to tell Mike her suspicions about Harvey. Maybe he could tell her where Chris's brother was now living. Harvey knew something, she was sure, and she was determined to find out.

* * *

159

The smell of coffee and home-baked muffins lured Eda out of bed early the next morning. She found her two friends already at the table.

"I wish I could eat like this in New York," Eda said, buttering a large, flaky muffin. "The bakery near me just doesn't make 'em like this."

Chris managed a smile. "You told us once Tim Becker's quite a cook."

"He never made me breakfast," Eda said, "but his cheesecake's incredible."

Lucille wanted to ask Eda if she missed Tim, but it didn't seem right. How could she bring up Eda's partner when Chris would never see her husband again? As if she'd heard Lucille's thoughts, tears welled in Chris's eyes as she unrolled the morning paper. Photos of Josh and Vicki were prominent under the headline: LITTLE VICTIMS: THE SEARCH FOR THE WANDER CHILDREN.

"Josh is so much cuter than this school picture," Chris said.

Lucille took the paper from her.

"I'm glad to see them on the front page," Eda said. "The more people who see this, the better chance of finding them."

"Like they found Teddy and Adrian Gammel?" Chris asked bitterly.

"That was thirty years ago," Eda reminded. "Forensics has come a long way. We have computers now, sophisticated analytical techniques and more. Mike can use the fax machine at the station to send these pictures all over the country. There's a much better chance of

160

finding Josh and Vicki than there was for the Gammel boys."

"They *will* find them," Lucille insisted.

Chris's shoulders heaved in a sigh of frustration. "It's been days," she said. "I feel so helpless! I hate sitting around doing nothing while my babies could be in terrible danger. What if they're hurt, or sick?"

She recalled hearing Josh cough the other night. "I think Josh was coming down with a cold," she said. "And I'm not there to help him!"

Lucille stood up and left the room. A moment later, she returned with a pad of paper and some drawing pencils she'd found in Jerry's room. She lay them on the table. "There is one thing you can do right now," she said. "Do you think you can draw a picture of the man who was following you years ago?"

Chris stared, momentarily shocked by the request. "Why? I don't want to remember that horrible man!"

But Eda understood at once. "I think it's a great idea. Chris, it will give the police something to work with. Right now, they have no real suspects."

Chris gave it a moment's thought, then nodded. It would be difficult to conjure up images of that hideous face, but she would do anything to help get her children back.

Eda excused herself and went upstairs to get dressed. She planned to drive to the police station for a talk with Mike. As she was pulling her belt

161

through the loops of her slacks, Lucille entered the room.

"I wish there was something *I* could do," she said.

"Giving Chris safe haven is a lot."

Lucille shook her head. "I was thinking about my mystery books last night, and trying to recall the different ways my detectives worked. But this is real life, and I don't know where to begin."

"Maybe there is something you can do," Eda said. "When we were talking, we recalled wondering why the Gammel house was still standing several years after the murder. Now it's been *thirty* years, and the place is still there. Someone must be paying property tax on it, or it would have gone into foreclosure. That's a nice piece of land someone could have developed years ago. Can you find out who owns the house?"

"That sounds easy enough," Lucille said. "I'll bet it's Irene Gammel."

"Then we'll have another clue. We'll find out where she's living. And when we find her, you can bet I've got a lot of questions to ask her."

Later, when Eda started telling Mike her suspicions about Harvey Burnett Jr., he gave her his full attention. She related the memories that had come back to Chris, Lucille and herself.

"I have to agree Harvey looks suspect," Mike said, "although tormenting his sister would hardly make him a murderer."

"Living with that father and mother might," Eda said. "But I'm not suggesting he came back

162

and killed Brian, the brother-in-law he never met. I'm just saying he seemed to show up at odd times. He was always a troublemaker. I'd be curious to know just where he is nowadays."

Mike jotted a note. "That shouldn't be too hard. I wouldn't be surprised if a guy like that ended up with a record."

There was a knock at the door, and a young policeman came in. He handed a file folder to the sheriff.

"Another sighting was reported, sir," he said.

Eda glanced from the young cop to the sheriff. "Sighting?"

"A few people claim to have seen the Wander children," Mike said. "But you understand that we take these reports with caution. Some are from people who are really concerned, but even in Aberdeen we have our share of mean-spirited bastards."

"That's right, sir," the young cop agreed. "Until we see those kids ourselves, we can't believe a thing."

Mike signed a form and handed the folder back to the younger man. He left the office, and the sheriff resumed his conversation with Eda. "This kind of thing happens when a story is all over the news," he said. "In a way, publicity helps our cause. Having people aware of the Wander children may help find them. On the other hand, too many interested parties muck up the investigation."

"It's hard to decide between useful and useless

163

information," Eda said. She stood up. "Speaking of information, you said I could have access to the old files."

Mike got up, too, and led her out of the office. "We've gone over them carefully," he said, "but it never hurts to have someone fresh take a look. Just the way you women are trying to make connections between events of your childhoods and what happened now, I've been trying to connect the few facts we have in this case with the old information. So far, I've come up with nothing helpful."

Eda followed him through a small reception area filled with four desks. When she was a child, there had only been one desk equipped with a little black rotary dial telephone. Now the office was filled with high-tech equipment and very busy people. She hoped each one of them was dedicated to helping Chris find her children.

They entered a large room. Tall windows striped the back wall, letting sunlight pour over a long conference table. There were several large bulletin boards hung on the walls, covered with scraps of paper, newspaper clippings, and announcements. Two file cabinets flanked the door. Mike went to one and pulled it open. "Here's the old file," he said. "You can sit in here and have a look."

The fact that only two file cabinets were needed to keep track of crime in Aberdeen reminded Eda just what a quiet town this was. Or at least, seemed to be. She wondered if Harvey Burnett, Jr. was in there somewhere. And what about Chris's father? Was there a file on him, on the way he drank and abused his family? She doubted it. People hadn't discussed those things back then.

And one thing leads to another. Maybe if they had talked, Chris's husband would be alive.

"Eda?"

She blinked and realized her mind was wondering. "Can you get me some coffee?"

"I'll have someone send it in," Mike said, and left.

Eda sat down with her back to the windows and opened a thick folder. Her first sight was a grainy black-and-white photograph of Darren Gammel's remains. Although his back was to the camera, and his arm thrown up over the empty space that should have been his head, the picture was gorey enough to send a shiver down Eda's spine.

She wondered what it had been like for Chris, finding Brian. With a sigh, she put the old photographs aside and started to read.

Before Eda and Lucille had left that morning, Lucille had repeatedly asked if Chris minded being alone for a few hours. Chris had insisted she was okay, but now she wasn't so sure. She had been sitting at one of the desks in the twins' bedroom, a blank pad of paper before her. As if she were a child again, she felt terribly afraid of being alone. How long had her friends been gone?

It was difficult to draw the man's face. Every oval she sketched for his face, every shadow she rubbed for his beard, sent such chills through her that she crumbled up each effort. She buried her head in her hands and sighed deeply. Except for a faint hum from the refrigerator, the house was still. She could hear an occasional car pass on the road below, and once a dog started barking. It was the kind of stagnant silence that filled a movie a split second before the murderer jumped out.

She tried to hum a Randy Travis tune, just to hear something. She was getting nowhere. She had to stop being so afraid! *You're not seven now, Chris. You aren't a helpless little girl.*

But her kids *were* helpless, and she had to do what she could to save them.

Hoping to clear her head, she went to the window and looked outside. A yellow police banner had been stretched between the trees that flanked the front yard. There were still a few people there. A police woman sat guard in her squad car. Two television trucks were parked at the curb. One was marked CABLE 75, Tiffany's station. Chris tried to find the woman in the crowd, but it seemed she wasn't there.

Even more surprising was the second TV van, which had come from North Dakota. Had her story spread that far so quickly? Good. The more people who knew about Josh and Vicki, the better.

She turned abruptly and headed back to the desk. With determination, she picked up a pencil and started to sketch again. People had seen her children's pictures. Now they'd see a likeness of the man who'd probably kidnapped them, of the murderer who'd taken Brian away from her.

Her hand flew over the page, the picture forming in a matter of seconds. When she finished, she recognized the devil eyes she'd been so afraid of as a child. Was this really him? Had he come back again?

She stared at the hateful portrait for a long time, her teeth set. She wanted to tear it up, stomp on it, set it on fire. No, she wanted to do those things to the man himself. How could he have done that to her, to her family? Why was he so full of hatred? Her only involvement in that long-ago crime was the blood Irene Gammel had smeared on her blouse. So why had he stalked her? Who *was* he?

She stared at the picture. Suddenly, she pushed it away. There was something too familiar about the face she'd drawn. It wasn't only that she'd seen him years before. It was more than that.

It's impossible, she told herself with a wide back-and-forth sweep of her head. It can't be! Just coincidence!

But in her heart, she was disgusted to realize it might not be coincidence at all. She had seen eyes like that in another face. Softer, kinder eyes, but with the same shape. And probably the same colour. Chris *knew* where she'd seen those eyes, but she didn't want to believe it.

*   *   *

While Chris drew, and remembered, and Eda studied police files, Lucille visited the town hall. Many years ago, it had been part of the building that also housed the library. That was where she'd first met Chris. But Aberdeen's growing population of school children prompted the town fathers to separate the two establishments. Now the library was a huge glass and stone building situated on the opposite side of town. The town hall remained in the old brick building, although it had expanded over the years to fill the void left when the books were removed. The records room was located where the children's library had once been. Instead of Dr Seuss and Nancy Drew, the room held birth certificates, death certificates, blank marriage licenses waiting to be filled in, and tax records.

Lucille hadn't been here since her divorce was finalized, and she was both surprised and pleased to see an old schoolmate, Stephanie, behind the desk. Stephanie had gained a good fifty pounds since graduation and had a lot of grey in her hair. But she still had the same nice smile and friendly manner Lucille remembered.

"Lucille Danton!" she cried. She frowned. "Oh, I'm sorry. It's back to Brigham again, isn't it? I was so sorry to hear about you and Sydney."

"Thanks," Lucille said.

Stephanie leaned forward. "How are you doing now?"

"I'm fine," Lucille insisted. She didn't want

to talk about her divorce. "I need a favour, Stephanie. I need to find someone's taxes."

"Income tax?"

"Property," Lucille corrected. "I was wondering if you could tell me who's been paying tax on the old Gammel place."

Stephanie's eyes widened with understanding. "Oh, this has something to do with the Wander family, doesn't it? I couldn't believe it when I heard Tiffany Simmons on the news. It sends chills through me."

"We're all concerned," Lucille said. "Can you get me that information?"

"Well, property tax is usually paid with a mortgage," Stephanie said. "You might do better at Western National Bank."

"I'd be surprised if there was still a mortgage on that house," Lucille said, a little shortly. She wanted work done, not conversation. "Will you please look it up, anyway?"

"All right," Stephanie said, a slight hint of hurt in her voice. "Wait here. Taxes paid by individuals rather than banks come in twice a year. The last pay period was May 31st. That shouldn't take too long to find."

Lucille sat down on one of five ladder-backed wooden chairs that lined the wall. She picked up a pamphlet and glanced at it without really seeing the words. Then she simply watched the clock for the next five minutes.

Stephanie came back with a thick book. She was shaking her head as she plonked the volume down onto the counter. "You didn't have to come here to find out who's paying tax on that property," she said sharply.

Lucille stood opposite her, perplexed. "What do you mean?"

"You could just ask Chris," Stephanie said.

Lucille looked at her with bewilderment. Stephanie turned the book around and pointed halfway down the page. Lucille read the words. Then she read them again, certain she'd made a mistake. But it was there all right, in black ink. The name of the person who'd paid the tax. Brian Wander.

Eda and Lucille had planned to meet each other in two hours. Eda hadn't had time to read all the reports from the Gammel investigation, but she was beginning to agree with Mike that there was no way to make a connection with the Wander murder and kidnappings. She'd read through all the autopsy reports, and now she was reading Darren's a second time. She had a feeling she'd missed something, but she just couldn't be sure what it was.

Although she tried to read the faded, blurry pica type with a clinical eye, Eda could only see Brian's name, instead of Darren's. The coroner had suggested the lines of the cut through Darren's throat were clean enough to suggest a quick blow. There were numerous other blows, but the autopsy concluded he'd died quickly. Had Brian's death been quick?

Again, she had the feeling she'd missed something. She went back to the second report. This man's name was Basil Horton, a bachelor who seemed to have no family. Irene Gammel had been released because this murder had taken place while she was in jail. Eda thought it was sad that no one talked much about this crime. She guessed that the Gammel murder was stressed because it involved the disappearance of children. But maybe, within Basil Horton's report, she'd find the clue that was eluding her.

The young deputy who'd been in Mike's office earlier knocked gently and opened the door. "Are you expecting a Lucille Brigham?"

"Sure," Eda said with surprise. Had two hours passed already?

Lucille came in, her face ashen. The dark hair she usually kept so neat had come loose from her braid. She looked as if she'd run all the way to the police station, and the wind had had its way with her. She took a deep breath and dropped into the chair next to Eda's.

"What happened to you?" Eda asked. "You're all flushed."

"Got here as fast as I could," Lucille said. "Eda, this is worse than we imagined."

"How could it be worse?"

"You'll never believe who's been paying taxes on the Gammel property," Lucille said. She didn't wait for her friend to prompt her. "Brian Wander!"

Eda opened her mouth to reply, but nothing came out.

"You heard me right," Lucille said. "*Brian* was paying the property tax. He's been doing so for about eleven years now."

"About as long as he was married to Chris," Eda said. "Somehow, Brian is connected to all this, and not just as a victim."

Lucille's eyes narrowed in suspicion. "You know, he was always going on business trips. I wonder about that."

Eda closed the file she'd been reading. She wanted to go over the autopsy reports again, but decided this was more important for now. "Maybe you should go to the department store," she suggested. "Find out just what he did there and where he went on those trips. Somehow, I wouldn't be surprised if Washington came up."

"Washington?"

"Washington State. That's where Irene Gammel moved after it all happened."

Leaving the files to be put away by someone who knew where they belonged, Eda stood up and left the room with Lucille. She knocked at Mike's door. There was no answer, so she left a message that she'd be back later. Outside, the blue sky was overcast with the promise of rain. The day was thick, muggy. She wondered how Josh and Vicki were doing. Were they cool enough, and dry?

"I could drop you off at the store," Lucille said, "then head home. Someone needs to be with Chris." She unlocked her car doors. She'd never felt it necessary to lock them before, but in the last two days it had become automatic.

Once inside, Eda answered her. "We don't have time," she said. "I want to visit the Gammel house. If Brian was in charge of it, maybe he left a clue there. It shouldn't take too much time. When I'm done, I'll swing around and pick *you* up. *Then* we'll go home."

The women drove in silence until they reached the shopping mall where Brian had worked until a few days before. Lucille got out and Eda moved into the driver's seat. As she pushed through a glass door, Lucille confronted one of the posters of the missing children. It made her heart ache.

Brenley's Department Store was at the end of a long corridor of shops. Inside, Lucille passed cosmetic counters, ignoring a beautiful young woman who wanted to spritz her with perfume. She cut through the accessories department, her long legs giving her a stride that was purposeful, businesslike. Just beyond the jewellery island, she stepped onto the escalator. It took her to the third-floor offices.

A few inquiries led her to the store manager. A young man, perhaps in his twenties, introduced himself as Jamie McEntire and shook Lucille's hand. She pulled up the chair he indicated.

"Brian Wander?" he said curiously. "But I've already spoken to the police."

"I just need some questions answered," Lucille

said. "I'm a friend of his wife, and there are things she needs to know."

McEntire closed the ledger he'd been studying. "I can't tell you much. I don't remember him very well. I've only been on this job six months and haven't gotten to know everyone who works here."

He made himself taller in his seat, as if daring Lucille to challenge him. Lucille had the feeling he was holding back, perhaps because he was resentful of this interference in his work day.

"If you don't mind my saying this," she commented, "you seem young to be in such a high position. That tells me you have brains. Someone so smart should be able to remember a man who made that kind of money."

"I wouldn't call twenty-five thousand dollars a year a lot of money," Jamie said.

Lucille stared at him for a few seconds.

"There must be some mistake," she insisted. Chris had told her Brian made a lot more than that.

"No, that was his salary. After all, he only worked part-time."

"Part-time?" Lucille echoed. This was getting harder to understand by the moment. "Brian worked a forty-hour week. More, when you consider the business trips he took."

"I think someone's been lying to you, Ms Brigham," McEntire said. "No *part-time* employee of Brenley's makes business trips. I don't know where he went, but it had nothing to do with us."

Lucille sank back in her chair, staring into space as she tried to sort things out. Brian had lied to Chris, but why? Where had those bogus trips taken him, if not on business? She wondered if he'd been having an affair.

She turned her gaze back on McEntire, who was watching her patiently as he drank from a mug that said: World's Best Daddy. Brian had been one of those, too, Lucille thought.

"Could I see Brian's resumé?"

"Sure," the manager said. "I haven't had a chance to refile it – it's right here." He pushed aside some papers to unearth it. "Good report on the guy," he said, handing the sheet across the desk. "A model employee, always on time. His resumé doesn't say much."

Lucille took the paper and read it carefully. She was hoping it would list his place of birth, but that information wasn't there. She did, however, find the name of the first company that had employed him when he came to Aberdeen. "Thanks for your time, Mr McEntire," she said as she stood up.

"Hope I was of help," he replied.

Too much help, Lucille thought. *I'm not sure I want to know all this.* She glanced at her watch and realized Eda wouldn't be picking her up for a while. Though she wished she could talk to Brian's first employer in person, she didn't want to wait that long. She opened her purse, collected as much change from the bottom as she could find, and headed for the nearest pay phone.

175

Information gave her the number of Mooney's Fine Furniture.

The line rang twenty times before someone finally answered, in a voice that was out of breath. Lucille introduced herself and explained what she needed.

"Brian Wander?" the man on the other end said. "What a shame about that guy, huh? Nice fella. He worked here for about two years."

"Could you possibly tell me where he came from?"

"I think he used to drive a UPS truck."

"No, I mean, where did he live before he came to Aberdeen?"

There was a hum on the wire. "I don't recall, exactly," the man said. "Wait here."

Lucille heard the buzzing sound of saws and pounding of hammers in the background. A recording cut in and asked for "twenty-five cents, please". Lucille dropped a quarter into the slot.

Finally, the man came back. "Got his papers right here," he said. "Took a few minutes to look it up. Yep, yep, here it is."

"It says where he used to live?"

"Sure does," came the reply. "Brian Wander came all the way from Washington State."

Lucille nearly dropped the phone. "What?"

"Washington," the man repeated. "Don't know what brought him all the way to Montana just to make furniture. Guess he must . . ."

Lucille cut him off, thanked him, and hung up the phone. Her stomach was starting to feel sour. Her surroundings became a blur of light and colours as she walked slowly to the mall entrance.

She'd thought they'd grown wiser over the years. She'd thought Chris had earned her happy place in life after the nightmarish childhood she'd had. No one had been happier than Lucille the day Chris announced she was getting married. Brian was such a nice guy. Eda had even called him "Chris's knight in shining armour".

It made Lucille sick to think that knight had more than a few chinks in his armour, chinks cut there by the swing of an axe.

Chapter Nine

Josh came to in the middle of the night, but without windows he had no way of knowing the time. Vicki was curled up in a ball next to him on the floor, her back pressed tight against his side. She had her thumb in her mouth. She'd taken a blanket from one of the cots to cover them both.

Slowly, Josh sat up. His head hurt badly, and when he touched it his fingertips came back dotted with blood. It took him a few moments to remember he had fallen from the ladder. The ladder – their only hope of getting out of this place. He shook his sister. "Vicki, wake up," he said. Vicki stirred, then sat up. "You're not dead," she mumbled, her eyes still half-closed.

"Of course not," Josh said, "but my head hurts enough to kill me."

Vicki opened her eyes and brought up a chubby hand to scratch her head. Her red hair was a mess of tangles. "You banged your head real bad," she said. Her voice was tiny, distant. "I tried and tried to wake you up, but you wouldn't. I thought it killed you."

"Well, I'm alive, all right," Josh said. He tried to stand up, but the room started spinning. It was a lot like the Tilt-N-Flip ride he'd gone on the previous summer. He put his head in his hands. For a few moments, he did and said nothing, just letting his brain steady itself. As soon as he could speak again, he said: "Vicki, check those shelves. Mom always gives me medicine when I get hurt. See if there's a bottle of Tylenol or something."

Still half asleep, the little girl stood up and padded over to the shelves of food. The cans and boxes seemed to swim in front of her. Although she couldn't read, she'd recognize the box right away. But there was none to be found.

"Sorry, Josh," she said. "Does your head hurt real bad?"

"Is the Pope Catholic?"

"I dunno," Vicki drawled. Why was he talking about the Pope, anyway? She reached up and pulled down a box of cereal. "I'm hungry," she said. "Is it time for breakfast yet?"

Josh shrugged. He wished he had the watch Lucille had given him on his last birthday. But he'd taken it off when he had got ready for bed . . . however long ago that was.

He closed his eyes. An image of someone running through his house filled his mind, so frightening he opened his eyes again. "I'll fix that," he said, walking to the table where Vicki stood with the cereal box. "We'll need milk. See that can over there? It's powdered milk. You have to mix it with water."

Vicki got the can while Josh filled a metal pitcher from the water tank. This time, he let it flow for a few moments, hoping to get rid of the rusty taste. He prepared the milk, then filled two bowls with cereal.

Vicki took a bite, then turned and spat it on the floor. "Ugh! It's disgusting!"

"I did the best I could," Josh insisted.

Vicki pushed the cereal bowl away. "I don't want any disgusting milk in my cereal," she whined. "I want the nice cereal Mommy makes. When are we going home, Josh?"

"In two minutes," Josh said sarcastically. "Like I'm supposed to know?"

Vicki climbed up on to the table, still pushed against the ladder. She looked up towards the trap door. "Hey, you! Open the door. I want out!"

Josh rubbed his head. "Owww! Your big mouth is giving me a worse headache."

Vicki swung around, tears streaming down her cheeks. "But I wanna go home," she said. "I want Mommy and Daddy. How come they don't come to get us?"

Josh opened his mouth to make another smart-aleck remark. But he realized he was just as scared as his sister. He wouldn't cry in front of her, though. No way, José! It wasn't her fault they were stuck down here. He guessed he didn't have to be such a creep.

"Vicki, they must be looking for us real hard," he said softly. "I'll bet the whole Aberdeen Police Department is looking for us. Maybe the Montana State Police. Maybe even the F.B.I.!"

Vicki stopped crying and stared at her brother in wonder. "Really?"

"Yeah," Josh said, pushing his own cereal away. He took the box and started eating dry cereal. He handed it up to Vicki to share. "I'll bet our pictures are in the news. Don't worry, Vicki. Someone is looking for us, for sure."

Vicki sat on the edge of the table, legs swinging. She thought about this a moment. "Josh, how can they find us? How can they see us?"

"What do you mean?"

"They can't see us," Vicki insisted. "There's no windows in this place."

Not far away, the stranger slept fitfully on a cold wooden floor. He tossed and turned as his dream self thrashed about on a bed.

A man was looking down at him.

"You'll get over it, kid. We'll be a big, happy family."

"Where's my daddy?"

"I found just the playmate for you. It's a girl, but there's something special about her. I'm going to get her for you."

"Where's Mommy?"

"She's with Adrian. You want a toy, kid? A ball? I've got a nice one. A special one with eyes, and a nose, and teeth . . ."

The man snapped himself awake, but the image of a severed head floated in the darkness for a millisecond before it vanished. He looked up at the small window over his head and saw it was still night. His nightmare was instantly forgotten as he wondered what his little prisoners were doing.

He found his shoes tumbled against a box, pulled them on, and went downstairs. He was standing over the trapdoor within a few moments. When he unlocked it and pulled it open, he was surprised to see bright light below. A little face turned up to him. It was the girl. This time was better than thirty years ago. This time, there was a boy, *and* a girl. Pretty kid, too. Not like Christy, but pretty in her own way. He was proud of his achievement.

"Hey!" Vicki shouted.

"Hey, yourself," the man shouted back. He knew the surrounding darkness would keep him invisible. "Why are you awake?"

Now the boy came into view. The man noticed blood on his head, but it didn't faze him. There had been plenty of blood, that other time, and everyone had come out okay.

"Who can sleep in this dump?" Josh demanded. "When are you gonna let us out of here?"

The stranger didn't answer. He stared into the unnatural light of the room, studying the two kids. He wondered how he'd be able to get them out of Aberdeen, get them to their new home where life would begin again. Christy would surely come with him if he had the two kids. That's what had happened before, too.

He could see part of the table from up here, and

noticed cereal floating in a bowl of bluish-white milk. "Did you eat?" he asked.

"I wouldn't eat this crap if you paid me," Josh snapped.

"Did you open anything?" He had to know that. He had to know exactly what they'd taken, so it could be replaced.

"Some powdered milk and some cereal," Josh told him, begrudgingly. "What's the big deal?"

"That's all you opened?"

"I guess so."

"Be certain!" the man yelled, his anger rising. Didn't they understand how important it was to keep things just right? He'd replaced the food they'd eaten earlier, while they slept soundly. Now he'd have to replace more food.

"I'm certain, for cryin' out loud!" Josh said.

Vicki started to cry. The man stared down at her, and his heart began to race. Something hot moved through his blood, pooling in his joints. He remembered crying like that, so long ago . . . No! He didn't want to think about that! He slammed the door shut and locked it, ignoring the children's protests.

He had to find an all-night store. He had to replace the food. Having things out of order too long would ruin his plans. There had to be fifteen of everything. Fifteen. It was a very important number.

The stranger hadn't been gone long at all when Josh and Vicki heard the overhead door squeaking open again. They ran to stand beneath it, shouting as loudly as they could. The door clanked back on its hinge, and Vicki pointed. "Josh, the sky! Look at the sky!"

Josh could see a circle of gray dotted with dark spots. There were storm clouds up there. But why was there sky? Weren't they in a basement. "HEY!" he yelled.

This time, their captor didn't answer. Josh moved around to get a glimpse of him, but only his hand and forearm came into view. A paper sack, tied to a string, came down into the room. "Untie it!"

"Come do it yourself!"

"Yeah!" Vicki agreed with false bravado. She didn't want that man down here for even a second.

"Untie it, or I'll chop off your stupid little head!"

Josh froze. The now-familiar, if vague, image of his father running through the house filled his mind again. And something more. Something bright and metallic flashing through the air.

"Are you doing it?"

Vicki gave Josh a shove, and the boy snapped out of his stupor. He quickly untied the knot. "Y-yes," he croaked.

"*What*?"

Josh's voice, congested with fear, hadn't carried. "YES!"

The string snapped up, and while the children

yelled the door slammed shut. They heard a lock being thrown across it.

"You *creep!*" Vicki yelled. Then she began to cough. "Josh, I don't think I can yell any more. My throat hurts a whole lot."

Josh put the bag on the table and started to open it.

"Don't!" Vicki begged. "It's something scary. I just know it!"

"No, it isn't," Josh said. He pulled out a can of powdered milk and a box of cereal. "How come he's giving us more food? We didn't finish what we opened." *How come he said he'd cut off my head?*

Josh shook the thought away. He took the food to the shelves, and for the first time noticed how neat the rows were. He counted the cans of powdered milk. Fifteen. There were fifteen juice cans next to them. Fifteen chicken noodle soups, fifteen tomato soups, fifteen cans of ham. "Fifteen," Josh said out loud. "There's exactly fifteen of everything."

Vicki reached around him for the bag of chips they'd opened the day before. She started munching on them. Josh counted the bags of chips. Not counting the opened one, there were fifteen of those too. For some crazy reason, the guy wanted fifteen unopened cans or boxes or bags of everything down here.

An unexpected pain flashed through his head. He touched the bruise over his eye. For a second, he thought he'd throw up. He held fast to the metal rack.

"Josh, are you okay?" Vicki's voice was full of worry.

"I think I'm gonna puke," Josh groaned.

Vicki made a face and backed away. She didn't want any yucky stuff on her.

Josh drew in a long breath and straightened his head. The pain was gone. Something new replaced it, an idea that spread a grin across his face. "You know what, Vicki?" he asked. "I think I know a real good way to get back at this scuzz."

"What, Josh?"

Josh took down a few cans and began to build a pyramid. "This is our arsenal," he said. "We're going to fight back."

"Our what?"

"Never mind," Josh said. "Just pretend we're going to have a snowball fight. Only instead of snowballs, we're gonna use cans. See the way I'm putting them here? You make a pile like that across the room."

Vicki began working eagerly on her own pile. Josh picked up a can of corn, hefted it up a few times, and pretended to throw it.

"We can get him coming down the ladder," he said.

"But he *never* comes down," Vicki protested. "And I can't throw that high."

"He'll come down, all right," Josh said, his plan almost completely worked out. "He'll come down, and we'll get him. Then we'll get out of here."

"Really?" Vicki asked hopefully.

Josh didn't answer. There was nothing he could say to reassure his sister. His plan seemed to be a good one, but he was praying it would work.

It had been years since he was last here, but the man felt he knew every sound of this house. The wood had a certain creak when it swelled and contracted, the glass windows rattled a particular way in the wind. He knew every scratch of a tree; every skuttle of a rat's feet. Hidden in the shadows of the attic, he slept peacefully through the day, until the sound of something *wrong*, a noise that didn't belong, jerked him into instant wakefulness. He sat up and cocked his head to one side to hear a car's engine being shut off. He ran down the hall and looked out the front window. Someone was parked out there!

Terrified someone would discover his secret, he raced into the bathroom. There he found the small bottle of chloroform he'd used to knock out the children a few nights ago. He hadn't planned to use it again until it was time to leave, but he couldn't take the chance of the children being discovered. He soaked a rag and hurried out the back door to the house.

The yard had been neglected for years, and the grass had grown as tall as his shoulders. He pushed through it like an old-time hunter. But he wasn't the hunter now. He was the tiger, every muscle tense, every nerve tuned to the world around him. He heard squirrels chipping, rabbits bounding through the thick growth. Above these, from far away, the sound of a car door slamming. The enemy was approaching the house . . .

It was beastly hot out here, stagnant with the pledge of a storm. Mosquitos nipped at him, drinking blood undisturbed. He only thought of his goal, getting to the kids and making certain they didn't alert the intruder. When he reached a round metal door set in the middle of the field, he unlocked it and flipped it open. There was no time to waste. "ARE YOU AWAKE?"

Josh put a finger to his lips, signalling Vicki to be quiet.

"ARE YOU AWAKE?"

Making him wait for an answer gave Josh a little satisfaction. But he needed him down here. "Yeah, I'm awake," he said. "And you know what? We opened up all the bags of chips! And the cans of soup!"

There was a long pause. Above, the man wondered which was more important. Replacing the fifteen items in each group, or silencing the children? "How many?"

"All of 'em!" Josh said. "Come down and see! Come down and count for yourself!"

He had planned to go down, anyway. But now he'd also have to take inventory. The kids had screwed things up. They'd be sorry about that. Slowly he started to climb down.

Vicki gasped. "Oh, Josh! It's the bad man from the fireworks!"

"Let him have it, Vicki!"

In seconds, cans were sailing at the man from every direction. He roared at the children to stop, throwing his arms over his head. The barrage impeded his descent, and one hit him so squarely on the head that it nearly knocked him from the ladder.

"Let us out, scuzz!" Josh cried.

"Yeah, let us out, scuzz!" Vicki echoed. She turned to get another can, but her eyes went round with dismay. "Oh, I'm all out of snowballs, Josh!"

The man stopped midway down the ladder to glare at her. Vicki was standing clear across the floor from her brother. Josh seemed to understand what was in the insane green eyes that studied his sister, for he flashed across the room. But the man was quicker, and with a jump and two strides he had Vicki up in his arms. The little girl screamed and kicked. The man shoved the cloth on her face, thinking how much easier it had been the other night, when she was asleep.

"Leave her alone!" Josh shouted.

The man let Vicki's limp form drop to the ground. He lunged for the boy, but Josh dodged him as easily as he'd pull away from another kid playing football. Josh raced for the ladder and was actually halfway up it, yelling, when the stranger grabbed his ankles.

"Quit kicking!"

"Lemme go! Help me! *HELP*!" Josh thought his voice might carry clear up to the darkening clouds. He felt a sharp pull, and then was falling back. His headache came back as gravity seemed to tug at his brain harder than the rest of him. He screamed, but never hit the cement floor.

The man kept his arms wrapped firmly around the boy and took the fall for him. But not before shoving the poisonous cloth over Josh's mouth and nose.

Chapter Ten

Eda stood on the front porch of the Gammel house, much the way she had when she was a child. Things were different now, though. There were no longer boards on the windows, and the porch had been swept clean. The building was a sharp contrast to the dilapidated condition of the surrounding acreage. Grass and weeds grew shoulder-high as far as she could see. Numerous animals had made their homes here. Wasps' nests hung from old tree branches, gopher holes dotted the ground. A few squirrels raced boldly across the porch.

Eda wondered who had maintained the place. Brian? That would explain the terrible shape of the yard. He could hide his work near the house, but someone would see him doing yardwork.

Though some work had been done on the house, Eda was tempted to walk off the porch and look for a broken window as a means of entry. But she took a chance on the front door and was pleased when it opened. It didn't creak, a sign the hinges had been recently oiled. The silence was almost eery in itself.

Eda thought an old door like that should scream in protest.

She stood in the foyer and looked from the living room to the dining room. The place was swept and dusted. It was downtrodden, to be sure, but clean. She moved along the hall to the kitchen.

The window over the sink had been left open, perhaps by a careless investigator. Eda could hear thunder promising a downpour. And something more.

She moved closer to the sink and curled both hands around its rusty ledge. Turning her ear toward the open window, she listened again. Someone was shouting! "Josh?" she said out loud. Her voice resounded through the empty room. God, it had sounded just like him.

She hurried to the kitchen door and tried to open it, but unlike the front door, it was locked. She rushed back to the main entrance, nearly crashing through it in her desperation. She had to get to those kids!

Outside, she raced to the back yard, shouting "Josh! Vicki!"

Only thunder answered her, a loud clap that immediately preceded the rain. Eda stood, shouting, oblivious to the fact she was getting soaked. No voices answered her.

She pushed through the tall grass, squinting as rain pelted her face, until she reached the barn. The weeds were so tall that it was difficult to open the door. She grabbed the broken handle with both hands and braced her feet in the mud. With a jerk, the door fought the thick weeds and won.

The barn was big, airy and empty. There was no hay here, no equipment to hide two children. With a sigh, Eda put her hands over her face. It had been only wishful thinking that made her hear Josh's voice. Of course the children weren't here, or Mike would have found them days ago.

She turned to walk back to the house. As she did so, she spotted something small and white on the ground and bent to pick it up. It was a card from one of Aberdeen's two real estate companies. Eda tucked it into her pocket. Now there was someone else she could talk to. But first she had to have a look around the old house.

Although it was July, the house was so cold that her wet clothes made her shiver. Her hair was plastered to her head like a yellow swimcap, water dripping over her face. She wiped it away with her hand and proceeded to check the basement. Finding it completely empty, she went to the second floor.

Like the main floor, it had been recently cleaned. There were no cobwebs, no dust. She wondered how Brian had managed to remove all the furniture without being spotted. To her modern cop's eyes, it seemed strange the house hadn't been sealed, kept the way it was found when Darren Gammel was murdered. Eda reminded herself that had been thirty years ago, and that the forensic technology used today hadn't been available. If the crime had happened today, there would have been much more done than dusting for fingerprints and taking photos. The investigators would have taken minute samples of dust, hair and blood. The house would have been sealed off in the chance a jury might want to come look at the crime scene.

She wondered how long Chris's house would remain sealed.

Eda came to the master bedroom, and here she finally found evidence of that long-ago crime. Though it had faded, there was no mistaking the spray of bloodstains on the wallpaper. In places, the wallpaper was coming loose, drooping nearly to the floor. Obviously, Brian hadn't worked on this after moving the furniture out.

Finally, she headed for the attic, slowly ascending the wooden staircase. Halfway up, she could see the entire attic. There were a few boxes that merited investigation, but nothing else. Eda opened them all, finding old clothes and a few toys. It was much warmer up here than in the rest of the house, and the combination of rain and heat made the air unpleasantly musty. She was about to leave when she spotted a pad of paper in the corner. She pounced on it, careful to touch only one corner. Bringing it over to the window, she held it up to the light and read:

Houghton Psychiatric Hospital
Spokane, Washington
Dr Marion Niles

Eda could not help a triumphant cry. Tucking

196

the evidence into her purse, she hurried down-stairs. How had Mike's people missed this? Perhaps it hadn't been here a few days ago. She'd take it right to him, as soon as she picked up Lucille.

Getting into her car, she was momentarily discouraged as she remembered the voice she'd heard earlier. Wishing she could have found the children, she drove away from the old house.

She never noticed the blue BMW parked across the street. If she'd looked into her rearview mirror, she would have seen Tiffany Simmons climbing out. The reporter had been trailing Lucille's car ever since it left that morning. Unable to follow Eda into the police station, she'd continued on to the town hall, where she'd seen Lucille in the records office.

Tiffany kept reminding herself that she'd tried to ask for information in a professional, civilized way, but Eda turned out to be the same little bitch she'd been years earlier. Tiffany couldn't imagine why a grown woman would try to start a fight. She knew Eda hated her, but she didn't care. She was after a story, and if it took clandestine methods to get it, the end justified the means.

She couldn't believe her luck when she walked into the office and spoke to her old sorority sister. Stephanie was full of gossip, pondering what Brian Wander had to do with the Gammel house. Tiffany meant to find out for herself, so she'd driven to the site of that long-ago crime. She'd almost run into Eda, slowing up at the last moment when she saw the other woman getting out of the car. While Eda poked around inside the dark house, Tiffany waited impatiently, tapping her perfectly manicured nails on the seat beside her. She wore sunglasses despite the rainy weather, but she knew it wasn't much of a disguise. Eda would know at once who she was. But Eda never looked her way. She came out of the house some time later, a serious expression darkening her face. From the unkempt look of her, Tiffany guessed she'd been caught in the sudden downpour.

As soon as Eda had left, Tiffany hurried to do some investigating of her own. She was as surprised as Eda had been to see how clean the place was. "It's still horrible," she said out loud. Her voiced bounced around the empty living room. "What could Christy's husband want with a place like this?"

Like Eda, she was disappointed to see the house was not only clean, but completely devoid of clues. Even so, the second floor was still exciting. Tiffany caught her breath when she entered what seemed to be the Master Bedroom, the site of the original murder, and saw the faded bloodstains. "Have to figure out a way to get a camera crew up here," she whispered out loud. "Too bad there's a rule about tres – " She was turning around as she spoke, but her last words turned into a scream that bounced crazily around the empty room.

A man was standing in the doorway. A man with wild green eyes, an unshaven face, and a vicious aura about him. "You don't belong here! This is Christy's room!"

Christy? What the h . . .? Tiffany's thoughts were sliced off as the man lunged forward with a rag soaked in chloroform. She collapsed to the floor.

For a few moments, he stared down at her. There was something familiar about this woman, and it didn't make him feel good. He wished he could think what it was. He'd used up all his sleeping drug. Filing away a mental note to buy some more when he had the chance, he bent down and gathered Tiffany into his arms. Throwing the unconcious woman over his shoulder in a fireman's hold, he lumbered down two flights of stairs to the basement. Outside, the sky had grown even darker. The earlier downpour had been a mere herald of the storm to come, and now the only light came from flashes of lightening. He dumped Tiffany on the floor, then looked around for something to use to tie her up. He saw some mouldy old books wrapped in twine, and used his pocket knife to free them. He took the twine and bound it tightly around Tiffany's wrists. Then he wrapped a piece of the cloth he'd used to knock her out around her eyes. He kept her mouth free, though. He wanted to talk to her.

There had only been a small amount of drug on the cloth, and he guessed she'd be waking up shortly. Sure enough, Tiffany soon began to struggle. The blindfold was unnecessary in the near-total darkness, but when she let out a scream he wished he'd gagged her. At least until he could trust her – if he could trust her.

He clamped a big hand over her mouth and nose. "Shut up!" he said. "I could hurt you now, so just shut up!"

Tiffany whimpered beneath his hand.

"I want to talk to you," he said. "I just want to talk. I wanted to talk to Brian, too, but he gave me a fight. That's why I had to kill him. You don't want me to kill you, do you?"

With a small cry, Tiffany shook her head.

"Can I pull my hand away?"

She nodded. *Pull it away, you bastard. The first chance I get, I'm going to kill you. Because; God help me, I know you'll kill me if you get the chance.* Tiffany thought about the gun she had in her purse, probably on the bedroom floor upstairs. If she could only loosen the ties around her wrists . . .

Slowly, he moved his hand away. Tiffany had to bite her tongue to keep from yelling. She had a feeling no one would hear her anyway, not only because of the storm outside, but also because this seemed like the most deserted street in all Montana. For a split second, she wished she hadn't followed Eda here. She put that thought away with annoyance. Investigating was her job!

"Now, let me talk," the man said. "What's your name?"

"Tiffany Simmons," she said, her voice strong.

"Tiffany Simmons, Tiffany Simmons . . ."

He seemed to know it.

"I'm an anchor on the TV news," she offered.

"Don't watch TV," the man said. "But I know you. Oh, yes! I remember now! You're the little girl who thought she was so much better than everyone else. So much better than Christy. But you can't be better than Christy, because she's an angel. And angels are perfect."

That little sleaze is no angel, believe me. Somehow, Tiffany knew that was dangerous to say out loud.

"You were mean to Christy, weren't you?"

"I don't recall – "

"Of course you recall," the man said. "You were the one who spread rumours about her being crazy."

"No!"

"I have to do something to make that right." The man's voice was strangely, dangerously, calm. "You'll have to pay for hurting an angel."

"I never did!" Tiffany cried. Suddenly, her false bravado fell away like a flimsy outer shell. Her stomach twisted into knots. He reached out and grabbed her.

"I've seen men get their heads chopped off," he said. "But I've never seen it happen to a woman. What do you suppose it's like?"

Tiffany said nothing.

"Do you suppose they bleed differently? Hmmm, why don't we find out?"

He spoke in strange, lilting tones now. Tiffany

was crazily reminded of a schoolteacher. "Please, don't – "

"Be quiet!" the man snapped.

She heard him moving around.

"I have an axe outside. You be patient, okay? It'll take me a few minutes to get it."

Tiffany listened as he thunked up the stairs. When the back door slammed shut, she began to scream, and scream, and scream. Even though she knew there was nobody to hear her.

After she had picked up Lucille at the mall, Eda headed back to the police station. She wanted to give the pad she'd found to Mike, and to hear if he'd learned anything new in the past few hours.

The rain was pouring down in sheets now, slowing driving considerably. It gave the women time to fill each other in. Eda was fascinated to hear how Brian had lied about his job, but she couldn't figure out why he'd do such a thing.

At the police station, the women dashed through the rain to get inside, where they found Mike talking on the phone. He waved at them, and they pulled up chairs to wait until he hung up.

"I was talking to the sheriff in Belfield, Washington," he said. "That's the last known address for Irene Gammel. I had a theory that the killer might have made contact again, the way he's come after Chris."

"Is the sheriff going to find her?" asked Lucille.

Mike shook his head, his expression weary. Eda knew at once what that meant – she'd seen the look enough on fellow cops in New York City. He'd hit a wall.

"Irene Gammel is dead," he said. "She's been dead since last August."

Lucille was thoughtful for a moment. Then her head snapped up, her eyes wide. "That's about the time Brian started going on those business trips!" she said, excitedly.

Mike looked from one woman to the other, curious. Eda handed him the pad of paper she'd found. "This was in the attic of the Gammel house," she said. "You did check the place out, didn't you?"

"Hell, yes," Mike said. "We didn't find a thing, which tells me someone's been there since. We noticed the place had been fixed up a bit."

"I think it was Brian Wander," Eda said.

Mike leaned back in his chair and crossed his arms. He looked like a man settling in for a good story. "Fill me in," he said. "It sounds like you two have come up with some interesting information about our victim."

Eda and Lucille took turns telling what they knew about Brian. The information, they all agreed, only led to more questions. But it established a connection between the victim and perpetrator.

"You know, Eda," Mike said when they'd finished. "I wish I could lure you back from

New York. We could use someone like you around here."

"I love Aberdeen," Eda said, "but my home is in Queens now." She thought about Tim Becker and felt a slight twinge. How much quicker would things go if she had her partner's professional input along with her own? She was reminded of the autopsies she'd read. Once again, the feeling she'd missed something important washed over her. Tim had a good eye for detail. Would he have seen what she missed? "I think you should check the autopsies again," she said. "I don't know why, but I have a feeling there's something there we overlooked."

Mike nodded. "I'll have someone get on that."

Lucille tapped Eda on the arm. "I think we'd better be going home. We've left poor Chris alone long enough."

After a quick goodbye, the women drove back to Lucille's. When they walked inside, the found Chris sitting on the living room couch, the drawing she had made held tightly in white-knuckled fists. Behind her, the picture window offered a view of the rain, slowing down now, but still virtually obliterating the yellow-roped scene across the street.

Chris's red eyes were an ugly contrast to the ashen hue of her skin. The last few hours had obviously been a terrible ordeal for her, and Lucille felt guilty for leaving her so long. She hurried to sit next to her.

Eda settled in the armchair, leaning forward with her hands clasped together. A look of concern crossed her face as she said: "Chris, what's wrong?"

Chris stared at the picture and said in a dull voice: "I know these eyes. Do you know who this is?"

Both women studied the picture a few moments before shaking their heads. Lucille shuddered, and Eda said: "Whoever he is, he's evil-looking. Is that the guy who was following you?"

"Yes."

"But it was so long ago," Lucille protested. "And you never saw him up close. How could you get such detail?"

"Oh, I've seen him up close," Chris said. "He stood right behind me once, in front of the bakery. You thought it was that old guy who used to walk around town drunk, but it wasn't him at all. But look at his eyes. Don't you know his eyes? He has Brian's eyes."

"Chris, that's impossible!" Lucille cried. Even with all the evidence she'd uncovered, she still wanted to believe Brian was an innocent victim. Hearing Chris's words shattered her last hopes. And Chris was right. The eyes *did* look like Brian's. In fact, they also looked like Vicki's eyes, only bigger and with the added dimension of meanness.

"Is it?" Eda wondered aloud. "It would explain a lot of things. Maybe Brian was related to the killer."

Chris turned to her, blinking a few times. "What?"

"Chris, we have a lot to tell you," Eda said. "The first is that Brian came from Washington State. Did he ever tell you that?"

"So?" Chris asked, feigning nonchalance. She knew the significance of Eda's statement.

"Do you remember?" Lucille said gently. She felt as if pushing Chris too far would be dangerous. "Irene Gammel moved there, after – "

"Brian was an orphan," Chris cut in. She was trying to break any connection between her late husband and that crazy woman. "He was brought up in a foster home, and he was very happy. His living there is just coincidence." *Like the eyes in that portrait are coincidence*?

As if in reply to her unspoken question, a soft chiming filled the room from an anniversary clock that sat on an end table.

"It's time for dinner," Lucille said.

"I'm not hungry," Chris insisted.

Lucille stood up. "Maybe not, but you should eat. I'll just put together soup and salad." She left Eda and Chris in the living room. Chris turned over her sketch so she wouldn't have to look at it. "What else did you find out about Brian?" she asked. There was a slight hint of annoyance in her voice, as if she resented her friends checking up on her husband.

Eda sighed. "Chris, maybe we should have dinner first – "

"Tell me!" Chris demanded. "I want to know

what else you learned! Those business trips – something was happening then, wasn't it? Brian was in some kind of trouble, and I have a right to know what it was."

"We didn't find out that much," Eda said apologetically. She wished they hadn't found out anything at all.

"Then tell me what you do know," Chris said. She saw Eda hesitate, and leaned forward. "Eda, my husband is *dead*. My children are missing. I don't want them to be missing thirty years! Please!"

"All right," Eda said. She'd wanted to protect Chris, but saw now that holding back the truth would only hurt her. "But we'll talk over dinner. Let's go into the kitchen."

There, over a simple meal of salad and vegetable soup, they told Chris what they'd learned that day.

Some time later, Chris was surprised when she looked down at an empty soup bowl. She'd been listening so carefully that she was unaware of eating at all. Now she regretted even this small meal. The unexpected news about Brian was enough to turn her stomach.

"Are you going to be all right?" Lucille asked, concern vivid on her face.

"I don't know," Chris said softly. "This is so much to take at once."

Lucille looked across the table at Eda. "We shouldn't have told her. We should have held back a little."

"No!" Chris said. "I want to know everything. Somehow, the fact that Brian was taking care of that house is a clue to finding my children. I only wish – " She felt heat behind her eyes and blinked a few times. She didn't want to start crying again. "I only wish Brian was here to explain things," she said. "I can't believe he was deceiving me on purpose. There must be an explanation to all this!"

"Of course," said Lucille.

"Brian really did love you," Eda insisted. "That was no lie."

Chris thought for a few minutes. "Before he – " she began, then had to stop to collect herself. "The other day, he told me he had his eyes on a five bedroom house. We talked about needing room for another baby."

"Oh, Chris!"

Lucille's voice was full of sympathy.

The phone rang, and Eda volunteered to answer it. Lucille said she'd take care of the supper dishes, pushing Chris gently back into her chair when she tried to help. When they heard Eda greet the sheriff, they both turned to listen.

"Really?" Eda was saying. "Blueriver Jail? That's just two hours from here, isn't it?"

Chris and Lucille looked at each other. Who was in jail?

"Did he kill his wife?"

"Who?" Lucille whispered.

Eda sighed. "I'm glad. Chris seemed to think

208

she was a nice person. So what are you going to do now?"

A few minutes later, Eda hung up, then said: "Well, this doesn't surprise me. They found your brother, Chris. He's in the jail up in Blueriver, doing time for manslaughter."

Chris brought her fingers to her lips. An image of Felicity, dreamy-eyed as she toyed with her love beads, came to her. "You . . . you asked if he killed his wife?"

"Felicity left him twenty years ago," Eda said. "Nobody knows where she went, and she took her daughter with her."

Chris sighed, feeling a loss for the niece she'd never meet. Still, she was glad Felicity had had the sense to get away from Harvey.

"Good for Felicity," Lucille said.

"The creep probably beat her," Eda said. "Anyway, Mike wants to ask some questions. He thinks Harvey may know something about the man who was following you years ago."

Chris shook her head. "Harvey didn't believe in him. He thought I was crazy, just like everyone else." She stood up, and wasn't surprised her knees felt weak. She yawned and rubbed her eyes. "I'm overwhelmed. I'm going to lie down for a while."

"That's a good idea," Lucille said. "A rest might clear your head and help you sort things out."

Chris's legs were so heavy she could hardly face the stairs. Still, somehow, she got to her room. Her mind was a cauldron of thoughts and questions, all jumbled together, with answers rising like elusive steam. Brain would have told her everything in due time, she thought as she lay down on the bed and closed her eyes. Brian loved her . . . She was asleep within moments.

Brian was standing on the banks of Lake Aberdeen, the wind tousling his red hair. "I'm not like them, Chris. I'm one of them, but I'm not like them. I got away soon enough."

"I don't understand, Brian!"

"I love you, Chris. That wasn't a lie. I love you!"

Chris came closer to him and reached out to touch him. He backed away. "Don't touch me! I'll break if you touch me. Here, you forgot this." He held out his hand. Something glimmered in the sunshine. It was a chain, and it turned slowly as it dropped to the grass.

Chris bent to pick it up, and found the charm bracelet the Crispins had given her one long-ago Hanukkah. "Oh, Brian, how . . . ?"

But Brian wasn't there. Harvey was there, and beside him stood an older man with red hair and green eyes. Red hair and green eyes like Brian's – but there was malevolence in those eyes. "No!"

"What're you gonna do?" Harvey asked.

"Take her to the boy. Take her to stay with Teddy, forever. She saw. She knows. They have to stay together."

"Leave me alone!"

"Christy, it was just a joke . . ." The man started

laughing. He came close to her, a rope stretched between his two big hands. Chris screamed and fell to the grass. But it wasn't grass at all. It was snow, deep and cold. The sunshine had vanished, replaced by a darkness so complete its only purpose could be to hide evil.

The man picked her up as if she was a little girl. No one heard her scream. Harvey just laughed at her. The man opened a door, and she could see a pit of darkness. She didn't want to go in there. She knew it was going to . . .

. . . hurt.

Chris opened her eyes and rolled over onto her side. She hurt everywhere. She rubbed her face and felt tears on her cheeks. The dream should have faded, as dreams do, but this one stayed with her in complete clarity. And she knew it had to be a sign. The bracelet, the evil man, Harvey – Brian had been trying to tell her something.

"Harvey," she whispered. "He was trying to tell me about Harvey. But what?"

Though she lay awake for a long time, nothing came to her. Sleep came before she found an answer, and the next thing she knew she was gazing out the window at the morning sun. Her hand went to her wrist in search of a charm bracelet she hadn't worn in decades. And instantly, she knew what Brian had been trying to tell her. Something had happened that Hanukkah night, and Harvey knew exactly what it was. She had to talk to him.

When she got out of bed, she saw it was only

211

eight o'clock in the morning. It was a two hour drive to Blueriver, and she wasn't sure about visiting hours. Would they even let her see Harvey? She didn't give herself another moment to think. Quietly, not wanting to wake her friends, she washed and dressed. Part of her said she should wake Lucille and Eda, but she ignored it. She moved stiffly, still a little disoriented from her nightmare, but successfully found Lucille's keys and slipped out of the house.

This was something she had to do on her own. She doubted either Eda or Lucille would be permitted to see Harvey. They weren't family. And Harvey would certainly refuse to talk to them. But she'd make him talk to *her*. She'd make him tell what happened when they were kids.

There was nobody near her own house as she pulled out of the driveway. Only the yellow police banners, flapping in the wind, gave witness to the horror that had occurred there. Harvey might know something about that.

"I've been terrified of that Hanukkah night all my life," Chris said out loud. "But now I'm going to face it. Damn it, if it means finding my babies, I'm going to find out what Harvey did to me!"

Chapter Eleven

The gag that blocked Tiffany Simmons' mouth was wet with tears of fear and outrage. Her captor had removed the blindfold, using the cloth to stop her from screaming. It hadn't really been necessary. She'd figured out quickly enough that no one could hear her.

The man had propped Tiffany up against a cold metal pole, then had taken a seat across from her, his back to an ancient oil burner. He sat cross-legged with the axe across his lap. Tiffany couldn't tell if he was staring at her, but imagined that his eyes could bore right through the dark shadows. She glared back, for what it was worth, all the while using the cover of darkness to try and untie the twine around her wrists.

About twenty minutes after leaving he'd come back, carrying the axe, and after propping her up he'd moved to his current position. He'd been sitting there, without moving, long enough for the sun to begin to set, bringing even more darkness into the damp, cold cellar. Somehow, his silence unnerved Tiffany more than the axe could.

When he finally spoke, it was so sudden

that Tiffany gave a small cry, muffled by the gag.

"I was thinking," he said. "You said you were a news reporter, huh? I don't watch TV, I said. But you want to hear a good story? You want to know what Brian did to me?"

Tiffany's answer was a quiet whimper.

"See, it's all his fault he got killed," the man said. "If he'd left things up to me, I wouldn't have hurt him. Like I'd never hurt Adrian. He got away from *her*, when I had to stay. She put him out for adoption, you know. That's cause *he* said he wouldn't take care of the two of us. I was worth something 'cause I was big 'nuf to work, but Adrian was only four, too little. *He* told my mother Adrian had to go or he'd go to the police and tell everything they did. You know what they did, don't you?"

Tiffany didn't move or make a sound. The reporter in her was absorbing every word, fascination taking over fright. What the hell was this crazy man talking about?

"They killed my father, they did," he said.

Tiffany straightened up.

"Chopped off his head," the man went on. "Cut him up in fifteen different places. Fifteen is my favourite number, you know. I gave it to Brian fifteen times. Maybe it was number five or six that did his head in. I don't know. I wasn't so good at it as she was."

She?

"They never knew I was hiding in the closet,"

the man said. His voice was distant, cold as the surrounding darkness. "Mother went screaming out of the room, and the man ran after her. Then he was carrying my little brother under one arm. I said: "How come Adrian ain't moving?" But then he hit me hard and shoved something up against my face. Same thing I did to you, I guess. Same stuff. Knocked me right out."

Tiffany struggled against her bonds. Her head was spinning, full of disbelief. Was this who she thought it might be? He'd mentioned an Adrian. Hadn't one of the missing Gammel boys been named Adrian? And what did Brian Wander have to do with them?

"I woke up in a dark room," the man continued. "Adrian was screaming and crying, but I just looked around and made sure of where we were. I knew the place right away. It was a fall-out shelter my father had built when the Cubans was causin' so much trouble. I wasn't afraid, then. There was plenty of food and water, and even a place to go to the bathroom. So I told Adrian to shut up and let me think. But Adrian wouldn't, so I hit him, and knocked him out. Stupid little kid."

Is this Teddy Gammel? Tiffany wished she wasn't gagged. She was full of questions.

"I had a plan," the man said. "I thought everything would be okay now that Daddy was gone. They took care of him okay. He wouldn't be beatin' up on Mother or me or Adrian any more, no sir. So things were gonna be okay. I figured Mother and *him* was just hidin' us until

215

it was safe to move. That man said he had a farm in Washington. He was a truck driver. He helped Mother with a flat tyre once, she said, and that was how they met. Mother said he was gonna rescue us from Daddy. Daddy said he was a Commie, and he was gonna kill us all if Daddy didn't stop him. He built that fallout shelter to protect us, he said. He made us practice 'Duck and Cover' to protect us, he said. Only trouble was, Daddy said I couldn't get it right, and he'd have to *show me* how it was done."

The more he rambled, the closer he moved to Tiffany. She could just make out his face. His eyes seemed to glow with malevolence. She shrank against the pole, working hard against the twine, wishing to God she had her gun.

His hands came up. Tiffany saw he no longer held the axe.

"Daddy said he'd show me how," the man went on. There was a choke in his voice, which had risen half an octave. "He threw the blanket over me . . ." His hands lurched forward.

Tiffany started, but realized he wasn't aiming for her. He was throwing an imaginary blanket, she guessed.

"And he held it there and held it and held it and I couldn't breathe and I wanted him dead and then *he* came and they had a fight and Daddy called him a Commie and *he* said: "I got a Purple Heart in Korea, what did you ever do for America?" And then Daddy came with the axe and there was a big fight, and Mother, and Mother, and Mother . . ."

He stopped then, his words choked off by big, racking sobs. As if Tiffany wasn't there at all, he threw himself around the cellar like a caged animal gone mad, crying with the memory of that horrible, long-ago day.

And Tiffany realized her hands were free.

When the shuffle of her captor's footsteps seemed farthest away, Tiffany bolted for the steps and raced up to the door.

He was after her in a flash. "NO!"

She felt him grab at her legs, but she was fast. She didn't hesitate or look back. She crashed through the door to find the room with her purse, the purse that held her gun. She heard him lumbering after her, and screamed as he touched her arm. There was fire where he touched her, and she realized to her horror that he hadn't *grabbed* her after all. He'd hit her with the axe!

"Stop it!" she screamed, stumbling up the next staircase.

"You weren't supposed to be here!" the man yelled. "You're Christy's enemy! I have to stop you!"

Tiffany reached the upper floor. She turned back just in time to see the axe swing toward her. It connected with her foot, slitting her shoe but hardly injuring her. "You *bastard*!"

There were too many doors in this hall. Which one led to the master bedroom?

The axe swung into the wall, fragmenting old sheetrock.

Tiffany pushed open the first door – a bathroom. She rolled against the wall, looking back as Teddy gained on her, stumbling toward the next door. With a scream, she finally fell into the master bedroom. Her purse was in the middle of the floor. She slammed the door shut to give herself a moment's extra time, and hurried to find the gun. But Teddy – if it was Teddy Gammel – was just a few seconds behind her, and the door crashed open as she pulled the weapon out.

With a yelp-like cry, Teddy flew at her. The axe came down as Tiffany rolled onto her back, the blade connecting with her shin. She screamed, pulled the trigger, and nothing happened. *The safety*! *The friggin' safety*! "Get away from me!"

She fumbled until the gun was operable, then fired again. She missed, but Teddy's aim was better. He swung the axe at Tiffany's hand, cutting through three of her fingers, knocking the gun across the room. Tiffany screamed in horror and pain, staring at the mess of her hand. She scrambled to her feet and tried to get to the gun. But Teddy blocked her path. He stood with the axe gripped in both hands, his green eyes wild, his shoulders heaving. The gun was a few feet behind him.

"You bastard . . ." Tiffany whimpered. Fire seemed to engulf her arm.

Teddy stared at her, a look of dismay coming over his face.

"Nobody ever got away before," he said. "You threw me off count. How many was that? How many? It has to be fifteen total. How many times did I hit you."

"Fuck you," Tiffany growled.

"How many times did I hit you?" he said louder, harshly. He took a step toward her, the axe held high. Tiffany screamed. She squeezed her eyes shut, waiting for the next blow to fall.

But nothing happened. Slowly, Tiffany opened her eyes and saw that Teddy had moved to the window and was looking out. "There's a car coming up the block," he said quietly. "I have to finish now. Hold still."

Tiffany glared at him.

He glared back.

Then the axe went up again. Tifany screamed as the weapon came flying towards her head. Everything went black.

A short time later, Teddy was sitting in the bedroom, his back pressed against a mix of old and new bloodstains, the axe laid carefully to the side. He was proud he'd remembered to have a backup plan. The grown-ups had had one when they took him away so long ago. They thought he'd grown up slow, but he knew they were wrong. He was smart enough to have backup plan.

Slow people couldn't remember things they did yesterday, but he remembered what happened thirty years ago. He remembered how the man had hidden Adrian and him in that underground shelter. It was just for safekeeping, he had said, until the police went away. The police wanted to take them from their mother. No one knew about the fallout shelter. Daddy had built it at night, using a bulldozer he had rented. No one saw it in the daytime because it was so far back from the road. The top was flush with the ground, and Daddy had covered it with sod to make it completely invisible until you were almost on top of it. The police had probably looked out over that vast stretch of yard and saw nothing at all. They never knew Teddy and Adrian were almost literally under their noses.

When he was a kid, Teddy remembered, the grass had been cut short and neat. Now the shelter's hatch was surrounded with tall weeds and thick tangles. Once he unlatched it, he could grab a thick handful and pull the lid back. But he understood it was just a matter of time before the police found the shelter. So, just as the man had moved the brothers after only a few days, Teddy knew he had to move these kids.

The man had paid a gas station owner to let him use an old metal shack with a lock. The owner had taken money without asking questions, so he never knew what the plans were for the shack. Teddy hadn't liked the cold metal place very much, but he hadn't complained. He knew the man was protecting them, saving them from the police the way he'd saved them from Daddy. Adrian, however, had screamed and cried so much the man had given him medicine to make him sleep.

Teddy wondered if the little girl would scream and cry. He worried that he didn't have any more sleeping potion. Well, if he had to, he'd stuff something into her mouth. In the meantime, he had to go to the gas station to see if he could borrow that old shack, too.

He decided he needed someone to keep an eye on the kids, in case they woke up before he got back. Of course, he had no friends in Aberdeen. But he did have someone who owed him, someone who hurt his precious angel, Christy. Tiffany still hadn't paid enough for that. She still had her head.

When he'd heard that car outside, he'd been so startled his swing had missed. Then he'd been afraid to go further, not just because he worried the owner of the car might come inside, but because he was terrified of passing the number fifteen. He'd decided he'd have time to count later, and if there weren't enough slashes he'd just have to add a few.

A search of the woman's handbag found car keys. He went downstairs and waited in the front door for a long time, making certain there was no one on the road. There were only two other houses on the street. One had a For Sale sign that was so old and faded there was no telling how long it had hung there. The other one was occupied, but Teddy knew the habits of its owners. They left for work early in the morning and wouldn't be back until late.

At last, he went out to Tiffany's car, keeping his head ducked low. Someone might see him, after all. People had binoculars, didn't they? Nosy people watched everything. Daddy had always said people watched you, waiting for you to make a mistake.

Quickly, Teddy opened the car door and got in. He drove the car a few blocks, heading to the outskirts of town, where he was less likely to be noticed. Then he went back home again, on foot. He didn't dare run, but he hurried as best as he could, wanting to be off the streets.

The walk gave him time to think, and he smiled as he got a brilliant idea. He'd make Tiffany watch the children! She owed Christy that much, at least. He went upstairs and hoisted Tiffany's limp form over his shoulder. Then he carried her downstairs and outside. In a few minutes, he was struggling down the ladder of the fallout shelter. Deeply drugged, the kids were still sound asleep. Teddy was very quiet, and neither child stirred as he moved around the shelter. He sat Tiffany up in a chair. Her head lolled forward. That wasn't good at all. She couldn't see the kids wake up if she was looking at the floor.

He found a very large sack of flour, big enough to fit on her lap, and wedged it under her chin. Her eyes were pointed directly at the children. Now they would be watched constantly, to make sure nothing went wrong.

Quietly, Teddy ascended the ladder and pulled

it up after him. Then, afraid someone might come to the house the way Tiffany had, he crept off to the woods to fall asleep under a tree.

Chapter Twelve

Aberdeen, Montana Proper was a small town, but its surrounding farmland stretched for miles. It took Chris nearly half an hour to drive beyond its boundaries. She was thinking about Harvey, and all the things that had come back to her through her dreams, ruminations, and discussions with her friends. Harvey figured in a lot of her memories, didn't he? He seemed to show up at strange times. When she got to Blueriver, she planned to confront him once and for all.

The endless stretch of sky and land that gave Montana the nickname Big Sky Country seemed to envelope her. In a state with barely a million in population, it wasn't unusual that Chris was alone on the highway for long stretches of time. It was a lonely road, without even the sight of mountains to break the view. Funny this state had been named Montana. Chris had seen the mountains only once in her life, on a camping trip with Brian.

Josh had been a rambunctious three-year-old back then, and it seemed she had spent every moment making sure he didn't run off the edge of a cliff. The whole trip had exhausted Chris, and she'd vowed she'd never go camping again. But seeing the beautiful Rockies had been worth it.

Chris realized she was crying. She suddenly felt more alone than she had in years. Brian had teased her for months about that trip, but he wouldn't do that again, would he? Damn, she didn't even have her friends at her side right now. She hadn't felt this alone since . . . maybe since before Eda Crispin had moved from Chicago to Aberdeen and became her best friend. She'd been alone at other times, too. All through her childhood and teens, when she often thought she saw that man stalking her, only Eda and Lucille believed her. Her own father had beaten her into silence, so she never mentioned her fears to any adult. Then, in her twenties, it was time for her two friends to move on in life. Eda had surprised everyone after graduation by announcing she wanted to be a cop – in New York. Lucille had already left Aberdeen after her own graduation two years earlier. She and her boyfriend, Sydney Danton, were sharing an apartment in Bozeman while they attended Montana State. Years passed with the women keeping in touch, mostly by phone and letter. Chris missed them terribly, but there was one good thing about that time. The man who had been stalking her seemed to have disappeared.

A few years later, Lucille announced that Sydney had finally asked her to marry him. Eda came back from New York to be a bridesmaid, and for the first time since they were teenagers the women were together again. Lucille's wedding was huge, as befitted the daughter of Aberdeen's "most important sugar beet farmer". Chris couldn't help smiling as she remembered how proudly Lucille had spoken those words. There had been eight bridesmaids. Lucille wasn't a show-off – she had six sisters in addition to her two best friends. Lucille's younger brother Stannie, who had grown dark-eyed and handsome, had been Chris's escort.

She looked up at the sky and thought the peach-coloured layer of sun shining beneath the clouds was very much like her bridesmaid's dress.

"I think I look ridiculous," Eda whispered as she tugged at the off-the-shoulder neckline of the batiste gown. "My mother is so happy I'm wearing a formal. She wants me to come to other parties while I'm here, but I'm never comfortable in that crowd."

"You look adorable," Chris had replied.

"No, I don't," she said. Eda had pointed to the flower girl, eleven-year-old Kim Danton. "Kim looks adorable. *You* look adorable. Maybe you'll get lucky and meet someone today."

Chris snorted. "Maybe I'll get lucky and leave Aberdeen. That's when I'll meet someone, Eda, not before."

Eda turned and busied herself with her blonde curls. She'd pulled them up into a circle of orange blossoms that Lucille had provided for all the attendants, but already her wild locks were coming loose in the misty Spring weather.

Chris waited for Eda to lecture her, telling her to put Harvey Sr in a nursing home. A few years earlier, he had had her mother committed, and soon after he'd had a stroke. Although she had a nurse come in every day to take care of the old man while she was at work, she had a lot to do herself. And Harvey Sr's last days had not been brief.

Chris reached into her glove compartment for a tissue. How had thoughts of her father's lingering death crept into her mind? Biting her lip, keeping her eyes fixed hard on the long stretch of road ahead, she steered her memories to the moments just after the wedding.

They were standing on the steps of St Gregory's Church, throwing birdseed at Lucille and Sydney. Lucille was a stunning bride, her black hair a dramatic contrast to the white silk and Chantilly lace gown. Chris's heart had been full of empathetic joy as she watched her beautiful friend race down the steps. Everyone was clapping and cheering the newlyweds.

Everyone but one man, who stood with the crowd on the other side of the church steps. As Chris scanned the group of well-wishers, her eyes met his; or rather, they met the black emptiness of his sunglasses. He smiled, and lifted a hand. Something bright gleamed in the afternoon sunlight . . .

He had come back, Chris thought as her hands tightened around the steering wheel. It was the man who had followed her, had chased her with a flashing knife. She'd seen that knife in so many nightmares. He was back again.

Twenty-three-year-old Chris, charming in her peach bastiste gown, froze. Was he going to plunge his knife into the neck of the old woman who stood oblivious in front of him? Chris let out a cry and pointed. The man ducked and disappeared into the crowd. Eda took hold of her arm.

Stannie tapped her shoulder. "What's going on?" he demanded.

"Chris, what is it?" Eda asked.

Chris was about to tell them what she just saw, but stopped herself. The man was gone. This was Lucille's day, and talk of evil would only spoil things. He couldn't hurt her with all these people around. She would try her best to put him out of her mind. It was only fair to Lucille. "Nothing," she said. "I thought that old lady was going to slip on birdseed."

Stannie laughed. "Her? That's my aunt Susannah. She may be old, but she's feisty as hell. I'm surprised she's not wearing roller skates!"

Eda laughed, and Chris forced herself to join

them. The next thing she knew, she was being herded toward a trio of waiting limos. Eda was nowhere near her, so there was no chance to discuss what had happened. And, to Chris's surprise, the day was so much fun she completely forgot about the man.

Eda had to return to New York the next day, so there was little time to talk. Dean Crispin's Mercedes pulled up outside her apartment in the early morning, and Eda had come up to say goodbye. She was running late, she said, but promised she'd call soon.

Then, once more, Chris was alone in Aberdeen. She was working at The Geode, a small shop that specialized in rocks and minerals. Dr Scott, her boss, was a retired professor from Montana College of Mineral Science and Technology. He often left her alone at the shop while he set off on geological expeditions. Today, Chris was planning to set up some Easter baskets in the window to reflect the upcoming holiday. She'd placed different coloured stones in them to represent eggs. As she was gathering things together, her eyes fell on a small, oval geode, sparkling under the track lights. Chris thought it would look cute with a baby chick coming out of it, as if it had just been hatched.

She was pulling out the previous window display when she saw him. He was standing directly across the street, just the way he had a few days earlier, at Lucille's wedding. Chris stared at him. His hand came up in a mock salute, silver glistening off the gleaming blade he held.

Chris dropped a slab of agate to the floor. The crash startled her enough to tear her eyes from the man, and she looked down at the stone. Carefully, she picked it up and checked it over. To her relief, the six-inch-long slice was intact.

She set it down and looked out the window again. The man was gone, having disappeared as he had so many other times. Heart pounding, Chris tried to concentrate on her work. When the bell jingled to announce the first customer of the day, she was so startled she almost dropped a whole basket of rocks. She swung around, half-expecting the stalker had come through the rough-hewn wooden door of the shop.

"Sorry!" a cheerful man's voice said. "Did I startle you?"

When Chris saw him, her heart stopped once more; this time, it wasn't out of fear. Her first customer of the day was one of the most attractive men she'd ever seen. She found herself making instant analogies to the minerals around her. His hair reminded her of burnished copper, and his eyes were like . . .

. . . well, like emeralds, Chris Wander thought as she sped towards Blueriver.

"No – no," Chris had faltered, back then, setting the Easter basket in the window.

The man gazed at her for a few minutes and

231

she realized he was studying her. Feeling a warm blush rush over her, she turned away and pretended to be busy. "I was just setting up a new display," she said. "I guess I was too deep in thought to hear you come in."

"You look like a woman who has many thoughts to think." He moved farther into the store and started to study some wares, displayed on rough-hewn wooden shelves.

"Are you looking for a gift?" Chris asked, trying to bring the conversation into familiar territory. He was probably married, anyway. "Or a souvenir?"

"Only looking," the man said idly. "I've just moved to Aberdeen and want to see what's here."

Chris laughed. "Not much. There are fewer than ten thousand people in this town."

"It's gorgeous," the man said. "The kind of homey, quiet place I like."

He came to her and held out her hand. Chris felt giddy when she took it, and was surprised she had developed a crush on a complete stranger. She hadn't dated much, but recognized the feeling of powerful attraction.

"My name is Brian Wander," he said, his smile gleaming.

"I'm Christine Burnett," she said. "Call me Chris."

"Hello, Chris."

It was that way she met her future husband. Brian came back to the shop a few more times that week, and actually bought something when Dr Scott was in. As Christy was wrapping a block of crystals, Brian leaned over the counter and whispered: "Would you like to have dinner with me tonight?"

Chris didn't know what to say. New relationships had never been easy for her. The thought of this handsome man meeting her father, all glassy-eyed and drooling in his bed, turned her stomach. She shook her head. "I can't."

Brian didn't push the matter, and that impressed Chris. He seemed both outgoing and gentle. But he wasn't the type to give up. He asked her out two more times, but both times she found excuses.

"Don't tell me you locals don't cotton to strangers," he said, pulling the last three words into a drawl."

"No, it's just that . . ." She couldn't explain.

"Never mind," Brian said patiently. "I'll try again."

After he left, a large number of people flooded the store. It was the biggest group the Geode had ever seen at one time, and they kept Christy very busy. They were tourists on a bus trip from Helena to Granite Park. By the time they left, the sun was coming down, and Dr Scott announced it was time to close up shop. Seeing him yawn and rub his neck, Chris volunteered to do the work herself.

"Thanks," the old man said. He looked down at his rough hands. They weren't a professor's hands at all. His dirty fingernails seemed proof of his hard work. "It was a rough day at the dig yesterday, and I've got another one tomorrow. I'd appreciate a good night's sleep." He said good-bye and left.

A few minutes later, the telephone rang. Christy answered it, but there was no one on the other end. The darkness outside the little shop suddenly seemed full of potential danger. Perhaps the stranger was checking up on her. Perhaps he was out there, waiting in the dark.

It was ridiculous, she told herself. She was a grown woman, not a frightened little girl. She flitted nervously around the store, finding work that would delay her, ringing out the cash register and cleaning up. She reminded herself that it was just a short walk home, and at this hour there would be numerous people on the street. She would be quite safe, of course.

As she was leaving the shop, locking the door, she felt a tap on her shoulder.

"So grown up and pretty," a terribly familiar voice whispered.

Chris screamed and tried to run, but the man was quicker. He pulled her close to him, covering her mouth with his hand. Chris thought frantically how alone she was, how isolated the little shop was.

"Please, please," she heard him say. The voice sounded different than she remembered, younger. But that was impossible! *Years* had gone by since she last heard from him. "He told me you were beautiful, but he didn't say how beautiful. I

234

won't hurt you, Christy! I've dreamed of you all my life. I only want to talk to you!"

Chris's teeth found purchase on a small pad of skin, and she bit down as hard as she could. The man let out a cry, and she broke into a run. She raced towards the corner, passing a small park-like area. Trees shadowed her path, trees that could easily hide a murder . . .

"Please, wait!" The pleading tones seemed incongruous with the rough voice. "Please talk to me!"

"Leave me alone!"

Chris ran to her apartment, heels clicking along the sidewalk. There were a few people on the street, and they turned to gape at her. But no one came to her aid. Why did she think they would? They were probably whispering that 'Crazy Christy' was at it again, the way they'd done all her life. Her fear mixing with a surge of hatred for all of them, Chris looked back over her shoulder. The man was about a block away, walking fast, gaining on her.

Suddenly, Chris crashed into someone. To her chagrin, it was Brian Wander. He took her by the shoulders.

"Hey, slow down!"

Chris tried to pull away. "Let me go! Can't you see he's after me?"

Brian looked behind her. "Who?"

Chris turned around slowly. The man had disappeared once more. "He was there," she said, a defiant tone in her voice.

"Well, he's gone now."

Chris's expression softened as she realized Brian couldn't know of her reputation. She blinked the last of her tears away.

"You're shaking like a leaf. Please, come into the coffee shop and talk to me. I'd like to hear what happened."

Grateful to have a sympathetic ear, Chris followed him down the street to Mayer's Luncheonette.

Her voice was soft as she ordered coffee, light and sweet. Brian took his black, but let it sit as he listened to her story. He interrupted a few times to ask pertinent questions, but mostly left the floor to her. With a sigh, she finally brought the strange story to an end.

She looked him straight in the eyes, challenging him to ridicule her. If he did, if he even suggested she was as crazy as people said, she'd walk out and . . .

"My God, you must have been terrified."

His sympathetic response was so unexpected that Chris simply sat there, agape.

"Wasn't there anyone you could tell?" Brian asked. "I mean, a little girl living a nightmare like that, all alone . . ."

"I tried to tell adults," Chris said. "But, since no one else ever saw this guy, no one believed me. I was punished for lying. But I wasn't really alone. I had my best friends, Eda and Lucille, to help me. I suppose I could have told one adult, a nice cop named Mike Hewlett, but I'd grown to mistrust

236

all adults. You see, my father wasn't very . . ." She sighed, taking a sip of her coffee, unable to tell this virtual stranger about her family.

Brian nodded, seeming to understand. "I can't say I blame you," he said. Then his expression grew more serious. "What do you suppose brought him back after all these years?"

"I don't know," Chris said. "It's been more than fifteen years since I last saw him. I can't think where he's been, or what he wants. All I know is that for some reason he can't put me out of his mind."

She felt an urge to start crying again, and pinched the bridge of her nose between thumb and forefinger. She tried to keep her voice steady, but there was a choke in it when she said: "He's had plenty of opportunity to grab me, if that's what he's after. Maybe he thought taking a child would be too conspicuous all those years ago."

"That didn't stop him from taking the Gammel boys," Brian pointed out.

Chris blinked, her eyes wet as she looked up. "They never found them, you know. Most people think they're dead. It was only some twist of fate that kept me from ending up like them."

The waitress came by and filled their cups at that moment. When she left, Brian spoke again. "Maybe you should report this incident. The police should know you're being followed."

Chris shook her head vehemently. "No! I don't want to involve the police. And besides, there's no proof. I was the only one running down the street. He was careful to walk." Chris shifted uncomfortably in her seat.

Brian reached across the table, took her hand, and held it tightly. His grip was warm and strong, supportive. "No one should have to put up with harassment the way you have."

"You don't know about me," Chris said. "You don't know what people have been saying about me all my life. I have a . . . well, people think I'm disturbed. My father and mother . . . uh . . . my mother . . ." She lowered her head and began to cry, unable to say more. How could she tell this kind, handsome stranger about her family's problems? About her mother, diagnosed schizophrenic and living in a home? About her father, who couldn't even feed himself?

"Hey," Brian said softly. "Hey." He came around to her side of the booth and took her in his arms. It felt good to have someone hold her close. "Come on. Let me walk you home."

Chris wiped her eyes with a paper napkin. "I'd appreciate that. I don't know if that man is waiting for me."

Brian paid for the coffee, and they left the shop. Keeping his arm around her, he led her down the street. It was dark out, and there were few people. No one looked in their direction.

"This is my place," Chris said when they reached the pizzeria. "I live upstairs."

"Should I walk you up?"

"No," Chris said. "No, thank you." *The last thing I want is for you to meet my father.*

238

Brian studied her for a few moments. "Will you let me take you to dinner Friday night?"

"I don't . . ."

"Please?"

Chris managed a smile. Why not? After all, she'd just poured her heart out to him. She owed him a little. "Okay," she said. "But it has to be an early evening."

She was grateful Brian didn't ask why.

On the lonely highway between Aberdeen and Blueriver, Chris looked up to see her destination was only ten miles away. She put thoughts of Brian aside for the time being, after allowing herself a quick memory of their first date together. But those memories were crowded out by a sense of foreboding. In a short while, she might be facing the brother she hadn't seen in years. "Oh, Brian," she whispered, tears streaming down her face. "I wish you were here to help me!"

Eda came into the kitchen with a towel wrapped around her hair. Lucille was draining bacon on paper towels and three places had already been set with sectioned grapefruits. Eda took a piece of bacon from the counter and sat down.

"Where's Chris?" Lucille asked. "Still sleeping?"

"She wasn't in her room when I looked," Eda said. "I thought she was down here already."

Lucille opened the refrigerator and took out a carton of eggs. As she cracked them into a bowl, she said: "Well, she's probably taking a shower. She'll be down in a minute. I'll keep some eggs aside for her."

"No, she's not in the bathroom. I just got out myself, and I didn't pass her in the hall."

A look of concern crossed Lucille's face. "I'm sure she isn't down here. Wait . . ." She parted the curtains behind the sink and looked out at the driveway. Letting them fall together again, she said: "The car's gone."

"Damn! Where could she have gone? We didn't even hear her leave."

Lucille looked up at the clock. "It's only eight-thirty. She must have gone out when we were sleeping."

Eda played with her grapefruit a few moments, thoughtful. "Blueriver," she said finally. "I bet she's gone up to see Harvey."

"Oh, no! I don't think that's such a good idea."

"I'm not sure it is, either," Eda said, standing. "I'm going to call Mike Hewlett. If she's on the highway headed up there, maybe he could have a state trooper find her."

When Mike heard Eda's suspicions, he promised to contact the state police. However, he thought it might be good for Chris to talk to her brother, and finally convinced Eda of this. He had some interesting news for her, too, and when she hung up she told Lucille. "They called the doctor whose notepad I found. It seems she had an appointment with a Teddy Eastman two days ago. He never showed up."

Lucille's eyes widened. "You don't have to be a scholar to figure out who Teddy Eastman really is."

"They're trying to locate his father," Eda said. "His stepfather, I mean. I guess Irene Gammel made a new life for herself in Washington. She married a man named Douglas Eastman."

"It's amazing to find Teddy alive after all these years. But it doesn't explain his connection to Brian, unless Douglas Eastman can answer that."

"Unfortunately, the Washington police have been unable to locate him. In the meantime, our force is on the lookout for Teddy. Mike put a guard on the Gammel house, but he said no one showed up last night. Unfortunately, it can't be a twenty-four hour watch. Aberdeen's police staff is small, and this case has them all working harder than ever."

"Do you think Teddy has been hiding in his old house?" Lucille asked. A shudder racked her tall frame. "To think you might have run into a murderer!"

"I'm okay. It's Chris we have to worry about."

Lucille packed the leftover breakfast food and put it in the refrigerator. "I just hate waiting!" she cried. "What if she isn't going up to Blueriver at all. What if, after all these years, the creep's finally decided to get her?"

For a few minutes, neither woman said a word. Eda was trying to put together the facts she'd learned over the past few days. Lucille was thinking about Chris, possibly in great danger. And, as if they were psychically linked, the two women thought of the children at the same time. Their eyes met, and Lucille said: "I'm scared. I'm so worried about those kids."

"So am I," Eda declared. "Dear God, so am I."

Chris had arrived before visiting hours, and sat impatiently in a small building just outside prison grounds. It was a sort of waiting area, where family members gathered until it was time for a little bus to shuttle them inside the penitentiary. Chris hardly noticed the others, except for a young boy with big brown eyes. He looked a lot like Josh. Chris couldn't help staring at him, and when he caught her he moved closer to his mother and buried his face in her skirt.

Looking down at her lap, she imagined that Eda and Lucille had discovered her missing by now. And she was certain they could guess where she was. So when a young cop came in asking for her, she wasn't much surprised. She stood up and went with him. He led her out to a car, opened the door for her, and explained that the warden wanted to see her.

The warden was a tall man with thick glasses and slicked-back hair that would have been more stylish in the early sixties. But he had a kind smile and called Chris "ma'am" when he offered her a seat. His name tag said Fitterman.

"Seems some folks in Aberdeen are quite

concerned about you," he said. "Sheriff Hewlett called to say you might be up here. Mike's an old friend of mine."

"I've come to see my brother," Chris said. "I think he has some important information."

Fitterman nodded. "Mike seems to think so, too. Now, the problem is that Harvey's been in solitary for nearly a week. Broke a plate over another inmate's head. Real troublemaker."

Chris shifted uncomfortably. "I know."

"He doesn't talk much," Fitterman said. "But Mike believes he'll talk to you. I thought you could talk better in private, so I'm having you go in a little earlier than the other families."

Chris tucked a lock of hair behind her ear. "How much did Mike tell you?"

"Just about everything," Fitterman said. "It's been in the papers, too. Damn, you are one brave lady. If it had been my family, I'm not sure I could be as strong."

Chris, anxious to speak with her brother, didn't say anything.

The phone rang, and Fitterman answered it. After he hung up, he stood and said: "Harvey's waiting for you."

Chris followed him out of the office and down a long hall. They stopped and waited for several gates to be unlocked and then relocked behind them. At last, they reached a room with a metal door and a small window. A police officer stood outside.

Suddenly, Chris froze. All she could think of

was her father, a man who had hurt her time and again. Had Harvey grown to be like him? Chris recalled he was in here on a manslaughter charge. Had he become the animal their father had been? When Fitterman put a hand on her shoulder, she jumped.

"Easy, ma'am," he said. "You're safe here. Officer Mascioli will be on guard the whole time."

Chris nodded mutely.

"Ready?"

"I guess."

Fitterman had the officer unlock the door, and he escorted Chris inside. Harvey was standing with his back to the door, his hands clasped behind him. He wore a white T-shirt with cut-off sleeves and a pair of khaki trousers.

"Burnett, your visitor's here."

"Yeah, yeah," Harvey sneered.

Chris felt a chill rush through her. He sounded so much like the boy she remembered!

"Who the hell would want to visit –?" His voice broke when he turned to see his sister. Chris, taken aback by his appearance, couldn't speak herself. She'd expected Harvey to be as big and mean-looking as their father. But this was a scraggly man, a wasted man. His eyes seemed huge in his sunken face, his hair more grey than brown.

"Oh, shit," Harvey whispered.

"Hello, Harvey," was all Chris could think to say.

Fitterman left. Slowly, Chris made her way to the table and sat. Harvey sat across from her, staring into her eyes with haunted eyes of his own. "Shit," he said again.

"Harvey, you know I never liked curse words," Chris said.

He said nothing for a few moments. Then a big grin spread across his face. "God, you turned out pretty," he said. "You look like Mom did when I was little, before stuff happened." He pushed his fingers over the top of his head, as if to run them through a phantom head of hair.

"Before she got sick, you mean."

They looked at each other, then both started to talk at once.

"Harvey, I . . ."

"You're really . . ."

They both took a breath.

"How'd you find me?" Harvey asked.

"Mike Hewlett found you," Chris explained. "Harvey, what happened to you? What happened to Felicity?"

Harvey shrugged. "She left. The baby changed her. She went to work and I started stealing money from her for drugs. Guess it was too much."

"You had a little girl, I heard."

"Lolani," Harvey said, looking at the blank wall. A wistful look came across his face but quickly disappeared. "Pretty kid. Looked a lot like you."

"Really?"

Harvey nodded. "Felicity couldn't take any

245

more of my shit. Not that I beat her or anything. I'd never do that. Too much like Dad. But I was dopehead."

Chris felt a momentary twinge of relief to hear Felicity and the baby hadn't been abused. But she quickly turned the subject to her reason for being here. All this small talk was just keeping her from the truth. "Harvey, do you remember the Gammel crimes?"

"Sure I do. Why?"

"A few days ago," Chris said, "my husband was murdered. Brian was . . ." She took a deep breath, concentrating on her brother's face to keep an image of her husband from her mind. "Brian was decapitated. The same night, my two children disappeared."

"Holy shit," Harvey whispered. He ran his fingers over his head again. "We've had a lot of crappy things happen to us, haven't we?"

"I need your help, Harvey," Chris said. "We – my friends and I – think you might know something about all this."

"How the hell could I?" Harvey demanded. "I've been in this dump for a year!"

Chris sighed deeply, trying to calm herself. "Harvey, I have to ask you about the night you walked me home from the Crispins' holiday party. I keep thinking something happened then, something you've kept secret for years. It might help me save my children. Please, Harvey, you've got to tell me what happened that night!"

Harvey stared at her for such a long time that

Chris began to feel hot. Finally, he nodded. "They told me someone working on a murder case wanted to talk to me," he said. "They said if I cooperated, I could cut my time here. You really want to know what happened that night?"

"Yes, I do," Chris said in a firm voice.

"Then you better brace yourself," Harvey said, "'cause you sure as hell aren't gonna like what I have to say."

"If it gets my kids back," Chris said, "that's all that matters."

"Boys or girls?"

"One of each," Chris said. "Josh is ten and Vicki is five."

"They know they have an uncle?"

Chris looked down at her lap. She had never mentioned Harvey or her parents to her children. They were part of a past she'd tried hard to forget. Strange how that past had caught up with her, overtaken her, and destroyed her family. But if Harvey would help her, she might still save part of her life. "They're very young, Harvey," she said.

"I get it," Harvey replied.

To her surprise, he reached over and patted her hand.

"Okay, listen," he began. "You have to realize something. I was a kid myself back then. I wanted nothing more than to get outta that hellhole we called a home. But where was I gonna go? I was only fifteen and I didn't have any money."

"You ran away that Christmas," Chris recalled.

"You were gone for three years. How did you live?"

"I managed," Harvey said. "You'd be surprised what a kid can do. But that night, the one you're talking about, I didn't tell the truth. That was no stranger who jumped us. At least, not to me. I'd seen him a few times, and I thought he was a worker from one of the ranches outside of town. One day he came up to me and started talkin'. He was no ranch hand, Christy. He had a wad of bills you could choke on. Gave me five dollars just to mail a letter for him. He started talking to me more and more. That was a little after Halloween, I think. He said he'd been watching our family, and he knew how badly we were being treated. He said he knew a nice couple that wanted a pretty little girl. I was supposed to get five hundred dollars if I turned you over to him."

Chris's eyes rounded. "You tried to *sell* me?"

"Well, don't put it that way, Christy," Harvey said. "It ain't like it was white slavery. I really thought that guy had a family that wanted you. But I knew something was wrong when he put that stuff over your face to knock you out. He said it was to keep you quiet, since what we were doin' was illegal. But then he started talkin' funny. He kept goin' on about an axe, and how good it worked, and how much 'the boys' would like you. I knew then and there that it was the man who'd murdered Basil Horton and Darren Gammel."

"Why didn't you ever go to the police?"

248

"Are you kidding?" Harvey asked. "With my reputation? And how could I explain I knew this guy 'cause I'd tried to sell him my kid sister? That night the bastard tried to cheat me – he only gave me two hundred dollars. That's when I got mad and hit him with a can."

"You said it was a hubcap," Chris recalled.

"A can, a hubcap, what does it matter? I saved you, didn't I?"

Chris buried her face in her hands and shook her head. The whole thing was unbelievable.

"Harvey, I can forgive you for what you did back then," she said into her fingers, her voice a steady drone. "Like you said, we were both kids. We were both desperate. But please don't insult me by pretending it was some noble act you performed. Because when you came back to Aberdeen, trouble started for me again. What made you return, Harvey? Did you plan to get more money from him, so you could beat the Draft?"

"That's right," Harvey said. "The first time I ran away, that same guy picked me up and drove me to Seattle. I worked for him for a while. He gave me the creeps, but I had no place else to go. Soon as I had enough money, I took off again. I finally ended up in San Francisco. But a coupla years later, both Uncle Sam and that guy found me."

"So you came back to Aberdeen," Chris said. "I could never understand why Dad was so glad to see you, after all the trouble you caused."

Harvey stared at the wall for a few moments before speaking again.

"That man followed me to Aberdeen," he said. "He had lots of money, and said he'd give me all I needed if I came back with him. There was one condition – you had to come along, too. I told Dad I knew someone who wanted to adopt a little girl, and was willing to pay lots of money for her. It made him very happy."

Somehow, this didn't surprise Chris. She felt no bitterness. Wanting to sell her was just one more flame in Harvey Sr.'s fire. Like son, like father.

"You keep calling him 'that guy'," Chris pointed out. "What was his name, Harvey?"

Harvey gave his head a rough shake. "No way. I ain't rattin' on him. The guy was a class-A weirdo, but he saved my ass back then. I couldn'ta survived without him."

"But, Harvey . . ."

"No!"

Suddenly, Harvey's expression changed. His eyes seemed to go a shade darker, and he stared at something Chris couldn't see. "That cop screwed it all up," Harvey said. "I didn't do a thing and he came up to the apartment to ask nosy questions. Well, I mean, I did have pot with me. He could have nailed me for that. But I was more worried he'd find the money my friend had given me and start asking where it came from. If Felicity hadn't faked labour pains . . ."

Chris nodded, understanding. So Felicity *had*

pulled a stunt that day. Something had been going on with *all* of them!

"We ran away from the hospital," Harvey went on. "We went up to Canada. But that guy found us and threatened to turn us in."

"You could have made the same threats against him."

Harvey shook his head. "This guy knew what he was doing. He was no drifter, Chris. He might have been crazy, but he was rich, too. He was crazy like a fox. So I had to do something to stop him."

Chris stared hard at her brother before asking: "Did you kill him?"

"Didn't have to," Harvey said. "He died in a crash."

"Then he couldn't have hurt my family," Chris said distantly.

"It would be a good trick," Harvey said.

It made sense, considering the man who'd stalked her would be very old by now. Who, then? She needed to know the man's name. Maybe then she could make a connection. "Please, Harvey," she begged. "You can't hurt him now. He can't hurt you."

"I said no!"

Harvey slammed his fist on the table, startling Chris so that her heart jumped. The guard outside the door looked in on them, gave Harvey a warning stare, and closed the door.

"All right," Chris said. "But tell me what happened when you came back to Aberdeen."

251

"He threatened to tell the authorities what I did to you,"

Harvey revealed. "Anonymously, so he wouldn't be implicated. I was already in trouble with the police, being a druggie. It was a pretty scary thing. But the prospect of Vietnam was worse. When he offered to pay me something to take off for Canada if I kept my mouth shut, I jumped at the chance. He still wanted you, Christy. He hadn't stopped thinking about you. So I was supposed to try to get you for him again." He shook his head ruefully. "What a mess it turned out to be! Mike Hewlett came to the hospital to talk to me. He said he'd seen me with a stranger and wanted to know who the guy was. Maybe he thought he was a pusher, I don't know. But I didn't tell him a thing. To this day, nobody's heard me mention the guy's name." He straightened his thin frame as if this were something to be proud of.

Chris felt herself growing angry, and forced calm into her voice. "What did you do after he died?"

"I went back to San Francisco, and me and Felicity and the kid lived on a commune. They left me even before my number came up and I had to run to Canada. I stayed about twenty years. That's all I can tell you, Christy."

Chris sighed, staring up at the wire-reinforced windows near the ceiling. "Nobody calls me Christy now," she said in a quiet voice.

She had been right. Harvey *had* been connected to the terrible man from her past. But unless she

252

knew his name, she might never find her children. Chris rolled her hands into tight fists and leaned forward. "Listen to me, Harvey Burnett," she said firmly, "I'm not the scared little twerp you remember as your sister. Something wonderful happened to me. A man named Brian Wander saved my life and gave me two beautiful children. Now someone's murdered him and taken my babies from me. And if I have to choke it out of you, I'll find out that man's name!" By the end of this tirade, she was shouting.

"Forget it!" Harvey yelled back. "I said I wouldn't betray him! He didn't kill your friggin' old man! How could he? He'd be seventy by now if he was alive!" He got up and started to pace the room.

"You owe me," Chris said. "For God's sake, what difference does it make now? The man's dead."

Her brother stopped, and Chris felt the old fears rising as a familiar snarl curled over her brother's face. He picked up a chair and threw it. "I don't owe you *nothin'*!"

The chair crashed against the wall. A second later, the cop came in, took Harvey by the arm, and led him out. "Sorry, lady. This interview's over." He twisted Harvey's arm behind his back. "You must like solitary a whole lot, Burnett."

They left Chris alone in that barren room, with the miserable realization the whole thing had been a waste of time.

Chapter Thirteen

Josh was aware they weren't alone even before he opened his eyes. Although his stomach was churning and his head ached, he could sense the presence of someone new in the room. Slowly, he opened his eyes to find Vicki curled up on her own cot.

Groggily, he turned his aching head. Through a sea of dizziness, he saw a woman sitting on a chair. He blinked and tried to speak, but his tongue felt ten times too big. His mind was a jumble of half-questions. Who are . . .? Where . . .? Why don't you . . .? It was too much to take, and the boy passed out again.

Vicki's screaming woke him up later, slicing through the drugged stupor that enveloped him. First he looked at his sister, beet-red and screaming. Then he looked where her finger pointed. And tried not to scream himself.

There was a woman sitting across the room, her head propped up by the blood-soaked sack in her lap. She was turned in such a way she seemed to be staring at them, but Josh knew at once she couldn't see. He turned to the other side of his bed and threw up.

"Josh, please!" Vicki whined. "Tell her to stop looking at me!"

Slowly, Josh got up. He took the blanket from his bed and walked towards the dead woman. Then he stopped cold, clutching the blanket tightly. What if she wasn't dead? What if she came to life? What if she grabbed him? "That's stupid!" he told himself firmly. Still, he looked at the woman only from the corner of his eye as he threw the blanket over her head. Now she was a shapeless form with legs, one ending in a heeled shoe, one cut and bloodied.

"Who – who is that, Josh?"

"I don't know," Josh said. "I – I think I've seen her on television. Just don't look over there, Vicki, okay?"

Vicki obediently turned away. "What happened? We were trying to stop that bad man."

"He jumped you," Josh said. "Then he got me. I think he poisoned us."

"I'm gonna be sick," Vicki said. She coughed a few times, then lost whatever food was in her stomach. The little girl began to cry softly. Without a thought, Josh went and put his arms around her.

"I wanna go home," Vicki said. "It's scary down here."

"I know," Josh said, staring at the trapdoor

overhead. "There's gotta be *some* way outta here!"

But there was only one way out – the locked trapdoor. And in order to get to it, he'd have to move that lady in the chair . . .

Chapter Fourteen

Shortly after hanging up with Eda, Mike decided to take another look at the Gammel house. It had been dark when he sent a surveillance team to watch it. Deputy Katherine Jackson had reported the place was empty.

Katherine and her partner were still parked outside the house when he arrived. He sent them home, sorry to hear that there had been no activity, but thinking he might be able to come across another clue or two in the daylight.

He never expected the clue would be fresh blood. There were spots of it on the stairs and trailing down the hall into a bedroom. Mike thought the search team should have noticed it, but reminded himself they'd been searching for a human being, in the dark, with flashlights.

The sight of reddish-brown stains made his heart stop for a moment. Slowly, he crouched down and touched a finger to it. It was sticky and cold. The sheriff got up and followed the blood spatters down to the cellar. He stopped halfway down the stairs, afraid of what he might find. Then, swearing softly, he took his gun out and continued down with great caution. He swung his flashlight around, but saw nothing unusual. A more careful search confirmed there was no one present, but Mike spotted a high-heeled shoe. Certain it hadn't been there when the house was searched earlier, he left it to forensics for study.

Quickly, he bounded up the stairs and out to his car, where he radioed headquarters for extra help. Eda Crispin had gone to the station and she joined the team that came to the house. When she saw the blood, a shiver ran down her spine.

"I don't think it's the kids," Mike said, trying to sound more reassuring than he felt. "I found a high-heeled shoe in the cellar."

"Maybe it was one of Irene's?"

"It looked brand-new."

The two were standing in the downstairs hallway, watching the flurry of activity as the forensics team worked on the house. A man in a grey suit sidled past them, holding up a plastic bag containing the single shoe. Eda recognized it at once, and stopped the man. "Mike, that shoe belongs to Tiffany Simmons."

"The reporter?"

Eda nodded. "She was wearing this last time I saw her. Those are designer shoes – there aren't too many people who can afford them."

Mike gave the bag back to the technician. "Have someone locate Tiffany Simmons," he ordered.

"Do you think something happened to her?" Eda asked, her gaze falling on the bloodstains.

"I don't know," Mike said. "But if there's been another victim, Chris and those kids are in more danger than ever. As soon as she gets back from Blueriver, I think you should make plans to get her out of Aberdeen."

"Mike, I had some thoughts. You probably figured this out on your own, but do you realize Teddy Gammel can't be the person who stalked Chris so many years ago?"

"Of course," Mike agreed. "He was only a child. But he seems to be our prime suspect right now."

"If he is, then the person who murdered Darren Gammel and Basil Horton is still free. Assuming he's alive, of course."

They walked out onto the porch.

"I was also wondering about Adrian," Eda said. "Have you been able to locate the boys' stepfather?"

"No," Mike replied. "But I've learned some interesting things about Douglas Eastman. He owns one of the biggest trucking companies in the West. Teddy's doctor, Marion Niles, was kind enough to provide some information. She said Eastman was a very unpleasant individual. She believes he's partly to blame for Teddy's problems."

"But not entirely," Eda said thoughtfully. "Not if he came into the picture after Irene left Aberdeen." She grimaced, feeling chilled despite the heat of the July morning. This house, with its tragic history, seemed to suck all warmth from the surrounding area. "Maybe she had the kids with her later in life," she said, "but she sure didn't have them when she left here. What kind of mother dumps her children that way?"

Mike didn't have an answer.

"Listen, I'd better get home," Eda said. "I want to be there when Chris arrives."

"Let me give you a lift," Mike said. "I've got things to take care of at headquarters."

Eda smiled at him. "Thanks. I walked to the station this morning. Chris took Lucille's car up to Blueriver."

After Mike dropped her off, Eda went in to hear the soft clicking of a computer keyboard. She guessed Lucille was working on one of her books. She decided to give Tim a call, but as she was dialing she heard a car pull into the driveway. She hung up and hurried to look out the window. Then she called: "Lucille! Chris is back!"

The typing noises stopped at once, and Lucille was in the kitchen a moment later. She opened the back door and hurried to the car. Unfortunately, one of the few reporters remaining at the house saw her, and Chris. He came hurrying across the street, followed by others.

"Go away!" Lucille demanded, putting a protective arm around Chris.

"Just a few questions, Mrs Wander!"

"Do you know anything about the blood found at the Gammel house?"

Chris swung around. "Blood?"

Eda stepped around her friends, flashing her badge quickly so no one could see it was from out-of-state. "Back off!" she snapped as the other two women raced for the back door.

"Freedom of the Press, lady!"

"Up your freedom," Eda mumbled as she went inside.

"Blood?" Chris repeated, as if she didn't understand the word. "What was he talking about?"

"They found fresh blood at the Gammel house," Eda told her. Chris gasped, and she held up a hand. "Mike doesn't think it's from the kids. For one thing, they found a woman's shoe that wasn't there a few days ago."

"Never mind that now," Lucille said. "Chris, we were worried sick about you! Tell us what happened this morning."

They brought her into the living room, where the drawn curtains gave them some privacy. Their friend's face was blotched red, her eyes shining. She looked from Eda to Lucille, then blurted: "He set me up! My own brother set me up just to get money!"

"Start at the beginning, Chris," Eda said.

"I wish you hadn't gone to see Harvey," Lucille said. "I knew he would upset you."

Chris shook her head. "No, I'm glad I went. This is something that's been a dark hole inside of me for thirty years. At least now I have some answers." She sniffled hard.

Lucille found a box of tissues and handed them to her.

"You know how I've always been so down around the holidays?"

Both women nodded.

"Now I know why," Chris said. "Harvey told me everything. That night of your Hanukkah celebration, Eda, when he came to walk me home, it was really to lead me into a trap. There was a man waiting in an alley for us. He'd told Harvey he'd pay five hundred dollars for a little girl. He said there was a family who wanted to adopt me."

She sighed deeply. "All the time, it was really the man who committed those murders. Harvey wouldn't tell me his name. There's some sort of strange loyalty there. I tried to reason with him, but he's so much like my father. He became so angry that a guard came in and took him away."

The women gave themselves a few minutes to absorb this new information. Then Lucille got up and announced she was going to make coffee.

"I could use a cup," Chris said.

Eda looked at her. "Are you okay? I mean, about Harvey?"

"Not okay," Chris said, "but not surprised. I should have known he was up to something. I kept dreaming that Harvey was talking to someone. That person said I'd seen too much. But I don't know what it is I saw. Only Irene Gammel with blood on her! Nothing more. What does it mean?"

Eda shifted her position on the couch. "We have some new information, Chris," she said. "We think the man who killed Brian and took the kids might be Teddy Gammel."

"Teddy!" Chris said with surprise. "You mean, he's alive?"

"Yes," Eda said. "Mike called the doctor on that pad I found. He's one of her patients. He's been missing for a while."

"What about Adrian?"

"He was put up for adoption," Eda explained. "Probably right after they left Montana."

Chris turned towards the closed curtains and parted them just enough to look outside. Since her arrival back at Lucille's house, at least two more reporters had shown up. "It's amazing how sick a family can be," she said, comparing her own nightmarish childhood to Teddy and Adrian's. "Maybe Adrian was the lucky one. Maybe he got into a loving family."

Lucille came back with the coffee. Chris finished half a cup before speaking again.

"If Teddy has come back to Aberdeen," she said, "it must be because someone told him to. That man who had been following me must have put Teddy up to this."

"If Teddy's that easily influenced," Eda said, "then he's more dangerous that we imagined. Only a very unstable person would do the evil work of another man."

* * *

265

Mike hung up the phone after talking with the station manager of Cable 75 News. Tiffany had been due on the set at 6 a.m., but she never arrived. The manager had called her house, with no answer. Mike suggested she might have overslept, but the manager adamantly disagreed. Tiffany was always punctual and dedicated. No, he believed she was sick, too ill to even answer the phone. He asked for an explanation, but Mike declined. Instead, he drove to Tiffany's house himself. No one answered his knock.

Even while imagining how loud Tiffany would scream foul if she knew what he was doing, he worked the lock open on the front door and went inside. Tiffany lived in a pretty little Cape Cod, nicely furnished in an ultra-modern style. The interior was immaculate. Every knickknack seemed to have its own place, every throw pillow was carefully fluffed. The place was so clean it looked as if no one lived here at all.

Mike went into each room, surveying. If anything so much as bothered him, he'd get a real search warrant. He found a huge trophy in the den, with the words "LITTLE MISS NORTHWEST" engraved at the bottom. There was a picture of Tiffany at a very young age near it; she was taking a bow in a frilly dress, showing off her new crown. Another trophy, only a foot high, sat on her desk. It was an Ace award for her work on Cable 75.

Pictures showed Tiffany with various celebrities, Tiffany with friends, Tiffany on the arms of a handsome man. Mike made a mental note to inquire about him. He was about to turn from the room when something jumped him from behind. He stumbled back against the fireplace, knocking down the big trophy. With lightening reflexes, he swung around as he pulled out his gun.

Then he laughed and holstered the weapon. His assailant was a cat. She rubbed herself around Mike's ankles, crying pitifully.

"You sound hungry." He went to the kitchen and saw the cat had neither food nor water. If Tiffany was so conscientious about her house, it wasn't likely she'd go out without caring for her animal.

Mike found some cat food and poured it into a dish. As he was filling a water bowl, worry about a new victim crept into his mind. He bent to set the bowl on the floor and noticed a scrap of paper. In this meticulously neat place, it was almost like a beacon. He picked it up and read: *Property tax on Gammel place – why was Wander paying it?*

So Tiffany knew about that. And if someone was aware that she knew, that person might have tried to stop her further inquiry. She could have gone to the house herself and ran into the suspect.

Mike pocketed the note and left the house. He drove to the station, planning to work through lunch. Douglas Eastman had promised to come

267

in from Washington to discuss his stepson, and Mike was hoping someone had heard from him. The man had refused to come by plane, and Mike knew the trip would take nearly a day by car.

Eda was in the records room when he arrived. "I couldn't stop thinking about the autopsies," she said. "Look, I've made some charts."

Mike came around behind her to study the papers. Eda had listed each characteristic of the murders in a column under the victims' names. She pointed to a description of the wounds.

"Look at Darren Gammel," she said. "The wound was very clean. The coroner felt it was made by a few sharp blows. But look at Basil Horton. His injury seems to have been made with a more sawing action. The edges are very ragged, downright sloppy, in fact. And he's the only one who took a blow to the back of his head. Brian Wander's was much like the first one, only there are bruises around his face to indicate he'd also been beaten. Other than a few scratches, Darren's injuries are concentrated on his neck."

Mike nodded. "I remember. We all believed Darren had been attacked too quickly to put up a fight. Basil and Brian must have tried to stop the killer."

"But it seems Basil was hit from behind," Eda pointed out. "The coroner stated he was bludgeoned first. He was probably dead before his head was taken off. And that's what bothers me. Why saw it off so haphazardly? Why not do it neatly, as in the first murder? A dead man wouldn't struggle."

"It's almost as if the killings were done by two different people," Mike said, reading Eda's mind. "But remember, the forensic equipment of that time wasn't very sophisticated. Back then, all the evidence pointed to one person."

"You thought it was Irene Gammel."

"After the second murder occured," Mike said, "we couldn't hold her without definite evidence."

Eda thought for a moment. "There were people who still believed she was guilty."

"We'll never know Irene's side, will we?" Mike said. "But the very fact this new crime occured after she died could be a clue. Her husband should be here this afternoon, driving all the way from Washington."

Eda started to gather up the papers and return them to the files. "What do you know about him?"

"Irene married him a few years after leaving Aberdeen," Mike said. "He's rich and powerful. Owns a huge trucking company."

"Powerful enough to keep Irene away from the police all these years?"

"Maybe," Mike said. "We'll get more answers when he arrives. In the meantime, I have some questions about Tiffany Simmons. She's definitely missing."

Eda went to the cabinet and returned the files to their places. She was frowning when she turned around.

"I never liked her," she said, "but I never wished her real harm. I hope we don't have another victim, Mike."

Chris hadn't slept or eaten much, in spite of Lucille's efforts. She'd given herself time to pity the little girl who'd been betrayed by her brother, but that tugging of her heart was quickly transferred to her own children. What were Josh and Vicki going through now? Did they think their own mother had betrayed them because she hadn't rescued them? The idea was so disturbing she quickly shut it away. That effort, combined with exhaustion, had rendered her almost paralyzed.

A newsbreak came on between shows and the children's pictures were flashed on the screen. The newscaster told of the blood found at the old Gammel house and speculated on foul play: "Police are not saying if Christine Wander is still a suspect," he said. "All efforts to reach the mother of the missing children have failed. Our own Tiffany . . ."

Chris didn't hear the last of it. She started wailing, great tears pouring from her eyes, blurring a recorded image of the police at the Gammel house.

Hearing her friend's cries, Lucille left her desk and hurried into the living room, snapping off the television. Without a word, she took Chris into her arms and held her until she calmed down. "God, this has got to end soon," Lucille whispered.

Chapter Fifteen

In spite of the blanket thrown over it, the thing in the chair looked like what it was: a person. There was no pretending it was a dummy or a robot. The blood that had caked on its shoeless leg was too real.

Vicki and Josh remained cuddled close together, not wanting to look at the body but not wanting to look away. Vicki thought it would get up and walk if they didn't watch it, and the thought of those cold fingers touching her neck kept her facing the hideous sight.

Josh looked at the ladder as he tried to plan their escape. Every few seconds, his eyes were drawn to the shrouded form, but he quickly averted them. This wasn't a video game, he told himself. You didn't win endless lives by typing in a secret code or picking up a number of gold pieces. Dead was forever, and dead didn't move. But he still didn't want to go near that thing. *Dead didn't move*.

He wondered how she'd gotten in here in the first place. *Dead didn't move*. She sure as heck hadn't come down here on her own.

"I know!" he cried out, so suddenly that Vicki screamed. "Be quiet!" he snapped.

"You scared me!" Vicki protested.

"Sorry, I just thought of something."

"What?" she said.

"Nothing . . ."

"You said it was something!"

"It's none of your business!" He didn't want to tell his little sister what he'd realized. That creepy guy had brought the woman down, the way he'd brought that extra food. Josh and Vicki hadn't noticed him because they were sleeping.

"Josh, this is boring," Vicki wailed. "I want my trolls, and my toy pony and my play dishes . . ."

"Quiet," Josh said. "I'm thinking. Open up a bag of chips and eat some."

Vicki looked worried.

"Don't worry," Josh reassured. "She can't hurt you."

"She isn't gonna get up and walk?"

"That's a dopey thing to say."

Vicki got up slowly, never taking her eyes from the cloaked figure. She sidled over to the shelves and grabbed the first thing she laid her hands on, then ran back to the cot, afraid the woman would chase her. She'd taken a box of cereal, and sat cramming it into her mouth.

"Cut that out," Josh said. "What the heck do you expect me to do if you choke?"

Vicki started making patterns on the cot with the cereal, trying not to think about the dead lady.

Josh was working out another plan. He had to trick that guy into thinking they were both asleep. Then, when he came down again, he'd be ready. He still thought throwing cans was a good idea. He could hide a big can, sneak up behind the guy, and let him have it. The only trick was to stay awake long enough, and have the strength to fight.

Teddy Gammel was scared. Almost more scared than that time when he and Adrian were kids. The sight of police cars around his old house shook him deeply. He stayed in the woods that wrapped around the back three acres of his family's property, sometimes climbing up a tree to watch the activity. From that height, he could just barely make out the difference in the tall grass that indicated the trap door to the fallout shelter. He wished he could run to it, climb down inside and hide the way Douglas had hidden Adrian and him so many years ago. But the police might see him, and take the kids away.

He knew the kids were the only way he was going to get Christy to come back to Washington with him. It would be just the way it had been with his mother and Douglas. He'd gotten the kids' daddy out of the way, the way Douglas had gotten his own daddy out of the way. That was what Douglas had told him to do. Douglas had told him to stop Brian from selling the old house. Teddy had felt nervous about it, but Douglas said: "Just do what I would do. Just get rid of him."

Teddy knew the right way to get rid of people. When you took off someone's head, they never came back.

Josh tried very hard to stay awake. Long after Vicki had given in to fitful slumber, he remained alert. He tried to remain awake by thinking of video game songs, doing multiplication in his head, imagining seeing his mother again. A vision of his father struggling with another man came to mind, but he snapped his eyes open to end it.

The blanket had fallen from the woman's body. She was staring at him. Josh was certain she could see him. In the strange light from overhead, her eyes were a horrid grey. Blood had caked around a wound in her shoulder and stained her blouse. Her mouth started working, her hand rose up slowly, pointing . . . She started to rise, moving ever-so-slowly, as if she were in pain. One of her arms, cut nearly to the bone, hung at a strange angle.

Josh screamed. And found himself sitting bolt-upright on the cot. "A nightmare," he whispered. "Just a nightmare." He was shaking all over. He didn't want to look across the room, but forced himself. The body was still hidden under the blanket, unmoved and unmoving.

Josh got up on weak legs and hurried to use the dry, rusted toilet. When he came back, he grabbed hold of the end of Vicki's cot. He began dragging it towards the room that had been locked that first day, the empty closet.

276

Vicki picked up her head, regarding him with bloodshot eyes. "Whatcha doin'?"

"I don't want to be near her," Josh said. "We're moving into the other room."

"Oh, good," Vicki said, and dropped off to sleep again.

The cot was just a fraction of an inch shorter than the door, and it was a ten-minute struggle to get it in. When he finally succeeded, he went back outside to pick up cans. Sometime when they were knocked out, their captor had gathered up their arsenal and stacked the shelves neatly again. Josh gathered as many cans as possible and brought them into the room. He piled them around the bed, within easy reach. This time, that jerk wouldn't win.

Chapter Sixteen

Lucille was glad when Chris finally fell asleep, on the living room couch. Eda had gone back to the police station, and Lucille didn't expect her to return until very late. She checked the doors and windows before going to bed.

Some time later, unusual noises from the back of the house stirred Chris awake. She bunched the edge of the afghan in her hands and shifted position, trying to get back to sleep. But the noise was persistent. At last, Chris pulled herself to her feet and went into the kitchen. She vaguely remembered Lucille saying Eda was working at the police station. It was probably just her friend returning home.

Too tired to think, she unlocked and opened the back door. He was standing there, her nemesis, her tormentor, her devil. Ugly green eyes. A big, glimmering knife. She opened her mouth to scream, but the sound froze in the back of her throat.

"I said I'd rip your face off if you told anyone," he hissed. And the glimmering knife flashed forward, so quickly it seemed part of his hand, cutting, ripping . . . But she didn't feel a thing.

She was lying on the couch in Lucille's living room. It had only been a horrible nightmare.

"Christy?" a whispered inquiry.

Chris gasped. He really *was* there. His eyes shone in the dim light, as evil as they'd been many years ago.

"Wake up! Wake me up!"

"You are awake, Christy! I've come back for you!"

Christy began to scream. She tried to get up, but the afghan was tangled around her legs. Malevolent laughter filled the room.

A knife flashed toward her. She rolled just in time, and the blade caught the cushion. He tossed the cushion aside as Chris freed herself, stumbling to the door.

"LUCILLE! LUCILLE!" Why wasn't her friend answering? *Because it's only a dream.*

"Christy! The game is over! I've come to finish you once and for all, and you lose!" He shot in front of her, blocking her exit.

"Please let me wake up!" Chris begged.

The sound of the kitchen door closing made both of them turn. Chris screamed as her assailant pushed her aside and ran to the front door. Lucille came running downstairs, her long dark hair flying. "Chris, what happened?"

Eda burst out of the kitchen. "I heard screaming."

Chris pointed to the front door. "He was

here! That man was here! He tried to kill me!"

Eda wasted no time. She shouted orders to Lucille to call the sheriff and took off after the man herself. Hidden in the shadows of the night, and a few seconds behind him, she wasn't certain at first which way to go. But training and instinct took over and somehow she sensed to run toward the Gammel house.

She was only a block behind him as he reached the corner. He stopped, and even from a distance she could see his shoulders heaving up and down. The run had been an effort for him, and she was certain she would catch him. He seemed to hesitate, gazing down the street at the old house.

"Freeze!" Eda shouted. "Police!"

He took one look at her and bolted again. As she raced down the street, she heard sirens blaring. A squad car pull up alongside her, and the woman inside opened the door.

"Get in, Officer Crispin," Lieutenant Noreen Royston said. "My partner's waiting at the house in case he doubles back through the woods."

Eda caught her breath. "There's a recharge basin there, right? He'd have to climb over barbed wire."

"That's what I'm hoping," Noreen said.

In seconds, they had passed the woods and came around the back of the sump. Another car came up from behind them, beacons flashing. Headlights, beacons and moonlight illuminated the fence and made the recharge basin as bright as day. They fell upon a man struggling to free himself from the barbed wire. Eda got out of the car and watched as Mike and his deputies took position with aimed firearms.

"This is the police," Mike boomed through his megaphone. "Come down from the fence, put your hands in the air, and turn around slowly."

Eda expected a struggle, but to her surprise, the man did as he was told. When he turned, she got a good look at him in the light, and gasped. He was a frail old man, his eyes bugging out of his gaunt face. More alarming was his right hand, for there was no hand. His arm ended in a stump.

Mike and the others hurried to make the arrest. As the beacons swung around, Eda noticed something glistening up in the barbed wire. She shouted for Mike and pointed. "It's a prosthetic device," she said. "It must have worked loose when he was up there."

Noreen read the man his rights. Mike went to the fence and worked the mechanical hand loose, handing it to one of his deputies.

"Do we have our suspect, Mike, after thirty years?" Eda asked.

Mike shook his head. "I just can't know, Eda. He's only got one hand. How can a man with one hand committ three beheadings?"

"And it doesn't tell us where Teddy is," Eda agreed. Until they could interrogate the man, there would be no more answers.

The old man's head snapped up. "Teddy saw too much! I shoulda killed that brat thirty years ago! I shoulda killed all of 'em!" He began to laugh maniacally.

Mike gestured toward one of the cars and he was led away.

"I'd better get back to Chris," Eda said. "You'll be wanting to talk to her. Do you want me to bring her down to the station?"

"I don't think that's necessary," Mike said. "I'll give you a ride and talk to her at Lucille's."

At home, they told Chris and Lucille the news.

"We caught someone," Eda said. "We don't know who he is, but he's in custody."

"It was that horrible man who tormented me when I was a kid," Chris said. "Eda, I remembered something! Something about the day Irene Gammel rubbed blood all over my school blouse!"

Lucille stood up. She'd changed into a nightgown and robe, and there were dark circles under her eyes.

"She's been talking ever since you left," she said. "Maybe you can make some sense of what she has to say."

Eda took Chris by the arm and led her back to the couch. Mike took another seat, got out his pad, and sat ready to write.

"Do you know this man's name?" Mike asked. "Now that you've seen him up close, can you identify him?"

Chris gave Mike a quick glance, but looked directly at Eda when she answered the question.

283

"I don't know his name," she said, "but when he grabbed me tonight, things came back to me! That day I rode my bike to your house, Eda, Irene came out screaming and grabbed me. I always thought she was alone, and couldn't understand why that man was after me. Now I know why! He came out of the house, too, and threatened to rip my face off with that claw of his if I told anyone what I saw."

Lucille groaned. Mike and Eda exchanged glances.

"He grabbed me and shoved that horrible thing into my face," Chris went on. "I was certain he'd gouge out my eyes."

"All those times you saw a gleaming knife," Eda said, "it was probably that prosthesis."

"I think so, now," Chris said. "But there's something more. Irene was all covered with blood, but that man didn't have any on him at all."

Nobody spoke for a few moments.

Finally, Lucille said: "How come we never saw him around town? How could a man with one hand remain unnoticed?"

"How could a man with one hand cut off someone's head?" Eda wondered aloud.

Mike leaned forward. "Your theory about two people is beginning to gel, Eda. I don't think this man killed Darren Gammel. I wouldn't be surprised if Irene did it herself."

"But another murder took place when she was in jail," Chris pointed out.

Mike and Eda looked at each other, remembering the differences in the autopsies.

"Irene killed her husband," Eda said. "But Basil Horton's wounds were sloppy. And it was a blow to the head that really killed him. This guy had to hit him from behind, then use one hand to saw, not cut, his neck. He did it to clear Irene's name."

Chris clutched at her stomach, feeling sick. She looked up with round eyes.

"Then he came back to kill my husband? Why? What did Brian ever do to him?"

Mike stood up. "I don't know, but I mean to find out. I've got to get back to the station."

Chris grabbed Mike's sleeve. "No, don't go," she implored. "There's more. That man threatened me another time, when my brother led me into a trap."

"But you said you were unconcious through most of that," Eda said.

Chris turned to her again. "Through most of it," she said. "But bits and pieces have been coming back to me. I remember being carried down into a dark room. We had to climb a ladder." She stopped, thoughtful.

"What else?" Lucille encouraged.

"I . . . I . . ." Chris said. "Sorry. It's starting to come back, but not fast enough. I think the ladder is a clue."

"There's a way to bring these memories out," Mike said. "Would you consider hypnosis?"

Chris's reply was instant, firm. "God, yes,"

she said. "You know I'll do anything to get my kids back!"

Some time later, they were all gathered in Lucille's bedroom with Dr Lloyd McKechnie, a psychiatrist. Chris had made herself comfortable in a big armchair near Lucille's window, a blanket on her lap.

Mike had explained the situation to the doctor, who had agreed to come to the house right away. When he introduced himself, he explained that he was good friends with the analyist Chris had seen years earlier when dealing with her childhood. That immediately established a basis for trust. Surrounded by her friends, and eager to find out the truth about what had happened so long ago, she went under very easily.

Dr McKechnie sat in a chair brought in from the kitchen, facing Chris. Lucille and Eda were on the edge of the bed, and Mike was in a chair he'd borrowed from Jerry's bedroom. In the quiet, dark safety of the room, Chris began to go back in time. And once more, she was Christy.

"Where are you now, Christy?" the doctor asked gently.

"Outside," Chris said in a voice higher than her own. Her childhood voice, Eda remembered. "The snow is so pretty."

"Tell me what you're doing."

"Walking with my brother," Chris said. "I was at a party at Eda's house. It was so much fun! I have a new bracelet." She held out her hand as if to show off the charm bracelet. Lucille found herself looking for it.

"But now you're going home," McKechnie said.

Chris shook her head. "No, Harvey says they're giving away toys. We're going to get some."

"Christy, I want you to move ahead a little," the doctor suggested. "You told me that Harvey took you down a shortcut. What happened next?"

"We turned a corner and . . . oh, no!" Chris's face twisted up, and she began to wriggle in the chair. She looked so much like a frightened little kid that Lucille felt tears coming to her eyes.

"What do you see?" asked the doctor.

"Oh, it's him! It's the bad man with those mean eyes!"

The psychiatrist gave her hand a squeeze. "Nothing can hurt you," he said. "These are just memories. Tell us what happens next."

"He . . . he's pushing something yucky in my face. I – " she stopped talking, her head dropping to her chest.

"What happened?" Mike whispered.

McKechnie held up a hand.

"Christy? Come out of it, honey."

Chris stirred again. "I hear voices."

"What are they saying?"

"He says he's gonna take me to be with Teddy," Chris went on. "He says I saw, I know. But Harvey says it's a joke. Oh, no! He's got a rope!"

"It's okay, Christy. The rope can't hurt you now."

Tears were streaming down Chris's face. She brought her hands up to her her neck. "He's tying me up," she said. "And . . . ugh! . . . he's putting me over his shoulder. I don't like hanging like this! Put me down!" She wriggled in the chair.

"Where is the man taking you?"

"Down a dark street," she said. "Oh, no! He's taking me to that terrible house! To the house where that crazy lady put blood on me! My daddy beat me up because of that!"

Eda bit her lip to keep herself quiet.

"Go on," the doctor urged gently.

"We're walking across a yard," Chris said. "It's hard, because the snow is so deep."

"Christy, why don't you yell for help?"

"Can't. He's got something around my mouth." Her eyebrows furrowed. "There's a funny door," she said. "A door in the ground. Why would there be a door in the ground?" She paused, as if watching something.

"He's pulling it open," she said. "It's dark down there. I don't want to go down there!" She began to wail. "Harvey! Harvey!"

"Christy! What is Harvey doing?"

"He's fighting with the man. He's kicking him. Oh! Harvey just hit him really hard with something. He fell down. Harvey's untying me. He's telling me to run, but I can't. I can't! I . . ." Once more, she passed out.

"She must have fainted at this point when she was a kid," Eda guessed.

"You can bring her around, Dr McKechnie," Mike said. "I've got my information."

Carefully, the psychiatrist helped Chris back to the present. She blinked and looked around at everyone's concerned faces.

"Is it okay now?" she asked. "Are we going to find my kids?"

Mike smiled at her. "You gave us a big clue."

"I don't understand," Lucille admitted.

Eda stood up and went to put a hand on Chris's shoulder.

"The door in the ground," she said. "That was 1962."

"So?"

"The Cuban Missile Crisis?" Eda prompted. "Chris, Lucille, there's a fallout shelter on that property!"

Mike was already heading for the door. "And I'd bet we're going to find your children there."

In her excitement, Chris stood up too quickly and became dizzy. The doctor and Lucille took either of her arms.

"Easy," the doctor said. "Just relax."

"No!" Chris said. "My babies might be trapped in a dark room underground! I'm not staying here!"

Eda looked at Mike, who nodded. "Then come with us in the police car," she said. "Lucille?"

"You aren't leaving me behind," Lucille said emphatically.

After a quick thank-you to the doctor, they left. Mike radioed ahead for backup, in case

Teddy was found. Within minutes, they were at the Gammel house again. As she stood looking at the eerie old house, armed with a flashlight she'd grabbed from Lucille's kitchen counter, Eda remembered something.

"I heard voices the other day," she said. "I thought it was Josh, calling for help." She sighed. "If I'd only known . . ."

To everyone's surprise, it was Chris who comforted her. "You did the best you could."

"Right," Mike agreed. "Now, let's finish it." He called to the two officers who were on watch and explained his suspicions.

"This is a huge piece of property," Lucille said. "It could take us hours to find that trapdoor."

"Not if each of us concentrates on a section," Mike said.

At his orders, they spread arm's distance from each other. They began to walk straight ahead, pushing aside tall grass that scratched at their arms and faces. Lucille mumbled worries about ticks.

"I have another idea," Eda called to Chris. "Maybe we can get a good look at the property from the attic."

"Great idea," Mike said. "Why don't you run up there?"

"No, I want to go," Chris said. "If someone's going to find that door, I want it to be me."

"Okay," Eda said, "but give us a call from the window when you get up there."

"What if Teddy's up there?" Lucille protested.

"He can't be," said one of the officers. "We would have seen him go into the house."

Chris raced back to the house. The old house didn't frighten her now. Her mind was too full of determination for fear to creep inside it. Aiming the flashlight, she hurried up to the old attic. It was so congested with heat that she found herself gasping for breath. Moonlight glowing through the window beckoned her, and she hurried to open it. But as she was reaching for the latch, someone grabbed her from behind.

"I can't wait for you any longer," a man whispered, his hand covering her mouth. "Adrian got to you first, but you're mine now. Douglas said you were mine!"

Chris knew that struggling would only make things worse. Somehow, Teddy had managed to sneak back into the house, and had been hiding up here the whole time. She prayed she could reason with him, bring out the boy who had been abused as much as she.

"Don't scream," he said.

She shook her head. Slowly, he pulled his hand away. When he was satisfied she'd keep quiet, he turned her around.

In the moonlight, his eyes were so much like Brian's she had to bite her tongue to keep from crying out. "Are . . . are you Teddy?" she asked. Her voice was even, gentle, but she was shaking inside.

"Uh-huh," Teddy said with a nod. He sniffled from the attic dust and ran a dirty hand under his nose. His cheeks were unshaven, nearly a week's growth of beard making him look like a ragged wino.

"Teddy, where are my children?"

"In a safe place," Teddy said. "I'm protecting them from the police. I know what the police will do. They'll take the kids away from us. But don't worry. I won't let them do it. And I won't let them split the kids apart!"

"The way they split up you and Adrian?" Chris asked. *Eda, why haven't you come looking for me? I should have opened the window by now.*

"Douglas made Adrian go away," Teddy pouted. "He said Adrian was too little to help and he couldn't afford to feed him. He wanted me to go away, too, but Mommy said no. They had a big fight. Just like the one Mommy had with Daddy, only nobody got cut up this time."

Chris felt her heart pounding. Somehow, she had to bring out the truth. "Teddy, what happened to your parents?"

Teddy licked his lips and stared up at the ceiling. "They were fighting one day," he said. "I went to their door to listen. I was leaning against it. I didn't mean for it to happen! The door opened. The door opened and I made Mommy slip and she had an axe in her hand and I made her slip and she cut off Daddy's head and there was blood everywhere and she cut him again and again and I counted fifteen times . . . fifteen is an important number . . . I cut up that man Brian fifteen times . . ."

Chris let out a cry of dismay. Teddy went on babbling, oblivious to her. Chris knew this was her chance to escape. She backed toward the wooden stairs, nearly stumbling over the top one. Then she turned and ran down, her heart pounding.

"You can't go away!" Teddy cried, lunging at her.

He caught her halfway down the stairs to the first floor. Chris screamed and struggled, but she couldn't escape from Teddy's iron grip.

"You can't have the kids until you say you'll be mine," he said. "Douglas said you were my prize. *Mine*! Adrian wasn't supposed to get you!"

Desperate, Chris blurted: "But I married Brian! Not Adrian!"

"No! *No*! Adrian got you! It was Adrian!"

Chris screamed again, and her voice blended with Mike's loud command: "Let her go!"

She stopped struggling to see Mike and two deputies, all pointing guns. With a loud cry, Teddy pushed her away and sank down on the stairs. Chris saw Lucille behind the officers and ran to her. "He killed Brian!"

"I know," Lucille said. "Chris, we found the fallout shelter! They're trying to get it open now."

Leaving Mike to make the arrest, Lucille led Chris out to the yard. Eda and a deputy were busy trying to pry the door open.

"I couldn't believe how well-hidden it was," Eda said. "If Lucille hadn't felt a strange rise in the ground, we might have gone right by it!" She looked up at Chris from her crouched position. "Are you okay?" she asked. "I was worried when you didn't open the window."

"Teddy was up there," Chris said breathlessly. But she only cared about getting the door open.

At last, the latch sprung free, and the door swung back with a loud clank. A soft glow rose from the room beneath them. The deputy looked at Eda. "Someone's sitting down there," he said.

Eda looked into the hole. She saw a woman's bloody foot.

Chris pushed next to her and leaned forward, yelling: "Josh! Vicki! Are you down there?"

And a few seconds later: "Mommy? Josh, wake up! It's Mommy!"

The deputy unlatched the ladder and let it fall to the floor below. He led the way, followed by the women. At the sight of the shrouded body, Lucille cried out in horror. But Chris was oblivious to anything but the sight of her precious children. She ran to them with opened arms, smothering them with kisses.

"I want to go home," Vicki said.

"Me, too," Josh agreed.

Both children kept close to their mother as she led them to the ladder. Lucille helped them up, leaving Eda and the deputy to deal with the body.

Carefully, the deputy pulled off the blanket, revealing Tiffany Simmons. Her once-beautiful face had begun to bloat, her skin was covered with patches of dried blood.

"She must have run into Teddy," Eda said. "Damn!" She couldn't help a twinge of guilt for the hatred she expressed toward Tiffany. The woman had been her enemy, but no one should have had to suffer like this. She moved quickly to the ladder. "I'll get Mike," she said, wanting to be away from the scene.

Blankets had been provided for the children, who seemed chilled despite the July heat. They were led to a police car, Chris carrying Vicki, Josh pressed close to her side. A policeman half-carried, half-dragged a man from the house.

At the sight of him, Josh cried out: "That's the man Dad had a fight with! He came to our house and said that Dad had taken Mom away from him! They had a big fight!"

"Shh," Chris said. "You can tell all that to the police later. Let's just get you home, okay?"

They piled into the back of Mike's car. The children pressed close to Chris as the seat belts would allow, as if afraid she might disappear from their sight.

Chapter Seventeen

"It was just a game," Douglas Eastman said.

"With Christine Burnett Wander as an unwilling player," Mike retorted.

They were sitting in a small interrogation room at the precinct, a table between them and a guard outside the door. A tape recorder on the table whirred softly. Mike regarded the man across from him. Douglas seemed too sick to carry on a conversation, but talking was what he'd been doing. A lot of talking.

He'd been read his rights, but had refused a lawyer, insisting he was smart enough to defend himself. He answered Mike's quietly determined questions with a steady voice. It was the mark of a man with a cool head, Mike thought. He could easily see how Douglas Eastman had come to own and operate one of the largest trucking companies in the West.

Anyone looking at this frail man, with his sallow skin and missing hand, initially would have felt pity. Mike, knowing his background, saw something profane in Eastman's eyes, the look of someone without morals. Chris had seen it, too. Even at seven, she'd known this man was evil.

"Tell me from the beginning," he said.

Eastman smiled, and Mike resisted an urge to grab him and make him see this wasn't funny at all.

"What beginning?" he asked. "When I met Irene? When Teddy and Adrian came of age and got their inheritance?"

"I suppose meeting Irene Gammel was the start of it all," Mike prompted.

"I changed a tyre for her," Douglas said. "She was standing against this Rambler in the middle of nowhere, crying her eyes out. I stopped to help her. I was driving from Spokane to Bozeman, and I was in a hurry. But she kept going on and on about how her husband was gonna kill her. She was so sweet, something got the better of me. I followed her home and made sure the bastard didn't lay a hand on her. But she was lucky. Or maybe I was the lucky one that day. He wasn't home. She showed me her appreciation in a special way."

"Special way?"

The prisoner looked at the sheriff with disdain. "We made love." He mumbled: "Dumb hick."

Mike ignored the remark. "Let's move ahead in time, to the day Darren Gammel was murdered. Did you kill him?"

"Yes," was the simple reply. "He found out about Irene and me, and the kids, and . . ."

"The kids?"

"Adrian and Teddy," Douglas said. "They're mine. You can tell by looking at them that they're mine."

Mike sighed. This was becoming more and more complicated. "Go on."

"That day, Irene was gonna tell Darren the truth," Douglas continued. "I went there to be with her, but the bastard tried to kill her. It was self-defense. She was defending herself."

Mike's eyebrows went up. "But you said you were the one who killed him."

For a second, the calm demeanor seemed to melt away. But Eastman quickly regained his composure. "That's what I said, all right," he said. "I killed him. But Irene didn't try to stop me. Anyway, I wasn't just defending her. It was the kids, too. *My* kids. I was sick of pretending they weren't mine. I was sick of hearing how that bastard beat up on 'em. It was time to put an end to that."

You sure as hell did that, Mike thought.

"You know what Gammel called me?" Douglas asked. "He called me a *Communist*. Me! A guy who lost his hand in the Korean War. Got a Purple Heart for that."

There was a great deal of pride in that statement. Mike couldn't help wondering what kind of man he'd been in the war. "What happened with the axe?"

"He tried to kill me," Eastman said. "But I got hold of it and let him have it. Irene got all messed up with blood, and she went running from the house like a crazy woman. That's when she ran into that little girl – Christy. I saw her, too. I told her to keep her mouth shut."

"Chris says you threatened to rip off her face."

The killer gestured as if to wave his hand, although there was no hand on that particular arm. "Right, right," he said. "I needed to make a big threat. Anyway, she ran off. I took the kids and hid with them. Irene was arrested. I didn't want her getting blamed for murdering Darren. I figured I could kill someone else to clear her name and get out of town fast enough. No one in Aberdeen knew about me. Sneaking around with a married woman taught me early how to lay low. I could clear Irene, and we'd all be on our way. Got a farm in Washington. Plenty of room."

"When did you go after Christy?"

"I watched her right from the start," Douglas said. "When I got a load of that crazy mother of hers, and the way her father beat her . . ."

"How do you know about that?"

"Takes an abused kid to know one," was the reply. "I could hear the screams and yells from the apartment when I was hanging around the street corner. I could see the kid's bruises. And I knew she wouldn't tell her folks about me. That's when I decided to make a game of it. I'd check up on her once in a while to make sure she wasn't telling anyone what she'd seen. I decided, when it was safe, I'd take her to live with my boys."

"What exactly did Christy see?"

"Irene with blood all over her," Eastman snapped. "Aren't you paying attention?"

"There was blood on you, too, wasn't there?"

"Well . . . well, of course . . ."

"You don't seem so sure about that."

"I'm sure! You want me to tell the story, or not?"

Mike nodded. "Go ahead. I want to hear everything."

With her arms firmly around the shoulders of Josh and Vicki, Chris followed Lucille into the house. Eda stayed outside to deal with the reporters who had come to talk to the newly reunited family. Chris had spoken briefly with them, politely asking for some privacy in the next few days.

Josh, pressed against his mother's legs, had remained quiet throughout the interview. But Vicki had charmed everyone with her straight-forward account of the ordeal. Although she understood her son's reserve, Chris was worried he was bottling up his feelings. She remembered her own childhood secrets, and how they had hurt her.

Lucille seemed to understand Chris's worries. Inside the house, she took Vicki upstairs for a bath. Chris sat on the living room couch with Josh cuddled against her. She kissed the top of his head, as she had kissed him a hundred times since she'd found him. "Are you ready to talk yet?" she asked gently.

"Vicki told everything that happened," Josh replied.

"But I want to hear your story," Chris said. "From what I heard, you were very brave. That was a smart idea, using cans as weapons."

"It didn't work."

"At least you tried," Chris said.

Josh sighed. Part of him wanted to forget what happened, but part of him wanted to tell his mother everything. She'd always said keeping bad things inside wasn't good. Dad had said it, too.

Dad . . . Josh fixed his eyes on a picture across the room and began to tell of that horrible night. "Someone rang the bell, and Dad went to answer it. I heard him say: 'I told you not to come here.' Then the other guy said: 'Daddy says it's time to end the game.' They got into a big fight. Vicki got scared and hid behind the couch, but I went to see. Dad punched the guy in the nose. Then the other guy picked up an umbrella stand and hit Dad real hard. That made Dad fall down. There was a lot of yelling. The bad guy saw me, and I ran. He grabbed me and pushed this gross-smelling stuff on my nose. That made me sleep."

"Then he took you and Vicki to the fallout shelter," Chris filled in. "You . . . you didn't see what he did to your father?"

"He hit Dad with the umbrella stand," Josh said. He looked up at his mother. "I know he killed him."

It was such a matter-of-fact statement that Chris

didn't know how to respond. She was only grateful her children hadn't witnessed the way Teddy had butchered their father. Without another word, she hugged Josh close.

The morning passed quietly, with Lucille fending off phone calls. Both children eagerly ate the pancakes Chris prepared. In the afternoon, Vicki took a nap without protest and Josh busied himself playing with Jerry's toys.

Chris was enjoying a game of cards with Eda when the doorbell rang. Lucille brought Mike into the living room. For the first time since she'd come from New York, Eda noticed just how old Mike had become. Or was it the ordeal of the past few days that put those dark circles under his eyes and the extra grey in his hair?

"I have some news," he said. "Eastman was more than willing to tell the whole story."

"Great," Lucille said. "Now we can find out the truth."

"I hope so," Mike said.

As the women listened, Mike related the story he'd heard, beginning with the day Douglas Eastman had come home with Irene Gammel.

"So they conspired to kill Darren Gammel," Eda guessed.

"Right," Mike said. "It seems Darren was going to kill Eastman, but somehow Eastman got hold of the axe. Teddy was hiding in the closet. He saw the whole thing."

"That poor child," Lucille said. Then she shook

303

her head, remembering how 'that poor child' had murdered her best friend's husband.

"No wonder the kid went crazy," Eda said.

Chris sat silently, staring at her wedding ring.

"Eastman took the boys to a fallout shelter," Mike went on, "until he felt it was safe to move them."

"I can't understand why it wasn't found thirty years ago," Eda said.

"Darren Gammel was terrified of Communist invasion," the sheriff replied, "even all the way up here in Montana. When he built that shelter, he was careful to do it at night, so no one would know about it but his family. He did such a good job replacing sod over it that it was virtually undetectable."

"Eastman took the boys to a farm he owns in Washington State. Irene caught up with them a few months later. Eastman's elderly mother was taking care of the kids. She was very strict, might even have been abusive. Teddy was submissive at this point, but Adrian had a defiant streak even at his young age. Eastman couldn't handle the kid, and forced Irene to give him up for adoption. Then he turned all his attentions to Teddy. He kept telling him about a pretty little girl back in Aberdeen, one who would be Teddy's when they both grew up."

"Me," Chris said simply.

"Right," Mike said. "But unknown to their families, Teddy was sneaking off once-in-a-while to visit his little brother. Teddy told Adrian about this girl, too, and he formed his own fantasies. But neither of them met Chris for twenty years."

"Darren Gammel had a will. He left all his possessions to his wife, but she couldn't collect until twenty years after the date of his death. It was iron-clad, and there was nothing Douglas or Irene could do to change it. By the time things cleared, Irene was too sick and old to travel. As blood relatives, only the boys could handle the deal."

"Wait," Eda said. "If Teddy or Adrian showed up, they'd have to explain where they'd been for twenty years."

Mike nodded. "But Eastman was clever. He knew the right way to get around that problem. He couldn't send Teddy, but he could make contact with Adrian. Under the new name his adoptive parents had given him, Adrian could pretend to be a representative of the family. Eastman knew he'd be loyal to his mother, and also knew he was more easily trusted than Teddy."

"Teddy doesn't seem like a smart fellow," Lucille said.

"And he was jealous that Adrian was returning to their old home," Mike went on. "He insisted on accompanying his brother. It was then that Eastman instructed him to begin stalking you, the way he had when you were little. The only difference was, Adrian was there, too. And he'd grown up to be a pretty decent guy. He didn't like what he saw his brother doing, and decided to rescue you."

Chris gasped. "I don't want to hear this," she murmured.

"But you want to know the truth," Lucille said.

"I can guess," Chris said. "I've known ever since I drew that picture. Adrian's adoptive parents were the Wanders, weren't they? They renamed him Brian."

Mike gazed at her, amazed at how well she was taking all this. She was truly a stronger, braver woman than she imagined.

"Brian was Adrian's middle name. Eastman explained that Adrian – Brian – told Teddy he'd stop him from hurting you no matter what it took. He really was in love with you, Chris. No matter what else you learn about your husband, keep that in mind."

"I will," Chris said, almost to herself.

"He married you to keep Teddy away from you," Mike said. "And for a long time, it worked. Teddy became so much trouble after he lost you that Irene and Douglas had him committed. But about a year ago, when Irene Gammel was dying, she begged Eastman to bring her son home again. After Irene died, Eastman sent Teddy back to Aberdeen to finish what he'd started twelve years earlier, when Chris and Brian married. You see, the house had passed from mother to sons. Eastman was afraid a search into the home's ownership would start a new investigation. He sent Teddy down here to warn Brian to keep quiet."

"But that was a year ago," Eda said. "Why did Teddy wait so long . . ."

Mike waved a hand. "I don't think Eastman meant for Teddy to kill his brother. But Teddy had been keeping his emotions bottled up for so long that he snapped. I think he was trying to resolve the problems of his own childhood by repeating the act that killed his real father."

Chris sighed, closing her eyes.

Mike stood up. "We have a confession. Both men spoke to us, although Teddy's statement is questionable. But we know now that Eastman killed both Darren Gammel and Basil Horton. And Teddy copied him by killing Adrian/Brian."

"No!" Chris spoke so loudly everyone turned to her.

"No, that isn't right," she insisted. "It isn't right at all. I *saw* them after the first murder. I . . . I remember that Irene had blood all over her. She did, but that horrible man with the metal claw didn't."

She looked up at Mike. "If he used an axe on Darren, why didn't he have blood on him?"

"Oh, my God," Eda said. "Mike, that theory about two killers . . ."

"The first was a clean wound," Mike said. "Hardly something a man with one hand could accomplish. The second was ragged and probably occured after a blow to the head killed Basil Horton."

"Eastman killed Horton to clear Irene's name," Eda said. "She murdered her own husband."

Lucille whistled softly. "And Teddy saw that."

Chris looked worried. "Could he be released on grounds of insanity?"

"Never," Mike said. "If he doesn't go to jail, he'll spend his life in an institution."

"Forever," Eda agreed. "Chris, I promise you, there's no way in hell those men will get away with what they did."

Lucille put her arm around Chris's shoulder. "They'll never hurt you again," she vowed.

Epilogue

The day after Brian's funeral, Chris, Lucille and their children accompanied Eda to the airport. Mike was there, too, and as they waited for the flight to board, he watched the children with amazement. Josh and Jerry were teasing Vicki, who, in turn, was flirting with the twins.

"It's as if nothing ever happened," he said. "How can kids bounce back like that?"

"We just do," Chris said. "Somehow, we just do." She smiled at her friends. "But having the best friends in the world helps a lot," she said. "I don't know how I can ever thank you."

"So you've said," Eda told her, "about a million times in the past few days."

"I'll keep saying it," Chris said. "You and Lucille helped me keep my sanity."

"Eda's detective work was really sharp," Mike said. "Why don't you stay in Aberdeen? We could use someone like you on the force."

Eda smiled, but shook her head. "Believe it or not," she said, "I miss the city. And I've got someone waiting there for me."

309

"Tim Becker?" Lucille asked. "Is there a romance brewing here?"

"Oh, Tim's been my partner for years," Eda said nonchalantly.

Lucille smiled at Chris. "I'd be willing to travel to New York for a wedding."

"Me, too," Chris said. "I'd like to look forward to a happy occasion."

Eda rolled her eyes: "Don't hold your breath. I'm still working toward my detective shield."

"You'll get it," Mike said, "once they hear how you helped crack this case."

An announcement invited passengers on Eda's flight to begin boarding. Chris threw her arms around Eda. She couldn't stop thinking that, if it hadn't been for her friend, she might never have found her children. "You hurry back," she said. "We didn't really have a chance to visit this time."

Lucille came to hug Eda, too. "I might visit my agent in New York this fall," she said. "I've got a great idea for a mystery story. Three women detectives."

"You can stay at my place," Eda suggested.

Mike came forward to shake Eda's hand. "I'm going to report your work to the governor," he said. "You deserve some kind of commendation for helping us."

The children came running over to say good-bye. Josh and Vicki trapped Eda in a bear hug. Eda knelt down to hug them back.

"Oh, I love you guys!"

"We love you, Eda," Vicki replied.

"Yeah," was all Josh would say.

Eda looked past the two little heads at her friends. "This is all the reward I'll ever need," she said.

Then she stood up, waved her hand, and boarded to flight to New York.